HAPPY AS LARRY

A NEW YORK STORY OF CULTS, CRUSHES AND QUAALUDES

A Novel by

Kaethe Cherney

HAPPY AS LARRY.

FIRST EDITION

Jacket Designed by Jamie Keenan
Interior Designed by Tim Osmond

www.kaethecherney.com

To the family I was born into and the family I made,
with a love supreme

first one thinks of himself as one
of a family, later as part of a community,
then as living in a city, citizen of such
and such a country; finally, he feels
no limit to that of which he is a part.

— John Cage

(as) happy as a sandboy (or as Larry):
phrase (British), extremely happy

— Oxford Dictionaries

Table of Contents

Author's Note

Acknowledgements

Author's Note

There was, there was, and yet there was not. That was the opening to a Georgian folktale my mom used to read to me, and in many ways, this contradictory notion holds true for my book.

There was an almighty chaos, which set in after my father died. In no particular order, my family's finances seesawed, routines went out the window, and my older siblings joined the Sullivanians, a cult that thrived on New York's Upper West Side until it disbanded in the late eighties. Our mom sought to reclaim her happiness with someone who made us children unhappy, and in my own blunderbuss fashion, I found my moxie with friends who are still my go-to people to this day.

Memory is an unreliable narrator. I wanted the freedom to condense time and not be beholden to biographic particulars, so I reimagined these events, firstly by making my fictionalized self eight years older than I was in real life when we were bereaved. I have written truthfully about my experience without necessarily being truthful to the facts. I have taken liberties with events I was not privy to or which I heard about secondhand.

By writing in the third person, I allowed Saskia to become a character who is me and not me. This in turn gave me the vehicle to be private in public. The only time I wrote in the first person is in the following excerpt, which was my very first stab at tackling this story.

Most importantly, I wanted to portray the exquisite peculiarities of growing up in a New York that no longer exists, and pay homage to a city that will forever make my heart skip a beat.

As in any good folktale, we eventually had a happy-enough ending. We pulled through it, and then some, with an abundance of love, red wine, and dark humor.

* * *

Some people have a bad hair day, but I had a bad hair decade. Looking back on it, I guess you could say that was the least of my problems. You see, my problems were of the chemical type. The fun, up-till-dawn, downtown, party-girl sort, and the sort where cesium meets water, and the world as you know it blows up in your face.

I've since traded in living on that little island off the east coast of America for another soggier one, off the northwest coast of Europe. Mostly I have good hair days now, thanks to brand-name products and the knowledge I've gained over the years.

But I'm getting ahead of myself. This isn't a story about hair care and island-hopping. It's about the time when we stopped being "we," after Daddy died. I think of my father when I smell turpentine and cigarettes. Baseball and highballs. Rothko reds and the blue notes of jazz. NYC is my DNA. Blondie and the great blackout are in my bloodline. Broadway is a river in me and my family are the rocks, worn smooth, which, no matter how far I travel, will always remain at the center of my being.

1.

No Place Like Home

Chelsea, New York, 1977

Right now, as the lights on the Empire State Building are being switched off, Saskia beholds the swagger of the city at dawn and feels her soul changing colors. For the second time that night, Manhattan has held her to its heart and shown her the impossibility of darkness in the light of day.

She crosses Seventh Avenue when the Walk sign changes, and starts down the stairs to the uptown local, but stops mid-step when a white limousine with a wilted bouquet of flowers on its hood cruises to a halt and double-parks at the corner of Twenty-Third Street.

She hurries back to street level, wondering if it's that very same limo from that night way back when, before the world as she knew it fell down. She cautiously traces her reflection in its darkened window.

It's as though only the pane of glass separates her from the past. True, she has the same curly hair and green eyes, but the scab on her thinned cheek and the faint red marks around her neck are as different as the girl she was two-and-something years ago.

She seems to reach into herself as she watches the limo pull off and disappear into traffic. Instead of continuing to the uptown train, she ducks into a twenty-four-hour deli where she selects a legal pad, a pen, a can of seltzer, and a box of Cracker Jacks. By the time she boards the downtown local, it's light outside.

It's not that her parents fight often, but Saskia can always tell when they do. There was one fight that was truly terrible. Daddy called Mom spoiled and she accused him of limiting her and then he slept in the maid's room for two whole nights. But that was a long time ago and thankfully has never been repeated.

She has friends in her eighth-grade class whose parents are divorced, but she never worries about it with the two of them. Even her aunt Tilly is divorced, which is why Daddy helps his sister as much as he can, and also why Mom sometimes gets annoyed by how often Tilly comes over for dinner.

Saskia's the last one up this morning since her big brother Toby has swim practice every day before school and Naomi, who is a year behind Toby, volunteered to help decorate the gym for the high school dance.

When she finds Daddy in the kitchen preparing a breakfast tray, there is a giddy second when she thinks it's for her. After all, he is the one who is going to be in the hospital for the weekend, and not just any weekend, but Valentine's Day weekend at that.

But when she clocks that Mom isn't there she figures something must have blipped while they were out last night. She had helped Mom pick her earrings and fastened Daddy's cufflinks, before waving them off. She knows it's corny, but she loves how handsome they look together. To her, Daddy is the Miles to Mom's Mozart. Their different styles make them tick.

Daddy is in his pajamas, brewing coffee, and listening to the radio, and instead of smelling like he always does of Royal Copenhagen aftershave, he has stubble on his chin and his springy dark hair is rumpled. He playfully groans when she sits on his lap. "No wonder I busted a gut."

"Are you calling me fat?"

"No sweetheart. I'm calling you trouble with a capital *S*."

He drops an Alka-Seltzer into a glass of water and with that burst of fizz, she can just about hear the high notes of the night before. It doesn't happen often, but often enough for her to know that when he gets juiced, Mom gets jangly.

"What?" Daddy protests when he catches her look. "It's not every day that your pal gets a promotion."

"You know she hates it when you do that," Saskia scolds, while twirling his wedding ring.

"Libby and Mom didn't exactly complain when we ordered that second bottle of champagne. Mom never usually rounds a third, but she did last night," he says. Saskia stares him down until he shrugs sheepishly and admits, "Then Tom and I put the ladies in a taxi and had a nightcap, or four."

Saskia pats his bathrobe pocket to see if he has a Valentine's Day card for her, but it's empty, so she reasons that he'll give her one when he gets home on Sunday. She wonders if she should give him his card now to open a day early, or put it in his overnight bag to have for tomorrow.

Valentine's Day is like an empty frame. She knows its shape, but not its content. She's never received a card from a secret admirer or been kissed by a boy. She's not as developed as some girls in her class who have the straight hair she longs for and already wear bras. She's not popular or unpopular; she's a second or third choice rather than a first.

The coffee finishes brewing so she gets up to pour him one with milk, no sugar, the way he always takes it. "What will your doctor say?"

"My hernia has nothing to do with my liver," Daddy laughs, then breaks a bloom off a potted poinsettia that adorns the windowsill to place among a saucer of grapes. "What are they teaching at that fancy place I send you to?"

Whatever it is, is going over my head, she thinks. She's not like her best friend Kathleen, who always gets straight As, although she never makes her feel dumb, or Toby, pianist and editor of his school newspaper, or even Naomi, who seems to have inherited Mom's good looks and her love of theater. She's the caboose on a fast train.

Daddy gets out the eggs to scramble while she finds him a bowl and the whisk. Then she puts butter in the pan and asks, "Can we go out for dinner Sunday?"

"On one condition. Promise to be home on time to say goodbye?"

"I promise, so long as you promise to take us to Luchow's."

"Deal." They shake.

When the eggs finish, Daddy motions for her to open the swing door that leads to the dining room. She picks up his coffee cup and follows him through the dining room and down the carpeted hallway, densely hung with the prints he sells at his gallery, to the sunny master bedroom.

Mom is propped up in bed, reading *War and Peace*, and surrounded by silk throw pillows. Her long, brown hair is loose, and the traces of last night's makeup cause her hazel eyes to look even more sultry than usual. "You're going to be late to school," she says, without looking up.

"No, I'm not."

"Just because some of us chose to come home in the small hours, doesn't give you license to be tardy." Mom signals for Saskia to turn around and gestures toward a spot where her shirt isn't properly tucked into the waistband of her pleated uniform.

"Here you go, Duchess." Daddy places the tray on the bedside table and sits down on her side of the bed. Mom moves away from him and slowly turns a page of her book.

"It won't happen again," Daddy continues, crossing his fingers so only Saskia can see.

He reaches over to move a loose strand of Mom's hair but she slaps his hand. He tries to kiss Mom, but she turns away sharply.

"This is no time to be hovering," Mom barks to Saskia. "You should be on your way."

Saskia hates to leave them all angry and tangled like this. She hesitates, spying their framed wedding photo. "Tell me the story of how you two met again?"

"Spare me. Besides, you know the gory details inside out," Mom replies tersely.

She sure does. Mom was doing summer stock. Daddy crashed an after-party with a friend. They eloped seven weeks later and then moved to a West Village walk-up.

Daddy throws Saskia a grateful look and picks up his cue. "If you won't tell, then I will. You asked me to hold your drink—"

"I live to rue the day," Mom interrupts.

Daddy continues, undeterred, "And then I asked you out."

"More fool I."

"Then lo and behold, our first date lasted three days."

"That's an inappropriate disclosure," Mom says, turning another page.

"Your parents were dismayed that you were marrying down and were convinced we'd starve. But I promised them there was a rich man in me, waiting to get out."

Mom puts her book down and fixes him with a haughty stare. "My father always said it's rude to talk about money."

"My pops always said twenty percent off is a bargain, fifty percent a mitzvah."

Mom stifles a smile and returns to her novel.

"I guess we could both agree that opposites attract," Daddy says, and holds out the grapes.

Mom brushes her fingers against his when she selects one and delicately peels it with her teeth. "Your transgression is going to cost you." Mom pauses to eat the grape. "A lot."

"Sweetheart, can you get some sugar for my coffee?" Daddy asks.

"But you don't take—" Saskia starts. And then realizes.

She closes the bedroom door behind her, and pauses to listen in to the laughter that gives way to that muffled language of nineteen years of them.

* * *

Much later that day, after assembly, after school, after hanging out at Kathleen's, she and her best friend hook arms as they saunter to Third Avenue, busily imagining what *he* thinks of them. *He* is Kathleen's new neighbor, who looks like a teenage Ryan O'Neal. *He* is the reason why she goes to Kathleen's every Friday, and *he* is the one they try to accidentally-on-purpose bump into while walking Kathleen's dog, every weekend when he arrives home in a taxi from boarding school.

Although she suspects that the boy prefers Kathleen, who is tow-haired and tomboyish, it's still fun to make eyes at him and imagine that he might, just might, like her.

While they are waiting on the corner of Seventeenth Street

for the Walk sign, Saskia hears the music of the city at night and wonders what riffs her future will bring. As if on cue, a white limousine with a bouquet of fresh flowers attached to its hood double-parks in front of them.

"I've never seen one so pretty," Saskia exclaims. "What I wouldn't give to ride in one of those."

"Maybe we'll rent one for our junior prom," Kathleen sighs dreamily.

"I don't want to wait that long. Come on, let's make a wish."

The girls touch their reflections on the glossy patina of the limo as though it were a genie's bottle. "I wish I get to ride around in limos when I grow up," Saskia says.

"I wish that new boy falls in love with me when I grow up," Kathleen proclaims, just as the lights change and the limousine glides off.

Saskia hastily kisses Kathleen goodbye and crosses the street to run down Irving Place, the cold night air chafing the skin between her knee socks and duffel coat. The windows of Pete's Tavern are cloudy with cigarette smoke from the Friday-night crowd, the bells in the Con Ed clock tower are chiming seven times, and the crescent moon looks like it's hanging from a bare tree branch in Gramercy Park.

Mikey, the ruddy-faced doorman, is outside having a smoke under the awning when she arrives, her nose running from the cold and her duffel coat dusted with the snow that has just started to fall. "You're in the doghouse, young lady. I just put Mr. Soyer in a taxi."

"Did he say anything?"

"He said you better not stay up too late watching TV, since he doesn't want you to end up with four eyes and an antenna where your brain should be."

Her mood slip-slides as she kicks herself for not seeing Daddy off to the hospital, but then she steadies her conscience with the promise that she'll make it up to him with a batch of her famous brownies when he gets back. By the time the elevator reaches their sixth-floor apartment, she's got that Friday feeling back again.

Toby is poring over a map in the living room with his best friend Arthur, both of them having already suited up for the dance. The cowlick in Toby's thick chestnut hair has been plastered down with Brylcreem and he smells of the Aqua Velva aftershave she gave him for his eighteenth birthday.

She knows they are planning their graduation trip to Paris. And that come July, they'll be gone for months. She knows, and this is the part that she'd rather un-know, that as of September, Toby will really leave, this time for college. That's the sticky part. He's the oil in their family machine, while Naomi is the accelerator. And as Daddy likes to tease, she's the one with a career in the Foreign Service, since she's the born diplomat.

Naomi must still be getting dressed, so Saskia drops down beside Toby and leans against his lanky frame as she tries to make sense of the upside-down mass of squiggles that constitute France.

"What's up, squirt?" Arthur asks when she sighs, his clean-cut blond looks marred by a rash of pimples on his forehead.

"Nothing," she sulks.

"Let me guess," Toby says. "Does it start with 'it's not fair'?"

"Well, it's not."

"Which part?" Toby continues. "Have you got a bad case of the I-wishes?"

Saskia nods and plays with his class ring. He always gets where her thoughts take her.

"Mark my words, when you graduate high school, Mom and Dad will send you to Europe on the *QE2*."

"And?"

"When I get home, I'll bring back so much French perfume you'll be swimming in it."

She hangs up his promise alongside the other shiny ones that he's made to her, like you'll outgrow your baby fat, and you're just as pretty as Naomi. You're the apple that fell far from the tree, Mom always says to her. Like she really needs reminding.

Naomi comes in brandishing three beers she snuck from the fridge. The red of her dress complements the garnet earrings she must have borrowed from Mom. Naomi usually has an Ali MacGraw-thing going on style-wise, but tonight her thick, dark hair is in a French twist, making her appear more grown-up than ever.

Toby takes one look at Naomi and groans, "People are going to think I'm your kid brother, again."

"At least she won't get proofed when we send her in to get a fifth," Arthur counters.

"I'm your gal Friday when it comes to buying booze," Naomi jokes. "Think of it, Saskia. By the time your day comes, I'll be legal."

"By the time that happens, you'll be in college," Saskia replies.

She is forever borrowing her sister's CoverGirl lipstick and peacock earrings, as though each item could instruct her in how to be prettier, worldlier, sophisticated-er, Naomi-er. She loves talking with Naomi in the dark before they go to sleep, and even though it bugs her sister that they share a room, it never bothers her.

She runs into the kitchen to say hello to Odessa, who is putting the finishing touches to dinner. Her appetite quickens as she smells burnt sugar and dives for one of the meringues that are cooling on the sideboard.

"Have you come in to tell me about your day or to paw at my food? Look with your eyes, child, not with your hands." Odessa's voice is stern but her eyes are not. They never are, and never have been in all the years she's cleaned for them. Her frosted orange lipstick and the burnished brown of her skin are as pretty to Saskia as a butterfly wing.

Odessa listens attentively while Saskia fills her in on how her pop science test went, while together they set the table for supper. Then Odessa puts the plates in the oven to warm and says, "Now go and call everyone for dinner."

Mom is in the bathroom, listening to classical radio while languishing in a Chanel-scented tub. Whenever she comes in to keep Mom company, Saskia feels as though she's entering a place where Mom is a woman first, and a mom second. Her mother's movements become sensual in the water, and she takes an almost girlish pleasure in her ablutions. Mom has a way of switching gears that can sometimes be abrupt, but she is always at her dreamiest here.

In the bathroom, they never talk about the boring day-to-day things like school, only the past. It's a door that Saskia never gets tired of opening. She's a junkie for Mom's stories about the horse she once had, the house she grew up in, and all the things she did before she and Daddy met.

Between Mom and Daddy, she has a world with two suns. Things can get overheated at times, but it never ceases to shine.

After dinner, Toby comes into her room to set up the portable TV in time for *The Wizard of Oz*. They usually watch something together on a Friday, but Naomi, Toby and Arthur are getting ready to leave and Mom is meeting Tom and Libby across the street for a party at the National Arts Club.

"Can Kathleen and me go to the movies tomorrow?" Saskia climbs under the covers.

"Kathleen and I." Mom strokes her daughter's forehead, her fingers cool to the touch. "I don't see why not."

The tumbling snow outside her bedside window makes Saskia all the more glad to be snuggled up in her flannel pajamas. She gazes at the bright stacks of windows that assemble her skyline and wonders which hospital floor Daddy is sleeping on tonight.

Arranging the pillows just so, she reaches for the graham crackers and cocoa on her bedside table as the credits on the TV screen roll. She drifts off to dream of Paris and peacock feathers as Dorothy clicks her heels and chants, "There's no place like home."

* * *

At 10:15 a.m. Saskia wakes with a start. For a moment, she panics about being late to school when she sees that Naomi's already risen, but then she remembers it's Saturday and lies back down. It's too early to call Kathleen, so she gazes outside the window at the sturdy troika of snow-covered water towers on the adjacent rooftop as the day begins to build itself around her.

She listens to find out who is up, but there's no breakfast radio or trace of voices, only the rhythmic rasp of a shovel scraping the sidewalk as someone clears a path on the street below. She stretches languidly, pushing her leg out from under the quilt to test the room's brisk temperature, then gets up to go to the bathroom that connects their bedroom to her brother's. Through the ajar door she can see Toby's empty bed, so she switches off his overhead light, flexing her toes as she walks to avoid the cold black-and-white-tiled floor.

The phone starts ringing but it stops just as she reaches the foyer. "Is anyone here?" she calls out.

Mom's pocketbook is gone. There's another in its place. But it's too matronly for Naomi and too cheap for Mom. She knows it's not Odessa's. She never works weekends and besides, she always uses the patent leather tote Saskia gave her for Christmas.

Confusion turns to joy when she spies Daddy's fedora and wallet on the hope chest. But her joy is disrupted by a glint of gold next to the hat. It's his wristwatch and wedding ring. Air seems to fall outside her body as she struggles to grasp why he's not wearing them. Her mind ripples in the space between seconds. Then a confused whimper escapes her.

The silence that follows curves her soul.

Her thoughts run cold as she whips around, trying to return to a moment that is no longer there.

She can make out that the dining room has been set for breakfast and food is on the table. But the scrambled eggs are hardened and the chairs are still tucked neatly in place. She bursts into the sun-spanked kitchen and promptly trips on the telephone cord that is stretched tautly from the wall socket to the inside of the maid's room.

She lands awkwardly and the space behind her eyes goes dark. From the floor, she sees the maid's room door open and cries out for Odessa. But the legs are white instead of black and the shoes aren't Naomi's or Mom's, they're Tilly's. As much as she loves Tilly, love has nothing to do with why her aunt is here, or why her face is wet with tears.

She instructs her mouth to form a question.

The answer is there, before Tilly says the two worst words, which Saskia doesn't need to hear anyway because she knows now that he's dead. Something older than existence itself has rolled over her life and rearranged it forevermore.

A garbled wail stuns the air. It's hers. As is the blood from her knees and the thud of her feet as she attempts to run from a day that has changed all her tomorrows.

Her legs leave her. Her ribs split with tears. Tilly wraps her in words that are useless. A door slams. Naomi and Toby are there now, their eyes leaking like stains, propping up Mom between them.

"What happened?" Saskia cries.

"There were complications—" Mom manages before collapsing as though drunk with despair.

"With the anesthetic and he never woke up." Toby finishes her sentence. The sentence finishes them. They've been plunged into a place where their grief has no corners.

* * *

If asked, Saskia couldn't recall when Oma arrived from Philadelphia, or where Tilly slept that first night after he died, or when Libby and Tom arrived, Libby in a fur coat flung over her nightie, having just heard the news. Saskia never saw a grown man cry until Tom broke down, and she never realized that crying could make your stomach hurt like it does when you laugh too much. She doesn't know what was said when her family grasped each other like buoys, as they weathered the wash of those liquid hours, where one world ended and another began.

Time behaves differently here. Hours no longer amount to days. Time has become units that she must bear, with each block heavier than the rest.

In this new place, promises are exchanged, love offered, loyalties pledged. Allegiances are formed. Oma, Tilly and Odessa work in unison to create order. Meals are prepared, baths drawn, arrangements duly made. She would laugh if it weren't so awful. As if she cared about what she wears, or who is notified.

Sorry becomes as predictable as *shocked*. Disembodied voices on the phone keep telling her, again and again, what a mensch Larry was. How friendly, how funny, how warm. She love-hates these people for telling her what she knows.

She is cold when indoors, hot on those few occasions when she ventures outdoors and is met with wet, sympathetic stares from Mikey or their neighbors. The Valentine's Day decorations in the lobby are a mockery. Love has no business flaunting itself in front of her.

Home is newly hollowed. It prickles with his absence and is rife with his presence. He is there and not there. In her head, he is everywhere. Fixing a highball. Listening to the radio while shaving. Watching the evening news.

Nights are restless. The images on the prints seem to move behind the frames. Shadows do ugly things when she wakes at odd intervals. She is too frightened by the sounds coming from Mom's room to brave going in there, so she takes to joining Tilly in the kitchen, where she invariably finds her drinking lemon tea while writing to inform their few remaining far-flung relatives of the news.

They wither in their grief. Mom's eyes grow fat from crying. Naomi's hair becomes lank and disheveled. Toby develops a spot that weeps with pus and Saskia bites her nails until they bleed. Oma, with the tenderness of a German Buddha, dutifully tries to nurture her daughter and grandchildren back into bloom.

Why? is the question that screams in her head and shrivels on her lips. *Why me,* is what Mom keeps asking through her tears. Only when the limousine comes to take them to the funeral service in Brooklyn does she see it.

She had let something loose by wanting to ride in one, and Daddy somehow paid the price for her terrible dream. A part of her is saying that's not logical, but a larger part is saying of course, that makes perfect sense, why would this have happened otherwise, with every thought hitting her harder than the next.

It is then that she swears to herself that she must do anything and everything to make them whole again. If she was responsible in any way for this, then her family's well-being is now her responsibility. For in letting the genie out of the bottle, she'd invited tragedy into their world.

* * *

On that first day back at school, when Kathleen waited on the corner to wordlessly hug her, Saskia said, "Watch me clear the room" before they went into their classroom. She was right. No one knew where to look.

She thought everyone would get used to her soon enough. Then she realized she was the one who couldn't get used to them. So she starts cutting school to walk the city instead.

It's so easy. She slips out of the house in her uniform

before Mom rises, with her jeans in her knapsack, and changes in the bathroom at a nearby coffee shop. Then she sets off for Kips Bay one day, Stuyvesant Square another.

She expects to be challenged, but never is, so she walks farther and farther, excavating the streets for traces of her dad, a Brooklyn native who once called this city his own. Often, she ends up in Central Park where the granite rocks protrude from the earth as though they were scattered vertebrae of the city. Once there, she spends her spare quarters on carousel rides, hugging the painted Arabian horse tightly as if it could carry her back to the perfection of her past.

But time is more patient than she can ever hope to be and Daddy is folded somewhere within it, leaving her to search alone for a New York that no longer exists.

2.

Make It a Double

Sundays, once Saskia's favorite day of the week, now seem a year long. Although it's been well over a month now since Daddy died, she still finds herself reaching for five placemats when it's her turn to set the table. Mealtimes are the worst. Everyone acting as though being a family of four were natural, when nothing is more absurd. This morning, no one has much appetite for bagels and smoked salmon, the *Times* goes unread, and at 4:00 p.m. she is still in her nightie, not having bothered to bathe. The rain, the shadow of her incomplete homework, and Toby's incessant piano practicing have made her edgy, yet listless.

She wonders if she can talk Mom into taking them to a movie at the Ziegfeld, and finds her on the phone in the dining room, with a near-empty wineglass in hand. Mom's eyes have that new mottled look that makes Saskia's stomach go all slippery. She crouches by the glass-paneled door to listen in, and hears Mom exclaim, "Stop living my life for me. I know what I'm doing."

She can tell that Mom is speaking to Oma, who took the train down from Philadelphia yesterday to spend the day viewing properties in Westchester, since she is of the opinion that New York is dirty, dangerous, and no fit place for a widow to bring up children.

Saskia liked some of the houses, particularly the four-bedroom in Croton-on-Hudson. It would be just perfect if they could transplant it to Manhattan, but Mom viewed it with her chin tipped in disdain. Oma was supposed to drive back with them and spend the weekend, but when Mom told her that she'd sooner grow a second head than leave the city—and besides, how could she be expected to run the gallery if they moved to the suburbs? Oma insisted that Mom should just drop her off at the train station instead.

The gallery is now the tug of war between them, and much as Saskia is loath to take sides, take sides she must. Mom has chosen to keep Daddy's business going and in doing so, she declines an offer to buy out the stock. And in doing that, Mom has sided against her mother.

The decision hasn't been easy. Saskia can feel Mom zip herself up every time she leaves for the gallery. She can see the effort that's involved in her getting out the door each day after a fitful night's sleep. Her porcelain skin breaks out in hives and her lips become jagged. She can hear the gravel in her voice when she exchanges pleasantries with their neighbors. Mom is still Mom in public, but the Mom who trudges in the door each night seems exhausted by her charade, and interested only in taking to bed.

Even the simple things that Mom used to enjoy doing at home, like making breakfast or overseeing their morning routine, seem to bewilder or frustrate her. The day she left the pan on the flame until the ceiling blackened became the day they stopped having eggs in the morning. How she keeps it together outside is one thing. How she lets go of pieces of their home life is another. On the occasions when Saskia has gone to pick up Mom after work, she's felt as though she were looking at a still life of someone she used to know.

Watching Mom getting all tangled once again makes her get tangled, too. She can't ask anything of this sad, strained stranger and keeps waiting for her lovely, feisty mommy to return. She trudges back down the corridor to her bedroom. She used to get splinters from dashing down the hall, but the thought of running is about as inviting as the algebra homework that awaits her, so she opens the lid of her dressing-up box instead.

She always let her reading list determine her course of play, imagining herself as a March sister after finishing *Little Women* or gazing at the sky outside her window like Anne in Amsterdam. But today, she's not after those clothes. She's after Daddy's button-down cardigan secreted in the bottom of the box. But it's no longer there.

Naomi comes into their bedroom to fetch a textbook from her desk and sees the open lid. It speaks without them having to. Naomi retrieves the cardigan from her bottom drawer, then they slump together, their thoughts enmeshed in the lifeless assemblage of wool splayed between them on the bed.

The phone rings; voices are raised. Toby stops playing the piano. A door slams. The bedroom air sags as they try to interpret these disparate signals.

"Do you think that's Mom?" Saskia asks, when she detects a muffled sob.

"No, it's Betty Ford," Naomi says tightly.

These days, conversations with Naomi are like climbing a rubber ladder. It never bends in the direction she thinks it will. "For real. Should we see if she's okay?"

"I can tell you the answer to that already."

"If you won't, then I will." Saskia gets up to sneak down the hallway to Mom's bedroom. From behind the closed door, she can hear Mom crying and Toby speaking in soothing tones. Frustration grips her. She wants to be the one who can comfort her mother, as well as the one who is comforted by her mother. If she can't have her *father*, then at least she wants her *mother*.

She runs back to their room, craving her sister's certainty. "Will she ever be like she was before?"

"Of course she'll be," Naomi says automatically, getting up to retrieve her textbook.

Her thoughts fall backward. She can't see above anything anymore, now that her world is on its side. She can't understand how Naomi manages to remain upright while she's still all inside out.

"Don't treat me like a baby!" Saskia exclaims. "Tell me what you really think, for once."

They used to talk in the dark before going to sleep most nights, but Naomi would rather fake-sleep than engage nowadays. Her outburst works. Naomi sits back down beside her and says, "I don't know what we are. I can't see it yet."

"Why doesn't Tilly come over any longer?" Saskia hasn't seen her aunt since the funeral, nearly five weeks now.

"Mom can't handle her."

Tilly was an aunt and grandma rolled into one, since Daddy's parents passed. It was Tilly who always took her shopping at S. Klein, and it was Tilly who took them to see the Rockettes at Radio City Music Hall. And now it is Tilly who is on the outs.

"How do you keep it together?" Saskia asks.

"Together?" Naomi chews a strand of her hair. "Hardly."

"But you seem the same around your friends."

"Apart from Arthur, I wouldn't call them my friends anymore. Their idea of being nice is to act like nothing's changed."

Saskia tries to arrange these notions in her head and feels them sliding away from her again. "Are we really going to move to Westchester?"

"Trust me, we're not going anywhere."

"What will Oma say?"

"Oh, she'll kick up a fuss until she comes up with some other idea. I know she loves us and wants what's best, but us? In the 'burbs? Shit stinks for a reason."

"I guess so." Saskia sits up and wipes her eyes. "I just want it to be like before."

"Just because it's different, doesn't mean we're different. This is still us." Naomi's voice grows husky. "And that will always be the same."

* * *

Saskia awakens to the news on her clock radio that the Vietnam War has ended. She always imagined it would be like a scene out of *Hair*, with hippies kissing hard hats and a Fifth Avenue ticker-tape parade. But it's like any other morning. She eats a bowl of Cheerios while watching breakfast TV, then calls Odessa, who will be thrilled since her nephew is serving in the armed forces. But there's no reply. Saskia loves Odessa and misses not having her around every day when she returns from school, now that they've had to save money by cutting her hours to just one shift a week.

She pictures how delighted Daddy would have been to see this day. Before their dog Pablo died of old age, they attached an "Out Now" button to his leash and went on many anti-war demonstrations. Daddy liked to rib his conservative mother-in-law by reminding her that he was responsible for registering Mom as the first Democrat in her staunchly Grand Old Party family. I should be happy for this, she thinks as she detaches the Peter Max *Peace on Earth* card, which graced the refrigerator for years, to add to her scrapbook in her bedroom.

She lies back down and plays the game she started weeks ago. She anticipates the moment she should start getting ready for school, then lets it slide. Another one slips by too. She wishes now she'd studied for today's math test, bathed last night, and bothered to untangle her hair. Units that once stacked neatly are no longer square.

Mom has already left to meet the bookkeeper at the gallery, Toby stayed over at Arthur's, and Naomi—who had Mom write her a bogus sick note—has crashed out in the maid's room. Her once on-it Mom is now working Mom, and that Mom has no compunctions about covering for her kids' skipping school, so long as they put in a few hours for her at the gallery.

Through the bedroom window, morning looks like dusk. The city roils in the gloom of the newly extended daylight savings time. An energy crisis exists outside, torpor inside. She realizes it's her third day without a bath so she anoints herself with Naomi's Jean Nate, then grabs a couple of Pop-Tarts and legs it to school, late again.

She envies her classmates who have a Pet Rock, a Hamptons beach house, and a father to tuck them in. Self-pity is the only subject now in which she shines. February's flurry of sympathy had dissipated by Easter. Spring may be approaching, but she feels cold with longing inside.

She misses Kathleen terribly. After her dad was mugged at gunpoint on the subway, he accepted a new job and they took part in the Great White Flight from Manhattan and upped it to San Jose. Mom lets her phone her only once a week, and only for fifteen minutes. Kathleen had been her best friend and her best chance at passing eighth-grade math. Without Kathleen there to generously supply the answers, any hope is gone.

The teacher circulates the exam paper. Variables and

expressions are meaningless. X equals gobbledygook. She's flunked before she begins. She can't stomach the idea of comparing test notes with her classmates in the cafeteria, so she surreptitiously eats her Pop-Tarts in the library as she peruses the fiction section for the latest Judy Blume.

After the last bell rings, she walks down Madison and lingers on the corner near the Browning School, hoping to maybe catch the eye of some nice boy—any boy, really. When she did this before with Kathleen it was all in fun, daring each other to strike up a conversation with a guy their age. But now that she knows the power of pity, she thinks if she could just get past the hello, she would be able to seduce them with her sadness. But so far, all of the smartly dressed boys in blue blazers have ignored her dumb, grey heart.

She continues down the avenue to Vidal Sassoon, where she watches a lady getting styled. She keeps looking for a sign that the war is really over, but all she sees is the echo of death—in the numbers tattooed on the elderly Jewish news vendor's forearm, in the hooded eyes of the Madison Avenue matriarchs being wheeled around on their assisted afternoon stroll, in the framed photos of the Vietnam vets that decorate so many liquor store windows in Manhattan.

Time gets tricky when she arrives at the gallery. Being there now never ceases to confuse her; the space seems to hold things that are no longer tangible. It even smells different, as though something old had been forgotten there.

She finds Naomi listening to her transistor radio while she minds the place on her own. "Where's Mom?"

"She's at Elizabeth Arden's Red Door Salon, having a cut and blow dry." Naomi slowly turns a page of *Rolling Stone* magazine.

"Really?" Saskia says, wishing Mom had invited her along. "That's nice."

"Yeah. Ten-dollars nice. Aren't we supposedly economizing?"

Saskia picks at the remains of Naomi's pastrami club. "Do you need me?"

"Does it look like I do? Being here is like being on board the *Mary Celeste*. The only person who came in today was the mailman, who made me sign for this." Naomi hands Saskia an envelope. Its lightness is deceiving. "Overdue" is stamped in red across it, making it heavy to the touch.

"I don't get it. How did Daddy do it?"

"Have you ever seen Mom try to make a sale?" Naomi pulls the club sandwich back. "She wasn't raised to talk about money. It's a foreign language for her."

"She's doing her best," Saskia says.

"Don't get me wrong. I know, but she doesn't have his know-how."

"Maybe she'll hire someone."

"And pay them with what, wampum?" Naomi shakes her head. "I saw the last bank statement. There're barely two sticks to rub together."

When money's not confusing her, it's troubling her. Dollars don't make sense. Old, new, ready money or not, somehow, they always had that in-between money that came from these very sheets of paper hanging on the gallery walls. Sure, some months were better than others, but even then, there always seemed to be enough.

"What difference does it make? Mom has money."

"You mean Oma has money."

Saskia's not sure what Naomi's implying, so she asks, "Doesn't that make it hers?"

Naomi sighs and starts again. "Were you dropped on your head when you were a baby? By that logic then, give me your amethyst ring."

"But it's mine," Saskia exclaims.

"You see my point?"

Saskia sulks, out-Naomied once again. "Didn't Mom get anything when Grandpa died?"

"That was ages ago and even if she did, you can bet your bottom dollar it's long gone."

This talk makes her head thrum. She downs the last of Naomi's soda and asks, "What's Toby doing later?"

"Your guess is as good as mine," Naomi replies, with her head down in the magazine. Saskia waits for the pulse of conversation to pick up. They flatline. So, she leaves.

When she gets home, she sneaks a long-distance phone call to Kathleen but gets no answer. Odessa telephones to invite Saskia to a dinner in celebration of her nephew's imminent return, but she knows Mom would never in a million years let her take a taxi by herself to Harlem.

She wanted the day the war ended to be outstanding, something she could tell her grandchildren about, but it was memorable only for its mediocrity.

* * *

Saskia is awakened by the sound of talking and creeps down the darkened hallway in her flowered nightgown to peer into the dining room where Mom, Toby, and Naomi are grouped around the table. Something about their hushed tone makes her draw back to observe them, unseen.

"How do you propose we tell Saskia?" Mom asks. "How can we break it to her that Daddy isn't really dead?"

"You should have thought of that before, shouldn't you?" Toby replies.

"Shut up, Toby," Naomi retorts. "Mom's right, for once. What are we going to say?"

"Give me a second guys. I'm almost there," Daddy calls from the kitchen.

Saskia cries out in ecstasy and starts running to him just as she awakens with a jolt. It's the second time she's dreamt he's still alive, until the realization that he's dead destroys her all over again.

Today is her fourteenth birthday. She's been dreading this for months and now that it's here, she's about as happy as a Kosher Jew at a crab bake.

She traipses to the kitchen to find that Mom has set the table with their best china and a vase of daisies in her honor. "Let me be the first to wish you a happy birthday," Mom says, but her upbeat tone jars with the shadows around her eyes.

Saskia sits down to eat the blueberry pancakes that Mom has made. By the time Naomi and Toby awaken, the second round of pancakes is on the table.

Mom had offered to take Saskia and her friends to lunch and the movie of her choice. But she's in-between friendship groups at present, so it's just going to be them. She asked Mom if Tilly could come instead, but Mom had chosen, in that way that she has, not to hear her. Max's Kansas City had been Saskia's favorite restaurant, but the dining area of the steak house was taken over by the bar the year before, so instead she decided they should go and see *The Return of the Pink Panther* and have lunch afterward at Serendipity.

Everyone helps clear the table, then Naomi and Saskia adjourn to get dressed, while Elton John's *Captain Fantastic* album plays. After spending ages in front of the mirror with a comb and a jar of Dippity-do, Saskia thinks she might even pass for pretty in her lavender culottes and neatly curled hair.

She goes to get Mom from her bedroom. The curtains are drawn and there's an empty wineglass by her bed. This is not good. Mom is lying down, clad only in her slip, with her dark hair looking liked dried blood against the white of the pillowcase.

Saskia can feel the sorrow hovering, piñata-like, and sets about to punch Mom free.

Mom sits up, with eyes that aren't there. "I was just having a lie-down."

"Don't worry. We have loads of time." Saskia goes to the closet and picks out the prettiest summer dress she can find hanging alongside Daddy's clothes, which have yet to be boxed and disposed of.

Mom pulls away when Saskia tries to feed her arms through the sleeves. "I'm perfectly capable of getting dressed by myself. You don't have to 'bring up' Mother."

"I'm sorry, I was just trying—"

"No. I'm the one who's sorry." Mom looks away, and then the words seem to slide from her mouth. "Promise you won't end up like me when you grow up."

"Don't ever say that again. You're the most beautiful, bestest mother in the whole wide world." Saskia hopes that one of her compliments will hit the mark.

One of them does. Those exquisite threads that are invisible to everyone but her, joins them once again. She has snipped Mom's sorrow and released her from her bind, for now at least.

Mom goes to the dressing table to fix her hair and says,

"Do you want to help me pick out some earrings?"

Saskia sifts through Mom's velvet jewelry box, like she's done a thousand times before, but not once since Daddy died.

"How about these?" Saskia holds up a pair of jade teardrops.

"You always know which ones go best with my outfit," Mom says, as if remembering her cue.

She slips the post through Mom's lobe. "When can I get my ears pierced?"

"Asking me again won't change my mind." Mom's smile is wan, but at least she's smiling. "You know perfectly well that I won't let you do so until you're sixteen."

Mom selects a pearl-embossed locket from her jewelry box and holds it up. "What do you think of this?"

Saskia nods, buttoning her excitement. "You know I've always loved that."

"I'm wondering what price it would fetch in auction." Mom puts the locket back and closes the lid.

Stupid me, Saskia thinks. Everything and every day is different now.

"Now, let's go and see about those presents in the living room," Mom says.

Saskia unwraps the parcels that are waiting for her on the coffee table, taking care so that they can use the paper again. There is a copy of *Jonathan Livingston Seagull* and the 45 of 10cc's "I'm Not in Love" from her siblings, along with a poster of Redford from *The Way We Were*. Then she opens Mom's package to find a secondhand copy of the complete works of William Shakespeare, a collection of postcards from the Met, and a comb. She stares at the items as though they're food stamps. They must really be poor now if it's come to this.

"I found the book in the laundry room," Mom says. "Can you believe someone would throw away such a treasure?"

Maybe it's really a treasure that she can sell at the Strand. Maybe Mom can't afford to take them out. Maybe she was wrong to ask for so much, when there is so little left to give. Saskia conceals her confusion with kisses and reminds everyone that they need to leave the house in five minutes to get to the movie on time.

Mom offers to get the station wagon and drive them, but since it's parked on Eighth they decide to take the Third Avenue bus to the Paris Theatre instead. Saskia secures a window seat next to Naomi and watches the sweaty-looking pedestrians avoiding the gusts of steam from the sidewalk grates. While the bus is stalled in midtown traffic, she thinks back to her birthday last June. Mom had brought her breakfast in bed, then let her pick out two pairs of shoes at Best & Co. They'd gone to see *Gypsy* on Broadway, and on the weekend, she'd had a slumber party.

She is snapped back to the present when Curt, her classmate Esmé's square-jawed brother, boards the bus on Forty-Fourth Street. Curt was always nice enough when she'd gone to Esmé's, but she's afraid of looking dumb as a box if she says hi. So she sits there, hoping he might notice her as the blocks tick by.

By the time they reach Fifty-Eighth Street, her thighs are so sweaty that when she stands up they rub against the seat and emit a loud farting noise. Curt looks up, catches her eye, and blanks her.

"Nice one," Naomi teases as they exit the bus.

"Shut up," Saskia retorts, wondering if the day will ever come when she won't feel like she is roadkill to the opposite sex.

When they reach the Paris, Mom spies the marquee and stops short. "Oh, goodness. They're playing *One Flew over the Cuckoo's Nest* instead of *The Pink Panther.*"

"Didn't you check the listings?" Naomi asks.

"Of course I did," Mom says with pointed pride. "What shall we do now?"

They decide to see it anyway. Saskia sits between Mom and Toby and is soon captivated by McMurphy's plight. She begins to sob when the Chief smothers him, horrified that a soul can be extinguished not once but twice. Her mind tips to Daddy and those seconds that yanked him away from time.

"It's just a movie, kid," Toby whispers, squeezing her shoulder. "Don't let it get you down."

When the lights come up, she's unable to control her tears, which threaten to develop into a full-fledged crying jag.

"Good call, Mom," Toby says as the theater empties and the usher starts sweeping up the popcorn from the aisles.

"It's not my fault the newspaper was incorrect." Mom sips her breath. "You can't blame everything on me."

"How old are you today?" Naomi ribs Saskia as they exit the Paris.

"Just leave me alone."

Saskia stops to tie her shoe while Toby, Mom, and Naomi cross the street before the light changes, leaving her on the corner of Fifth. Head humming from the humidity, she spots them waiting by a Good Humor truck, looking drained. She sees that the day is taking it out of them. It's taking what's left of them. The four of them keep eddying away. What joins them is fragile, and birthday or any day, she will have to work to keep them together.

When they arrive at Serendipity, the hostess tells them there will be a short wait for their table, so Saskia goes to the bathroom to coax her hair, with which the humidity has played havoc, into something resembling curls. "Today is the first day of the rest of my life," she intones to her mirrored reflection, trying to find inspiration in the Total breakfast cereal jingle.

"For god's sake, what took you so long? You just missed him," Naomi says breathlessly when Saskia rejoins her family.

"Missed who?"

"Your secret admirer," Toby says archly. "A little bird must have told him it's your birthday."

"*What* are you talking about?"

"Robert Redford was just here with his daughters. That's why our table was late," Toby replies.

Saskia bolts outside and scrambles past the delighted onlookers who have stopped to gape at Redford. She climbs an adjacent stoop and spots him in sunglasses, T-shirt and jeans, holding hands with Shauna and Amy, who are carrying Bloomingdale's shopping bags.

In the giddy balance of a second, Saskia believes that Redford—being the true star that he is—will see through the rusted universe of her soul and make her shine again. But Redford follows his daughters into a Checker cab and she's left with the awful knowledge that she'll never set foot in Utah, meet Paul Newman, or be anything other than the dull nobody that she is.

"Did you get his autograph?" Toby teases when Saskia returns to the table.

"Get lost," Saskia snaps, as she slumps back in her seat.

"Don't get sore, kiddo. I was just kidding," Toby cajoles.

"Come on," Naomi says. "He didn't mean it. Just—"

"Act my age and not my shoe size." Saskia finishes the sentence for her.

"Don't let a piece of paper get you down," Mom says and offers her a glass. "Here, we ordered you a root beer float."

"I don't like root beer anymore," Saskia pouts and shakes her head no.

"Since when?" Mom asks.

"Since ages now," Saskia says, without knowing why. "Please, we don't have to do this if it's too much."

"What are you getting at?"

"You know. Movies, lunch, the works. It must cost a lot."

"Meaning?" Mom smiles, but her eyes don't.

"Nothing." Something tightens and then rucks between them. "Just forget I ever said anything."

When the waitress comes to take the order, Mom asks for a scotch instead of food and then bristles when Toby gives her a look. "What?"

"I can't help but notice you've been drinking more," Toby says hesitantly.

"Says our resident pothead over here."

"I admit I like to smoke sometimes—"

"As in most times? Just 'cause I choose to turn a blind eye to your habit, doesn't give you the right to judge my little indulgences."

Toby flushes, then gathers himself. "Wise words, Mom. I'll remember that the next time I add another bottle of Mr. Walker to your account."

There's a choked silence when the waitress brings them their order.

"Are you sure you're not hungry?" Naomi asks Mom. "You could have some of my club sandwich if you like."

"Or my salad," Toby adds.

Mom gives them a waxy smile and thirstily sips her drink.

Saskia mechanically tucks into her burger, having lost her appetite. She wishes they were at the original Max's, eating their signature steaks served by mini-skirted waitresses in fishnets. When she was five, she wanted to be a waitress at Max's when she grew up. Now that she's fourteen, all she wants is to be back at the table where she sat when she was five.

"Hey, don't you think you should slow down?" Toby suggests, when Mom signals the waitress for a refill.

"If you insist." Mom demurely cancels the order. Then her expression recalibrates and she calls out to the retreating waitress. "On second thought, make it a double."

"But Mom—" Toby starts.

"No one tells me what to do. I'm not some sad sack you can push around," Mom exclaims. "You all act like I'm incapable of making an adult decision."

"He wasn't saying that," Naomi intervenes.

"Then what was he implying?" Mom asks.

"All he meant was that if Daddy were here—"

"But he's not, is he?" Mom's voice catches. "I didn't ask to become a widow. I never wanted this."

"We were just—" Toby starts.

"Oh, spare me your judgment and 'concerns.'" Mom turns on Saskia. "And that goes for you too."

"Who, me?" Saskia protests. "I didn't say anything."

"You don't have to. I can feel your anxiety rolling off you in giant waves." Mom knocks back her double when it arrives, then continues. "I know things aren't exactly up to par, but I'm trying my best. The least you can do is give me credit for that and stop fussing and clucking around me."

After they get the check, Mom springs for a cab and insists on sitting up front with the driver. When they get home, they scatter to their separate rooms. Naomi and Toby light a bong while Saskia looks for Redford articles in her back issues of *People* magazine.

When Kathleen calls to wish her a happy birthday, Saskia adopts an upbeat tone as she tells her friend about her celebrity sighting, but as soon as she gets off the phone she wads up her new Redford poster and throws it out.

* * *

Sure as shit, Saskia fails math, which kisses any hope of getting into Spence or Hewitt goodbye. Faced with the choice of attending summer school or being left back, she convinces Mom that it's more important to let her help pack up the gallery than to make her finish off the last three days of a school that she's flunked out of.

Their annual summer rental in Cape May had already been shelved when Mom admitted defeat and gave up the lease on the gallery. She'd put the remaining stock in auction, but it hadn't met the reserve so she ended up being lowballed by a fellow dealer who bought her out. There was even talk of placing the kids in public school, but after much discussion it was agreed that they'd drain what was left in their savings instead, and that Toby, who was supposed to be majoring in Journalism at Northwestern, would transfer to Columbia to save on living costs.

Toby's graduation trip to Paris, which he'd been planning with Arthur since they were sophomores, was also pulled at the eleventh hour. Toby bravely declared that it was no biggie, Paris will be there "Seine time next year," but he became sad-eyed, with a smile now faint as the Mona Lisa's.

So now, armed with a checkbook and her middling school report, Mom dons a linen suit and pearls and takes Saskia on an SOS tour of private schools that might, just might, accept her mathematically challenged daughter. Mom strikes a deal with the flirtatious dean at Dalton that Saskia can go there if she repeats eighth grade, but Saskia flat-out refuses.

After working their way through the A- and B-list schools, they taxi it to the Village to grab a burger at Joe Junior and then head to the Collective, a progressive school which is their last resort. As they walk past Saint Vincent's Hospital they gag from the heady whiff of garbage fermenting in the sunshine. All the sanitation services have been interrupted now that the city is poised on the verge of bankruptcy, and Saskia, like every other New Yorker, is still smarting from President Ford's recent decision to veto any emergency funding, resulting in the *Daily News* headline "Ford to City: Drop Dead."

"Mom, are you sure we have the right address?" Saskia regrets having chosen to wear her Laura Ashley pinafore when she sees a few straggly-dressed teens hanging out on a stoop. She detects the scent of pot as they wind their way through the sloped bodies on the steps, and blushes, convinced that these hippies and stoners are laughing at her girly getup.

Approaching the teachers seated around the communal desk in the front office, Saskia braces herself while Mom turns on her twin beams of class and charm. "Tracy, Emerson." Mom greets them and motions for her to come forward. "I'd like you to meet my daughter Saskia."

She nods shyly at Tracy, who is seated on the far side of the desk, wearing a burgundy pants suit with an air of easy élan. Then she shakes hands with Emerson, who has a hairy mole, silver ponytail, and nicotine-stained fingernails.

"Pleased to meet you, mm—I mean, the pleasure's mine," sputters Saskia, transfixed by this fiercely androgynous creature.

"We go by first names here. It's just Emerson. Come, I'll show you around while your mom has a chat with Tracy."

Saskia follows Emerson up two flights of stairs to the top floor. The Collective consists of three classrooms, plus a library-cum-music room, and an art studio. The middle floor is rented to a cooking school, so the entire building is permeated with the scent of burnt cheese.

"What do you think?" Emerson asks when they enter the art studio to find a nude man being sketched by the class.

Saskia blushes and averts her eyes from the model's mushroom-like prick. "It sure makes a change from doing still lifes."

"We believe that learning comes in a variety of forms and is best experienced in an atmosphere of self-respect and tolerance. At the Collective, the students are the school. They don't just go here." Emerson brings her into an empty classroom to continue their conversation. "The life model was the kids' idea. He's pretty nifty, don't you think?"

Saskia smooths the folds in her paisley pinafore and thinks, maybe I should repeat eighth grade after all.

Emerson lights a Winston and extends the pack to Saskia. "Tell me about yourself."

Saskia has never seen a teacher smoke in a classroom, let alone been offered a cigarette by one, and primly shakes her head. "I don't smoke."

"Aren't you a good girl," Emerson says with a chuckle. "Do you like school?"

She shrugs and discreetly focuses on whether she can

detect the outline of breasts under Emerson's button-down shirt.

"I met your father once," Emerson continues.

This grabs her. "What?"

"He helped me appraise a print I inherited. I found him to be a most pleasant and knowledgeable man."

"Did he say anything about me?" Saskia clutches at Daddy-sized straws.

"Well, not that I can recall."

The ivy outside the window blurs as hot tears swarm Saskia's eyes.

"But now that you mention it, I can see that you're your father's daughter. You have a way about you that speaks of him," Emerson quickly adds.

She blinks, trying to compose herself. After a morning of viewing private schools, potheads, and a prick, she's a nervous wreck.

"You must miss him terribly."

"Something awful," Saskia confesses.

"Benjamin Franklin said that many people die at twenty-five and aren't buried until they are seventy-five. You don't want that for yourself, do you?"

She shakes her head, as the tears find their well-worn exit and course down her cheeks.

"I'm not in the business of peddling big promises, but if you decide to come here, I can assure you we'll do our best to help you find your feet. Your life is never going to be the same again, and neither are you. Do you have anything you'd like to ask?"

She hesitates, then spies Emerson's gold band. "So you're married?"

"That wasn't the question I was expecting," Emerson laughs. "But yes, my husband and I have been together now for thirty-five years. Anything else?"

She shakes her head, having ascertained that her teacher-to-be isn't a man, but a hirsute and sympathetic woman.

* * *

Saskia watches from the hood of the family station wagon as a workman finishes scratching Daddy's gilded name off the gallery window and proceeds to paste an Under New Management sign in its place. She slides off the hood and goes to the driver's side window to check on Mom, who is staring ahead impassively from the front seat.

"Can't you see she needs a minute?" Naomi says and pulls Saskia toward the pile of boxes scattered on the curb.

"We have to put on a good face for Mom," Toby adds, as he wraps the cord around the radio and loads it into the trunk. "Go see if we left anything behind."

Saskia runs through the gallery to the office to look for any forgotten items, but the dusty bookshelves are empty and there are only luminous patches, as if marked by an invisible weight, where the lithographs and prints once hung. She rummages through Daddy's desk drawers, which yield some pencils and a dried-out rubber stamp, and feels a colorless subtraction in the stillness.

A moving man pushing a dolly comes in and starts wrapping Daddy's desk chair, which followed him from Brooklyn, where he started off in overalls as a framer's apprentice. Then he graduated to selling art books before working his way up to opening his own gallery on Madison Avenue and having his suits made. "Think Yiddish and dress British" had always been

Daddy's mantra for running his printed empire.

She presses the room's impression to her heart one last time and walks past the foreman, who has started ripping out the glass-fronted vitrines to make way for the boutique that has taken over the lease.

By the time she reaches their double-parked car on Madison, another piece of her life has been dismantled.

* * *

"For Christ's sake, Mom, you've got to signal before you change lanes." Toby recoils as their station wagon sweeps in the path of an oncoming sixteen-wheeler.

Mom, who is perched on the edge of the driver's seat clutching the wheel like it's a buoy, winces as the truck driver leans on his horn.

Saskia checks to see that her seat belt is fastened while she memorizes Toby's verbal instructions in case Mom needs backup. She has to go to the bathroom badly, but she's not about to admit this since they're already over an hour late. They're meeting Oma at her friends' house and spending the night at a local inn, since Oma thought a change of scene would do them good. They'd planned on having an early start to avoid the Fourth of July weekend traffic, but didn't squeak out of the house until past eleven.

Saskia had woken first and found Mom asleep in her room with the bedside light and TV on. With Mom's sleep patterns out the window, she's become a broken cuckoo clock who makes Jell-O at midnight, irons at 3:00 a.m., and listens to the radio at all hours.

Saskia ran out to the grocery store when she saw they were flat out of food. Then she came home and turned her radio on at full blast to get her siblings out of bed. Toby and Naomi used to be circumspect about smoking pot when Daddy was around to put his foot down. But the inmates are running the institution nowadays, so their bong keeps on burning like the eternal flame on Kennedy's grave.

They miss their exit and drive to the nearest Howard Johnson parking lot to turn around. Then they pull off the highway to pass through sleepy Pennsylvania Dutch townships, adorned with red, white, and blue bunting and American flags.

They stop at the traffic light next to a buggy carrying a Mennonite family. She stares through the window at a girl in a lavender-checked bonnet who looks to be her age, with a hefty toddler seated on her knee. The girl gazes back, with confidence. Her lucidity unnerves Saskia, who feels like a fish bumping up against the glass walls of a mucky tank.

The first time she saw Mennonites was when Oma took her to a farmers' market and she'd viewed their old-world habits with city-girl pity. But from where she's sitting now, their way of life looks good. She wishes she had a baby brother sitting on her lap and can practically smell the boy's musky hair as she imagines what his wriggling mass must feel like.

Mom crunches the gears when the light changes and stalls the car, causing Toby to sip his breath in exasperation. As the buggy pulls away, the Mennonite girl smiles sympathetically and raises her hand in parting. Saskia feels an inexplicable pang of longing. She used to think privilege was about what she had. Now she aches for the privilege of knowing where she belongs. A Mennonite who she once would have thought of as having nothing has more than her.

They finally locate the address of their Oma's friends and tumble out of the car, clothes crumpled from the journey.

Saskia is first to the porch, decorated with miniature flags, a dried-flower display, and an "Ain't God Good" sticker. She rings the doorbell and a bespectacled middle-aged man answers. Before he can even say hello, Saskia blurts that she needs the toilet and is shown to the bathroom.

After washing her hands and inspecting the toiletries, she retraces her steps to the porch. The man and his comely wife are deep in conversation with Mom, whose face is creased with worry. Saskia hurries over to join Toby and Naomi and to see what the problem is.

"But I simply don't understand. My mother should be here." Mom pulls a letter from her pocketbook and hands it to the man of the house. "This is the correct address, is it not?"

The man sucks his bottom lip while he adjusts his glasses to study the sheet of paper. "Well, according to this here address, it would appear that this is the right street. But I'm afraid that we're in Middletown, Pennsylvania. Your ma must be waiting for you in Middletown, New Jersey."

Saskia would like to leak through the floorboards and grabs Toby's arm to plug her embarrassment. She catches the man's wife taking in Toby's frayed chinos and Naomi's stained miniskirt with concern and, for the second time in an hour, senses a stranger's pity.

"Why, you must all be terribly hungry after your journey. Can I offer you some refreshments?" the wife says warmly, taking off her daisy print apron. "I made a fresh batch of cupcakes this morning."

Saskia's stomach rumbles at the suggestion of a sugar rush, but she tugs at Mom's arm, willing her to leave.

"That's very kind, but we mustn't keep my mother waiting any longer," Mom says, fumbling for her sunglasses in her pocketbook. "Thank you for showing such patience and hospitality."

Head held high, Mom marches back to the station wagon with her kids straggling behind her and even manages a jaunty wave goodbye, but wilts as soon as the car door slams shut. She starts the car without stalling, but as soon as they're on the main road, she pulls over and starts to cry.

"It's okay, Mom. It could happen to anyone. I bet you anything it happens all the time," Saskia beseeches from the back seat.

"What are you going to tell Oma?" Toby says, fiddling with his cowlick.

"I don't know what I'm going to tell her." Mom hits the dashboard in frustration. "I don't even know how long it will take us to get to New Jersey."

"But what about—"

"Gosh darn it, Toby. I don't have all the answers. Just give me a blessed minute."

Toby looks like he wants to say something else, but instead he gets out of the car and disappears into the cornfield by the side of the road.

"I better go see how he is." Naomi follows suit, stumbling in her haste to join her big brother.

Saskia clambers into the front seat and takes Mom's hand. "Everything is going to be okay." She feels like Pinocchio. "I'll always be here for you." Her nose recedes.

"It's far from okay. It's about as far from okay as it gets," Mom confesses. "Nowadays I feel like I'm never coming back and this is the state of things for the rest of my life."

"It will get back to normal soon, Mom." Words once large seem small. "I promise."

"Really?" Mom laughs harshly and takes off her sunglasses, allowing her to bury her head in her arms against the steering wheel. "Don't you get it? This *is* our new normal."

Saskia shoos a mosquito from Mom's neck. "There must be something I can do."

Mom shakes her head, overcome. Then she says in a pained tone, "Just need me less, and help me more."

Mom seems to detach herself. A cold rush of strangeness brushes their commonality aside. Saskia waits until she can wait no more, and then punctures the clammy silence. "I'm going to go and look for Toby and Naomi."

Mom acknowledges her comment with a weary wave of her hand.

Saskia gets out of the car and plunges into the verdant rows of corn that are taller than her. Rustling stalks and the occasional drone of flies soon surround her, yet no matter how far she walks, she doesn't seem to be making progress.

Her foot feels like it's being licked. She looks down to see a snake slithering across her sandal. She doesn't know a copperhead from a cottonmouth and breaks into a run, only to trip and cut her leg on a patch of dried bramble. The sight of blood makes her woozy but she gets up and staggers ahead, struggling to find her sense of direction, until she bursts screaming through the perimeter of the cornfield.

Toby, Mom, and Naomi look up from the map that's spread out on the car hood and run over to comfort her, but their concern soon gives way to teasing.

"Lions and tigers and bears, oh my!" Toby laughs at her dramatic account of perceived danger, while Naomi plucks corn sheath from her sister's hair.

"But it may have been poisonous," Saskia protests, relieved

that everyone's talking to one another again.

"My goodness." Mom dabs Saskia's cut with a moistened hankie before motioning everyone to get back into the car. "What a commotion over a harmless grass snake."

"Go left . . . I mean right . . . I mean straight ahead," Toby joshes at the junction.

"Yeah, Mom. I believe there's a Middletown, Connecticut, too, we might as well do a tour of the entire Eastern Seaboard," Naomi chimes in, ever her brother's Ed McMahon.

"If it's all the same to you, I've lost my appetite for this venture," Mom admits. "Why don't we just head back to the city and call it a day."

"We have to let Oma know. Otherwise she'll think the worst," Saskia says.

Mom pulls into a gas station and heads to the phone booth with a stack of dimes after giving the kids money for ice creams. By the time she returns, they've eaten the cones and pooled their change for a box of Ring Dings. Mom won't say how the phone call with Oma went, but her smudged mascara says it all. Then they climb into the car to boomerang back to Manhattan.

By the time they reach the approach to the Lincoln Tunnel, the first firework of the evening is etched between the distant silhouettes of the World Trade Center and Empire State Building. Once they pull up to their building, Mom announces she's opting for an early night instead of going to Libby and Tom's annual July Fourth party, while Toby and Naomi beg off to go say goodbye to Arthur, who is leaving for Paris the following day.

Saskia waits in front of their building while Mom parks the car and watches Toby and Naomi recede into the bustling city streets. Ever since Daddy died, they've bolted ahead. Her sister and brother have changed. But she's not changing with them. So much has changed between them that she's beginning to wonder if she'll always be the one who is left behind.

3.

It Was Meant to Be

Saskia is crouched on the living room window seat with her knees tucked under her nightgown, anxiously scanning the street below. Toby was supposed to be home over an hour ago from his first day on the job. It's only three stops on the Lexington Avenue local from That's Shoe Business to Twenty-Third Street, so she can't figure out what's keeping him.

She's starving, but doesn't want to eat the meatloaf that Odessa prepared earlier without Toby. When she called the shop there was no answer. She almost tried Arthur, before remembering he left for Paris ten days ago. Mom is out for the evening with Libby. Naomi is at a slumber party and most definitely doesn't want to hear from her. Saskia hates not knowing where Toby is. All she can imagine is a force majeure, a Bellevue psychiatric inmate on early release or a freak accident involving her big brother.

New York is so noisy on a summer night. She's never been in the city before in mid-July and can't get over how cranked up it is. A black-tie party is taking shape at the National Arts Club across the park, and a couple of teenagers are horsing around in front her building, their laughter ricocheting in the humid night air. She feels like an astronaut observing life on a distant planet, detached and solemn, the back of her eyes as wet as a sponge.

The shudder of the elevator sends her running to open the front door before Toby has time to get his key in the lock. "Where were you?" Saskia exclaims, recoiling from the bitter stench of beer on Toby's breath. "You were supposed to be home ages ago and didn't even call. I *hate* it when you're late."

She regrets her shrill outburst when she sees that Toby's brought a bearded someone home with him who, with his sleek ponytail, enviable eyelashes, and Afghan tunic, resembles a Jewish Cat Stevens.

"You see?" Toby nudges his companion. "I told you Saskia is like the Emily Post of the family."

"Isn't that sweet? Your kid sister's watching your back. Hey, I'm Manny."

No one remotely like Manny has ever walked through their front door. Certainly not her parents' friends, and even Toby's prep school friends look like *My Three Sons* in comparison to Manny, who appears to be a good five years older. He looks like he would know how to kiss, she surprises herself by thinking, and then instantly flushes.

"Geez Louise." Manny whistles as he does a 360-turn of the foyer. "You've got quite a setup here. My entire pad would fit right here in this entrance."

Saskia sidles toward her bedroom to change from her candy-striped nightie into something that will make her look like a teenager.

"What, off so soon? Is it my hair? My shirt? Green was never my color," Manny says jokingly. "My cologne? I'll scrub it off straight away." Manny takes Saskia's hand and escorts her to the living room while Toby goes to fetch more drinks.

She rushes ahead to remove the unfinished game of Risk on the ottoman, but Manny stops her. "Don't do that for me. I'll play with you later if you let me be the Soviet Union."

"That would be neat." Giddy from the turn the evening has taken, she searches for conversation and thrusts the near-empty snack bowl at him. "Do you like pretzels? I just love them."

Manny sits down next to her on the couch and takes a handful. Then he starts examining the ivory figurine on the coffee table. "Did anyone ever tell you that you look like Little Orphan Annie?"

Orphan. I'm halfway there, she thinks with a thud.

"What's the matter?" Manny's brown eyes are as rich as Hershey's Kisses. "Did I say something?"

"Nothing I haven't heard before," Saskia says, searching for a suitably nonchalant tone. "It's just that no one's called me that since my dad died."

"Please don't be sore with me." Manny's eyes now look like melted Kisses. "You poor kid, I had no idea that was the case. If it's any solace, my old man kicked the bucket when I was a little older than you, so I know where you're at."

"You do?"

"You've been dealt a rough hand, but you have to trust that the universe has a plan and everything is meant to be."

"You really think so?" She crosses her legs tightly, conscious that she's not wearing any panties beneath her nightie. "I always thought plans were when good things happened. I didn't plan on this."

"How old are you? Twelve? Thirteen?"

She straightens up to look taller. "Fourteen, actually."

"At the risk of sounding square, you're too young to get it yet. But the plan's out there. It's happening, right now."

"What's happening?"

Manny leads her to the window and gestures to the twinkling cityscape. "Don't you see?"

She nods uncertainly, wishing she'd washed her hair earlier.

"Look at all those people on the street, and in all those

buildings." Manny puts his arm around her shoulders. "And just try to figure the odds of us ever getting to know each other."

She nods again, hoping she doesn't look fat in her nightie.

"The plan is in place. Like today: meeting Toby, and now you. It was meant to be." Manny holds out his hand to make a bet. "I'll bet you that in two years—tops—you'll see this for what it is."

"Okay then, mister." Saskia shakes his crooked pinkie. "You're on."

"So we're friends now?"

"We're friends."

Manny goes over to open the Steinway's lid. "Do you play?"

"Not me. But Toby does."

Manny sits down and plays the opening of Rachmaninoff's Prelude.

"That sounds good."

"It should do. This is what I got into Juilliard on."

"You went there? That's neat."

"I was offered a place but my family couldn't get it together." Manny stops mid-chord. "I guess you could say that it wasn't meant to be."

"But you still sound really good."

"It should be so. Music isn't a dream for me. It's a way of life." He closes the spruce lid and goes to look at the photos on the mantelpiece.

"Do you want to see a picture of Daddy?" Saskia selects his portrait from the bank of framed pictures.

"He looks like a million dollars." Manny puts Daddy's photo back facedown when he spies another snapshot. "Is that really Barbara Walters?"

"My mom roomed in the same House as her at Sarah Lawrence." Saskia straightens Daddy's photo. "A whole bunch of them even summered together in Europe."

"You don't say." Manny whistles. "My mom went to Queensborough Community College and summered at Coney Island. Do you know how to get to Carnegie Hall?"

She waits for the punch line.

"You've got to practice, practice, practice!"

Her laugh sounds rusty from months of disuse.

"Did I tell you that I got into Juilliard on piano on the first round?" Manny says to Toby when he comes in, bearing their drinks, having changed from slacks and a Brooks Brothers oxford into jeans and a Mets T-shirt.

"Well, I'll be," Toby says and hands Manny a beer stein. "What was it like?"

"Oh, I didn't end up going there."

"Where'd you study instead?"

"I didn't have any formal training, but that hasn't stopped me from getting gigs around town."

"You're the real deal," Toby says, joining them on the couch. "Where've you played? Maybe I've seen you."

"It's more Borscht Belt than Birdland for now." Manny adopts Marlon Brando's accent. "If it weren't for my lousy day job, I could really be a contender."

"Let's drink to your success." Toby clinks glasses with Manny. "Hell, I'll drink to excess any day."

"Here's to music and friendship." Manny puts the damp glass directly on the coffee table. "Hey, you were in the middle of explaining why you didn't get to go to Paris."

Saskia slips a coaster under Manny's glass while he lights a joint from his cigarette pack.

"What do you know? A man after my own heart," Toby says when Manny offers him a hit. "Any-hoo, it's short and bittersweet. Our Dad died five months ago. Mom tried to keep our boat afloat, but then we went the way of the *Titanic* and couldn't afford my trip. And *fini*. End of story."

"What line of work was he in?" Manny asks.

"Dad was a print dealer," Toby replies.

"Nice. What happened to the business?"

"It went down the swanny." Toby swigs his beer. "So, I figured I'd get myself a real job and save up some bucks before I start at Columbia."

"It's just the three of you now?" Manny asks.

"No, I have another kid sister, so that makes me the man of the family." Toby makes quote marks in the air.

Manny puts his feet on the coffee table and turns to Saskia. "Let me guess. You're at an Upper East Side private school, majoring in driving the boys crazy?"

Saskia shakes her head and tries not to smile.

"Get out of here! You're pulling my leg," Manny exclaims. "She's bullshitting me, right, Toby?"

Saskia scurries to the kitchen to replenish their empty steins. Toby's laughter and the patter of conversation is making the apartment sound the way it used to. She prepares a plate of cold meatloaf sandwiches from their uneaten dinner and hurries back, hungry for more of Manny's magic.

* * *

"I wonder what Arthur's doing right now." Toby stacks the lunch dishes in the dishwasher while Saskia checks the brownies in the oven. "It's been a month now, *sans* a peep. I guess he's been too busy learning horizontal Berlitz."

"I bet he's on top of the Eiffel Tower," Saskia replies, picturing him on the pinnacle, King Kong-like.

"I bet that's not all he's on top of."

Toby dodges Saskia when she tries to swat him with the pot holder. "You've got a one-track mind," she says, as she wipes the counter and unplugs the electric mixer. She's been the self-appointed mess cook for the past twelve days, ever since Oma invited Mom on a two-week cruise of the Maine coastline to clear her mind. "Can you put this on the top shelf for me?"

Toby takes the mixer from her and sniffs, perplexed. "If you've just made brownies, why am I getting mayonnaise?"

"I don't know what you're talking about." She'd read in *Seventeen* that mayonnaise deep-conditions your hair, so she'd tried it out to make herself look nice for Manny. "I don't smell anything."

Toby pulls her closer to get another whiff. "It's you. You smell like a Waldorf salad."

Saskia pushes him away, blushing furiously. "Get lost. You're imagining things."

"Oh, no I'm not."

"Oh, yes you are."

"Cool it, coleslaw. I'm going to the store now."

"Don't forget my shopping list. And remember, Manny doesn't like cheese." She should know. She's made dinner for him almost every night since Mom left.

Toby scans the list. "You forgot something."

"What?"

"Limes for the margaritas. That's his favorite cocktail." He should know. He's been Manny's bartender.

Saskia takes the brownies out of the oven just as Naomi comes into the kitchen, fanning her hands, to get a drink of water. "Hey, where'd you get that T-shirt?" Naomi asks Toby. "I've never seen you in that before."

Toby looks down proudly at the Che Guevara image. "You dig? Manny gave it to me."

"I dig." Naomi handles the glass delicately so as not to smudge her fingernail polish.

Toby pockets the money that Mom left next to the sheet of emergency numbers and says, "It's Miller Time. Any special requests from the deli?"

"Pepperidge Farm, or else," Saskia says.

"Just some more Diet Dr Pepper," Naomi says, and then follows her brother from the room.

Saskia finishes putting the beer steins on ice so they're nice and frosted, just the way Manny likes them. Then she goes to her room to de-stinkify her hair, only to find that Naomi's already in the tub listening to Joni Mitchell on her tape player. She uses the wait to help herself to her sister's makeup and try on her cutoff shorts.

Naomi glides out of the bathroom on a moist cloud of Nivea and Jean Nate. "What do you think you're doing in my clothes?" she exclaims. "Take them off, this instant."

"But they don't fit you anymore."

"Oh, yes they do." Naomi critically inspects her naked reflection. Ever since Manny started making their place his home away from home, she threw herself on a crash diet and began doing a hundred sit-ups a day. "Besides, they're too tight on you."

Saskia sucks in her stomach. "What are you getting at?"

"I'm saying it might help if you laid off the Devil Dogs.

I'm also saying those're mine and I'm wearing them, so don't have a cow."

Saskia peels off the shorts and tosses them on the floor, inside out.

Naomi holds up a Revlon eye shadow that's missing its cover. "Are you going through my stuff again?"

"No." Saskia widens her eyes to hide the fact that she's wearing that very shadow.

"Bullshit. In that case, let me borrow your amethyst ring." Naomi grabs Saskia's jewelry box.

"No way," Saskia says, snatching the box back from her. "That's my special ring."

"Then get your hands off my special makeup."

"You're not the boss of me," Saskia retorts. "What are you getting so dolled up for anyway?" Like she really has to ask. Anyone can see that Naomi and Manny have been making eyes at each other.

"When the cat's away, the mice will play."

Naomi's attention returns to getting dressed when she hears Toby come back from his errand. Saskia uses that as an opportunity to sneak some of Naomi's Jean Nate before locking herself in the bathroom. She runs her head under the tap then towel-dries her hair, sniffing it to make sure there's not a trace of mayonnaise left. She applies Adorn hair spray for good measure and sprints to be the first to answer the doorbell when it rings.

"What's up, doc?" Manny greets her by way of his best Bugs Bunny accent. He holds out his clenched hands so that she can select a Pez dispenser to add to her growing collection.

"I made you walnut brownies again today," she says, pulling him toward the kitchen. The way to his heart is through his stomach.

"I got you another bottle of tequila today," Toby says, ushering Manny toward the living room. The way to his heart is through his liver.

Saskia runs to get the beer steins she's prepared and comes back to find Naomi reclined on the couch, rolling a joint on the cover of *Mad* magazine, her bare legs resting on Manny's lap.

Figures, Saskia thinks. There would be room for me next to Manny if Naomi weren't hogging the whole couch. "Hey, guys. Should I start the burgers?"

"Not now," Toby replies and pops open a beer tab. "Me and Mr. Miller have some catching up to do."

"Well then," Saskia stalls. "Should I get the *TV Guide* and see what's on tonight?"

"Maybe later, after Mr. Miller and Señor Blanco get acquainted." Manny pours three tequila shots and passes them around.

"How about a game of Scrabble instead?" Saskia persists.

"Not tonight, but I promise, cross my heart, I will next time." Manny touches his cold glass to Naomi's leg and makes her laugh.

Saskia goes Day-Glo green with jealousy. After the way they hit it off, she thought Manny was her special friend. But Naomi and Toby, with their combined advantage of age and panzer-like ability to party, have shoved her into no-man's-land.

There's no point in her cooking if all they want is a liquid dinner, again, so they can get drunk, again, like the three of them have been doing ever since Mom left. If only Mom knew what they've been getting up to, but that's too big an if, and she'd never have the nerve to tell on them.

Saskia gives up and goes to the kitchen to select a Birds

Eye TV dinner and fans herself with the freezer door while it cooks.

"Yuck," Naomi says when she comes in to find Saskia eating Skippy peanut butter straight from the jar with a spoon. "That's gross."

"I don't care. I'm hungry."

Naomi, balancing a six-pack in one hand and an ashtray in the other, shuts the fridge door with her foot. "Why don't you just chill out for once?"

"Make me."

Saskia sulks off to Mom's room with her meal to watch TV, slamming the hallway door in case the downstairs neighbors complain again about the stereo being too loud.

During the commercial break, she makes her way to the kitchen to get a brownie, and pauses in the foyer when she smells incense and sees the living room is now in darkness.

"Is anyone there?" she calls, wondering if they've gone out and forgotten to turn off the Marvin Gaye record that's playing.

She hears a muffled whisper and tiptoes in to see Manny and Naomi snuggled up on the coach. His fingers are playing with her hair. Saskia's chest feels like a melted candle. She's been a chump. Manny's not her special friend if he's getting this close with Naomi.

"Hey," Saskia says sharply and snaps on the overhead light. "What's going on in here?"

"Steady there, Officer." Manny holds his hands up in mock surrender. "A man is as young as the woman he feels."

"Where's Toby?"

"He—he—" Naomi is overcome with giggles. "He went out to get me some cigs."

"Since when do you smoke?" Saskia asks, hand on hip.

"Since none of your business, *Mommy*," Naomi retorts, face flushed with alcohol.

Manny pulls Naomi closer to him. "Easy now, tiger. Keep those claws in."

Saskia starts to sit down but Naomi's warning glare makes her leave.

"Saskia?" Manny calls when she reaches the door.

She turns expectantly.

"Be a good kid and turn off the lights on the way out, will you?"

Saskia pretends not to hear him and spends the rest of the evening in Mom's room, imagining what's happening next door. Her sister is being pieced back together, while her Humpty-Dumpty heart remains in a thousand pieces. She'd do anything to be in the arms of some nice boy, kissing her whole again.

She'd pictured being a teen as a benign process that would yield what she craves. To be loved, to belong. But *this* is not that. And *that* might never follow. Maybe love is as elusive as searching for a marble in the dark. Maybe it's out of her reach, and it's possible that she might never find it.

* * *

Saskia wakes up the next morning in Mom's bed fully clothed, hair sticky from the damp pillow and with crumbs from last night's meal glued to her cheek. Deciding a shower is in order, she goes to get a change of clothes and opens her bedroom door.

Manny and Naomi are sprawled in naked slumber, their lanky limbs haphazardly differentiated by the soft mound of his hairy ass. Their long dark locks blend together and cover the pillows, making it impossible to know where one head of hair ends and the other begins.

Within the space of ordinary hours, Naomi had been taken to that unutterable place where something timeless happened. Life had cried out right here in their room, but not for her. Her body feels mute amid the echo of sex. And so far away from the sister that Manny is now so close to.

Naomi's eyes flutter, and then snap open when she sees Saskia. "Get. Out. Now," she mouths, drawing the sheet up to her chin.

Saskia scampers to the kitchen and starts putting away the utensils in the dishwasher before realizing that they're still dirty. She gets out the milk for her cereal and turns on the radio, the music shredding the morning stillness.

Naomi pads in, wrapped toga-like in a towel, and sits down with her. "Well?"

Saskia's mind is crawling with questions. "Did you get to fourth base?"

"Not that it's any of your business." Naomi runs her hands through her tousled locks. "But since you're asking, yes."

"Does Toby know?"

Naomi lights a cigarette and coquettishly blows out the match. "What? Like I need his permission?"

"What will you tell Mom?"

"Sweet f-all. Manny's made me happy again and I want to keep it that way," Naomi replies, craning her neck to inspect a love bite on her shoulder.

Saskia grabs the cigarette from her and stubs it out. "He's like *twenty-three*."

"What's with you? That was my last one." Naomi picks the

end off the cigarette and relights it. "I'm old enough to do my own thing. And by the by? He's twenty-five."

Saskia's hands stop obeying when she pours milk into her cereal and spills it across the table instead.

Naomi pushes her chair back to avoid the mess and says, "Manny's been through what I'm going through. He gets me. In fact, he thinks he loves me. And if you care about me, you'll know better than to say anything."

It's not supposed to be like this, Saskia wants to cry out, wishing Mom was due home now instead of the day after tomorrow. The sight of Naomi's nipple, peeping out from the towel, makes her cross her arms over her near flat, chaste chest.

"Not all of us want to stay kids forever. This is what I've wanted, so be happy for me," Naomi says and saunters toward the swing door. "Be cool about this and I promise to play Monopoly with you later."

Saskia stares at the dry mass of cereal in her bowl as the milk continues to drip off the table to form a puddle by her feet. She imagines what it must be like to fall in love and pictures it as the rainbow of all colors that only two people can see, with herself inexorably consigned to its shadow.

* * *

Saskia flits and frets around the house, tidying up after Manny and Naomi leave to go out for breakfast. She finds a strand of what can only be his hair in her hairbrush, and promptly throws the brush out. She thinks she smells the sex in her bedroom, so she airs the room and sprays it with Mom's Chanel. She wants to change Naomi's bed, but is too grossed out about what she might find, so she covers it with a fresh sheet instead. She throws out the remaining package of Betty Crocker brownie mix, vowing never to make them for Manny ever again.

As soon as she hears Toby stir, she picks her way through the empty beer cans to join him in his bedroom where he's watching a rerun of *Jeopardy*. She is gagging to talk, but Toby still looks bleary from the night before, so she goes and gets him a cup of coffee and a bottle of Bayer.

"Well, well, What do we have here? A regular Florence Nightingale?" Toby gratefully downs the aspirin with his coffee, and moves over to make a space for her next to him on the bed.

"So?" she leads.

Toby burps but doesn't say anything.

"What do you make of this?"

"Of what?" He's toying with her. "Jimmy Hoffa's disappearance?"

She rolls her eyes.

"Or the Mets playoffs?"

"No. Them."

Toby groans and runs his hands through his hair. "I plead the Fifth."

"Come on. I mean it."

Toby turns off the TV and his mouth rearranges itself as he chooses his words. "You know how in journalism, you're constantly told to be fair and impartial?"

"Why would I? You're the writer guy, not me."

Toby grows more animated as he speaks about a topic he loves. "That, and truthfulness, independence, accountability, and humanity are the golden rules that apply to any given story. They hammered that one home the entire time I was the editor at school."

"What does that have to do with them?"

"Everything and nothing. I'm just trying to frame what happened." Toby pauses to finish his coffee. "And it's hard. Impartially speaking, should it bother me that he's older or that he was my friend initially?"

"What are you getting at?"

"Naomi's always been in a rush to get there first. Like Mom always says, she even walked before I did. I have to accept that she knows her own mind." Toby gauges her expression and continues. "And at the end of the day, I'm her brother, not her father."

There's a click as the word *father* hovers there, in all its invisible thickness.

"What do you think of when you think of him?" Saskia asks.

"What *don't* I think of? Stupid things mostly."

She hugs him, her rock in their ocean.

"I was supposed to go to Paris, and Mom goes on a cruise instead. I was supposed to go to Northwestern, now I'm not. I'm supposed to man up since I'm the eldest, but times like this I feel like it's never going to be my turn."

4.

Meredith Again

It's Saskia's first day of freshman year and she's having serious second thoughts about her choice of high school. The prospect of new people, no uniform, and co-ed classes has her up before her alarm sounds.

Saskia finds Toby in the kitchen making coffee in preparation for the long and often delayed subway journey uptown to Columbia. "Today will be the first of many firsts, so try not to get worked up," Toby says, tousling her hair. She waves him off and helps herself to juice.

"Do you want me to walk you to school?" Toby asks.

She vehemently shakes her head no.

"You'll be all right," he tells her. "Trust me on this one."

Saskia retreats to her bedroom to get dressed in the Gloria Vanderbilt jeans and Benetton shirt she chose after an anxious search for an outfit that didn't scream square girl.

Naomi, who still has a few more days of vacation, stirs in her bed and says, "Good luck."

Saskia meets her greeting with a tepid smile. Manny has definitely put a strain on their weary relationship. Ever since Mom got back, Naomi has taken to sneaking off to Manny's Hell's Kitchen apartment share whenever he gives the word. On those few occasions when they get together, she is electric with their jive. Saskia's mind is buckling with their secret, but she knows Naomi would brain her if she breathed even a syllable of this to Mom.

Toby joked about being the third wheel, and was all too happy to hang out with Arthur when he returned from France.

He even quit his summer job a week early so that he could drive with Arthur to Northwestern and take the Greyhound back. He insisted he was fine with seeing his best friend off to the college where he too was supposed to go, but Saskia sensed a Chicago-shaped scab forming on his soul.

Saskia kisses her sleeping mother goodbye and leaves to get to school on time. On the way out, she checks the mailbox in the lobby and finds it empty. Judging from the lapse in letters and the unreturned phone calls, she'd bet just about anything that Kathleen has a new best friend. She tries that thought on and is almost crushed by the prospect that even their forever-and-ever friendship has changed.

It's hard to believe that just this time last year she'd met Kathleen on the corner, racing to get there first in her haste to see her. She'd do anything to be on the Third Avenue bus with Kathleen right now, trundling uptown toward her old school. She used to love kvetching about the place, but now that she's no longer a part of that elite community she'd do anything to belong there once again. But death has dumbed her down, got her left back in math, and got her here.

She feels fat with nerves when she arrives at the Collective. She searches for a space to fit in. Eyes glance over her and move on. Her smile becomes squeezed as the weight of her insignificance sinks in.

"Welcome to the Collective," Tracy exclaims, throwing open her arms. "Here's to becoming a big part of our little family."

During attendance, the students introduce themselves and then break off into year groups. Saskia likes the look of Becky, who is freckled and fresh-faced compared to Florence, an edgy blond waif who has a camera slung around her neck, or Tabitha, a glamorous black girl with heavily kohled eyes. She tags behind Becky when Andy, a smartly dressed sophomore with an easy smile, leads the freshmen to a room filled with mismatched desks. When a boy whose name she can't remember bags the place next to Becky, she plumps for sitting alongside Tabitha and Florence, who are sharing a pack of Jelly Babies, but then Florence eyeballs her and puts her feet on the chair she was about to take.

Ears burning, Saskia sits beside Ethan, a handsome stoner with a pierced ear and thick shoulder-length hair who blanks her tentative greeting.

"This is the English lab where you'll meet Emerson for first period every day," Andy says. "Do you have any questions?"

Becky raises her hand. "What do we do for gym?"

"We don't have a gym." Andy inspects the dried gum on the heel of his Frye boot. "But under New York State law you have to do something sporty, so we go bowling once a week on University Place."

"What electives do we have?" Ethan asks.

"You can decide on whatever it is you'd like to take," Andy explains. "And Emerson and Tracy will set it up as long as six kids enroll."

"You mean anyone can choose anything at all?" Saskia queries.

"You got it. Hostage negotiations, clog dancing, basket weaving, it's your call."

Emerson comes in with a sheaf of paper and motions for Andy to leave, then studies her expectant students. "You look like a scared litter of puppies with shiny coats, wet noses, and big paws," she guffaws, before breaking into a smoker's cough. "Don't worry, I won't bite. Let's start by having you write a short piece about your summer."

Obediently, Saskia starts. Then the hugeness of it makes her stop. The summer has made her smaller. There is less and less of herself that she likes. She thinks of how she used to be—*not lonely, not cool, but not sad*—compared to who she is now—*lonely, weird, sad*. So, she erases what she started and writes an anodyne account instead.

Emerson scans the paper and asks her to stay behind. "Was your summer as 'wonderful' as you made it out to be?"

Saskia shrugs tightly.

Emerson waves her off. "You run along now. We have plenty of time to get to know each other, warts and all."

Saskia hurries to use the bathroom and is dismayed to find Florence perched on the sink smoking a joint while she fiddles with the lens on her camera. Saskia opens the stall door on Tabitha, and then hastily slams it shut. "Oopsie. I'm so sorry."

Tabitha comes out of the stall to take a drag of Florence's joint and says, "None of the locks work. Apparently, they took them out to discourage the students from getting stoned in here."

"But they failed to take into account how *highly* motivated we are," Florence adds.

"Was it like this at your last school?" Tabitha asks.

"Not really," Saskia says.

"Maybe that's 'cause she went to a finishing school," Florence smirks.

Tabitha studies Saskia quizzically. "You seem different. Are you religious?"

Saskia shakes her head no.

"Are you from the country or something?" Tabitha continues.

"No. The city," Saskia replies, suppressing the urge to cough when Florence exhales in her direction.

"Not a city I know." Florence checks the state of her eyes in the mirror and squeezes out some Visine. "Come on, Tabitha. Let's go."

* * *

Now that Mom gave up the gallery, she fitfully tries new pursuits. She digs up her cookbooks and prepares elaborate meals. Some mornings she's up, with breakfast on the table. Other days she doesn't get out of bed. She forgets to pay the electricity bill and they're temporarily disconnected. Mail goes unopened and the potted plants wither. Mom goes to visit Libby and Tom on Fire Island, and comes home a day early. Lunch with some of her old college alumni sends her into a funk that lasts for days.

"I don't know" becomes her mantra. I don't know what to do with myself, Mom laments. I don't know how to earn a living. I don't know how to file a tax return. I don't know how to make new friends. I don't know where I belong. I just don't know.

The "I don't knows" instill a queasiness in Saskia. For if Mom doesn't know, then who does?

* * *

When Naomi is picked from her drama club to perform a monologue from *The Little Foxes* for Scene Night at school, she starts speaking in a Southern accent to get into the part, and runs lines with Mom before bedtime.

"'I mean what I say with all my heart. There is nothing to talk about. I'm going away from you,'" Naomi drawls, looking to Mom for a clue for the next line.

Seeing them together like this, with the bedside lamp reflecting in their dark hair, is comforting to Saskia. Naomi, so ripened by Manny, regains an innocent desire to do justice to the part.

On the night of the performance, Saskia chooses a cerise shift and matching earrings for Mom to wear, but Mom selects a plain navy dress instead and applies some makeup only at her insistence. The Mom who used to turn heads seems reluctant to attract attention. Brisk showers have replaced languid baths, ChapStick is favored over lipstick, and the scent that Mom emits these days comes from bars of Ivory Soap instead of her bottle of Chanel.

Saskia takes her seat between Mom and Toby in the school auditorium, holding the bouquet of roses Mom purchased for Naomi. The lights dim, and early into the program, it's Naomi's turn. Saskia can never get over her sister's ability to shape her imagination so that she's the one in the room who stands out. Mom is the first to applaud when it's over and there is a replete moment where pride occupies the space in Mom's eyes that is usually reserved for sorrow.

But afterward, Saskia sees it start. The quick, cautious looks from fellow parents who knew Mom as one of two. The way in which the other mothers lock arms with their husbands, as if to hoard them. Their empty promises to call.

Mom keeps her best Mom-face on while Toby goes backstage to find Naomi, but it seems to be taking him forever so Saskia offers to get them drinks.

Her stomach curdles when she spies a man with a ponytail waiting in line at the refreshment table. It's Manny, who has dressed for the occasion in a corduroy suit, button-down shirt, and Hush Puppies. She ducks behind a pair of suited men, struggling not to spill the beverages she is carrying, but Manny spots her.

"Aren't you going to say hello?" he asks.

"Say hello," she mimics coolly.

She hasn't set eyes on Manny since the summer and was beginning to believe that he was just something strange that happened, like sleet in August.

"Ah, come on. Be nice. Like you used to," Manny says. "There's no reason why we can't be cool."

A snappy retort dangles beyond her reach. "I can think of many," she finally comes back with. "What are you doing here?"

"Take a wild guess."

Mom sees that Saskia is bearing drinks and breaks away from her conversation group to join them. The boundaries of her world crumble when Mom nods politely at Manny and says, "You must be the drama teacher."

"I've been called many things, but not that," Manny replies. "I'm Manny."

"I take it you're a member of staff?" Mom asks politely, sipping the fruit punch.

"Who, *him*?" Saskia snorts. "No way. He sells shoes."

Manny's expression twists tightly while Mom's unravels. "I'm sorry, my daughter forgot her manners."

"Well, it's true," Saskia says adamantly. "He's just someone Toby met at his summer job."

"Guilty as charged!" Manny throws up his hands in mock surrender.

"I apologize for my daughter's sorry manners," Mom says in disbelief, and puts down her unfinished drink. "Now if you'll excuse me." She yanks Saskia by the hand into the auditorium where they left their coats and the bouquet, then turns on her and snaps, "You humiliated me. What got into you?"

"Nothing," Saskia sulks.

"You acted like an oaf," Mom laments.

"I was just telling the truth," Saskia protests.

Mom silences her with a look and collects the roses along with her coat. When she strides back into the main hall with Saskia in tow, Manny is waiting with fresh drinks in hand.

"Flowers? You didn't have to," he quips.

Mom allows herself a wane smile when she realizes he's joking.

"Come on." Manny takes the roses from Mom and deftly leads her to a vacant bench by the staircase. "It looks like you could do with a breather."

Manny's done it again, Saskia bitterly marvels. He's shaped the moment and omitted me from its frame. She tries to round the circle by perching beside Mom, who pointedly puts her belongings on the seat between them.

"I think what Saskia was trying to convey in her best, most elegant teen-lish is that yes, I used to work with Toby. And yes, I sell shoes to support my music, and yes, I'm here in friendship," Manny says.

"They're lucky to have made such a friend," Mom says, stealing a glance at the parents she was just talking with. "At least they have some."

Saskia thrusts the bouquet at Mom. "We need to give these to Naomi."

Mom obligingly clasps the stems and cries out when she draws blood from a thorn. "Oh my days," she exclaims, checking her dress pocket for a tissue.

"I didn't mean to," Saskia says defensively, when Mom sighs in irritation and then sucks her finger to stanch the bleeding.

"For someone who didn't mean to, you sure seem to," Manny says archly as he offers Mom his handkerchief.

"You don't have to do this," Mom demurs.

"I know that. I never do what I don't want to do." Manny takes Mom's hand in his and tenderly applies the cloth to her wound until the flow abates.

"I forgot what that feels like." Mom blushes when she hears herself. "I mean the part about doing what you want."

"It's not that hard, Toby's Mom," Manny replies. "Or shall I call you Mrs. Soyer?"

"Come on. They're waiting for us," Saskia bleats impatiently.

"Please!" Mom tenses, and reaches for the punch. "Give me a minute."

"But Mom—" Saskia starts.

"No more Mom or Mrs. tonight," Mom interrupts, voice catching. "Just let me be Meredith again."

Saskia stomps off to sit on the nearby staircase to silently curse Toby and Naomi for taking so long, all the while pretending not to listen in.

Manny starts playing with a stray rose petal and asks, "Who is this 'Meredith again'?"

Mom ponders his question while savoring her drink. "It's the me, without him."

"I'm so sorry," Manny murmurs. "Toby told me."

"You're the first one to ask me *who* I am, instead of *how* I am." Seeing that Manny has finished his drink, Mom passes her cup to him.

Manny absently traces the outline that her lipstick made on the rim and asks, "Who would you like this Meredith to be?"

"I'd like her to be . . ." Mom notices that Saskia is eavesdropping, and lowers her voice. "I don't know what's come over me. It must be the punch."

"So long as it's not the company," Manny says intently.

"I can assure you it's not." Mom allows herself a bashful smile. "Enough of me. Tell me about your music."

"I was supposed to go to Juilliard but it wasn't meant to be. But that hasn't stopped me from making music, and it never will. I'll get there yet."

"At least you have a 'there,'" Mom says wistfully. "I did too, once."

"If you want to be Meredith again, then you have to let yourself find her."

"You make it sound so easy."

"Everything happens for a reason," Manny says. "Maybe it was meant to be because—" Mom opens her mouth to say something but Manny beckons her to listen. "There's more than one 'me,' and more than one 'him.'"

When Toby and Naomi finally join them, the air becomes oily and the conversation slick and fast. Naomi pinkens under her pancake makeup. Compliments and kisses are exchanged. Voices overlap, sentiments are repeated. Mom seems to have forgotten her own anger by the time she leaves with Saskia to taxi home, while the rest continue to a party.

It's later when Saskia goes to say good night to Mom that she realizes. They forgot to give Naomi the roses, and that Mom has just finished having a bath and smells of Chanel once again.

5.

My One and Only Love

Naomi throws herself a Sweet Sixteen costume party on Halloween, since her real birthday fell on a school day this year. On the night of, Naomi is in a bathrobe and curlers, barking orders from the kitchen table, where she is doing her nails.

Saskia carries a bowl of Utz potato chips into the living room, which Toby is party-proofing in anticipation of Naomi's entire junior year's arrival, while Arthur, who is east for the weekend, and has come dressed as Alfred E. Neuman, ferries ice to the bathroom to fill the tub for beer.

Saskia flops down on the couch beside Arthur to get away from Naomi, who has been busting her chops ever since Mom left after lunch to run errands.

"What are you guys going to do with your mom tonight? Slip her a Mickey and lock her in her bedroom?" Arthur asks drily.

"That won't be necessary." Toby is removing all the breakables from the mantelpiece. "Naomi made her promise she'll go to Libby's until midnight."

"And she agreed?" Arthur is all ears. "What, did she make her an offer she couldn't refuse?"

"Let's just say she signed on the dotted line," Toby says, as he starts putting the *objets d'art* inside the sideboard.

"How did she sweet-talk her into letting a bunch of tanked-up teens romp freely in the narcotic-filled woods?"

"Naomi asked for it as her present, since we all have to cut back now," Saskia sighs, sick of all the economizing-this and budgeting-that.

"Wow." Arthur whistles. "Impressive."

"I got to hand it to Naomi," Toby says. "She could talk a Catholic into using birth control."

Saskia hears the doorbell and fetches the candy bowl to go and welcome their first trick-or-treaters, the twins from the twelfth floor dressed as Raggedy Ann and Raggedy Andy. Now that the evening has landed, she wishes she could join them. Although Naomi gave her permission to invite someone to her party, the truth is she doesn't have anyone to ask. At fourteen, she's too old to dress up and trick-or-treat for UNICEF and too young to get wasted with her siblings.

After saying goodbye to the twins, Saskia places the candy bowl back on the hope chest and is sifting through for some Pop Rocks when the front door opens. It's Mom. But a different Mom with a look that is so out there, it makes her eyes hurt. "What happened to your hair?" Saskia exclaims.

Mom inspects her new shag cut in the foyer mirror. "Say hello to the new me."

Saskia has seen Mom looking classy and pretty before, but never pretty sexy. Mom left this morning looking like *That Girl* and returned as *Klute*.

Mom does a twirl on the living room step. "What do you think?"

Toby does a double take and says, "Holy crap. People are gonna think it's your party."

Mom puts down her Lord & Taylor shopping bags. "I decided to heck with Elizabeth Arden and went to Vidal Sassoon instead. I told them out with the old and in with the new."

"You look so different." Saskia's cheeks hurt from forcing a smile. "You look so young," she adds reluctantly.

"I got to say, Mrs. Soyer," Arthur declares. "You're a dead ringer for Natalie Wood."

"Do you really think so?" Mom dazzles Arthur with her smile. "And please, call me Meredith. I may be on the wrong side of forty, but I'm no fogey."

Naomi comes in to see what all the commotion is about. "Gee, Mom," she says, arms crossed and lips narrowed. "You didn't tell me Libby was having a costume party as well."

The air whistles as Naomi's red-hot shot fires through the room, piercing Mom to the quick.

"I say, you're quite the comedian," Mom coolly rejoins.

"And you're quite the consumer." Naomi disdainfully regards her shopping. "Where's my cake?"

"Cake?" Mom gathers her bags along with her ammunition. "I didn't have time to collect that."

"How could you forget to? It's the one thing I asked you to do today."

"Correction. I didn't forget. I said I didn't have time."

"But you promised."

"No, I didn't 'promise,'" Mom replies. "You made the assumption that I would just blithely do as you bid. If you're big enough to entertain on your own, you're big enough to do everything."

"Don't speak to me as though I'm a child," Naomi retorts.

"Then stop acting like one and get it yourself."

"I can't go out like this," Naomi fumes. "My guests are arriving soon."

Toby intercedes. "Don't either of you worry about it. I'll pick it up."

"That's good of you. Now if you'll excuse me, I'll go get changed for my night out. I know my marching orders and wouldn't want to let the captain down again." Mom clicks her heels and salutes Naomi, before marching off to her bedroom.

Toby beats a hasty retreat, whereupon Naomi steams into the kitchen with Saskia and Arthur in tow and explodes, "I can't believe she screwed up my fucking cake!"

"What are you so angry about? It's just a stupid cake." Saskia starts mashing the avocados, triple-time, for guacamole.

"She's our mom," Naomi replies testily. "It would be nice if she acted like one."

"You got to admit she looks about ten years younger with that haircut," Arthur says, filling a bowl with ice.

"How could you?" Naomi scoffs. "She looks like a frigging Miss Subways contestant."

"You got to hand it to the lady. At least she can pull it off." Arthur begins replenishing the ice trays. "My mom would be mistaken for a Christopher Street drag queen if she tried that one on."

"The party was my present, but she doesn't think twice about dropping cash all the way down Fifth Avenue," Naomi fumes. "She gets all Amish on us when we want something, but acts like Happy Rockefeller when it suits her."

"At least she gives you space. My parents would never let me have a party, and they'd sooner make a citizen's arrest than let me get high at home. You come from the cool house; I come from the Norman Rockwell one."

"Yeah, but . . ." Naomi trails off.

"But nothing. It's your birthday, you only turn sixteen once and it's your night to remember," Arthur says firmly. "Now where's that beer you promised me about three days ago?"

Saskia, having finished making the guacamole, skips off to Mom's room before Naomi can come up with any more jobs for her to do.

"Just a minute," Mom calls when Saskia knocks. Then Mom opens the bedroom door, now attired in a new pair of silver shoes and a cocktail dress. "What do you think?"

"I like it." *Not*, Saskia thinks.

Saskia sits on the bed and starts counting the empty shopping bags while Mom puts the finishing touches to her makeup. She calculates that if each bag represents eight dollars, Mom spent thirty-two dollars today. "Do you want me to choose your earrings?"

"I'm one step ahead of you. I picked these up today along with a bottle of Charlie." Mom dangles a pair of rhinestone hoops. "I'm tired of Chanel. It makes me feel ancient."

Saskia hugs Mom as an excuse to fuss with her hair to try to make her look older.

Mom playfully slaps her hands. "Don't muss it up. I want to look good. Between you and me, Libby is introducing me to her accountant tonight."

"Is her accountant a he or a she?" Saskia steps back and trips on an empty shoe box.

"He's a he, darling."

"So she's fixing you up?" Saskia goes flush-faced. "Like a date-date?"

"It's been nearly nine months now. It's time for me to get back out there. You kids have each other, but no one's looking out for me."

"That's not true. I look out for you every day," Saskia protests. "So do all of us. And your friends."

"It's not the same anymore. Either I remind them of their worst nightmare or they don't want to include me in case their husbands try to get me into bed."

"Does this mean that you're going to get married again?" Saskia's eyes sweat while she toys with the makeup on the dressing table.

"Don't be silly," Mom says, pulling Saskia toward her for a hug. "There'll never be another Larry, and I'll never bear another man's child. But you don't want me to rattle around on an empty shelf for the rest of my life now, do you?"

Saskia blinks rapidly as she plays with the paste button on Mom's dress.

"Do you?" Mom kisses Saskia's hand. "Can you picture me all covered in dust?"

"No, Mom," Saskia relents.

"Now try and have a good time tonight." Mom dabs Saskia's wrist with her new perfume. "You can stay up if you like, 'cause you'll never get to sleep in this chaos."

Saskia tags along behind Mom when she goes to call the elevator. She doesn't want to fend for herself tonight and she most certainly doesn't want Mom to meet another man.

In the past, Kathleen would have been her copilot on such a night. They would have laughed themselves silly watching the evening unfold. But now one continent, two time zones, three thousand miles and four letterless weeks separate them. "Can I come with you?" she asks impulsively.

"Don't be silly, you belong here with the youngsters." Mom tweaks Saskia's nose just as the elevator doors open.

Manny emerges dressed as Harpo Marx and honks his horn when he sees Mom. "*Ciao bella*. We have Sophia Loren in our midst."

Mom laughs and brushes past him to press the lobby button.

"Well, Saskia. What are you going to be for Halloween?"

Manny asks, like he's the self-appointed Mr. Rogers of the neighborhood.

"Sober," Saskia mutters. She's wary of Naomi's talk of spiking the punch with vodka and making hash brownies, and plans on eating only what she made herself. "Night, Mom."

Manny puts his arm out to block the elevator doors from closing. "Don't tell me you're going so soon, 'Meredith again.'"

"I happen to have a prior engagement." Mom presses the lobby button once more.

Manny leans against the frame. "But I just got here, and I haven't even set eyes on you since that night."

Mom fiddles with the clasp of her pocketbook, trying not to smile. "That may be. But you belong here with the kids while my place is with the grown-ups."

"Mom's got a date," Saskia blurts. "You're going to make her late."

"You don't say. Well, in that case, I don't want to keep the lucky man waiting." Manny steps back and lets the door go. "Just remember, there's always more than one fish in the sea."

Saskia waves to Mom as the door slides shut and watches the numbers start to descend on the panel. Then she camps out in the maid's room with the portable TV, a packet of Pepperidge Farm cookies, and the current issue of *People* magazine before the first guests arrive.

By ten thirty, the TV is competing with the noise from the rest of the apartment. Her cookies are long gone but she doesn't want to brave the crowd to get more. A partygoer, propping up his drunken date, stumbles in thinking he's found the ultimate make-out spot but backs out when he sees her. She turns up the volume on *Creature Feature* and drapes the quilt from the daybed over her head to filter out the music and laughter. But just as she gets comfortable, the door opens again.

"I'm busy here," she cries.

A coatless Mom comes in. "I thought I'd find you here. How's my night owl?"

"Okay I guess." Saskia scrambles to sit up. "You're back early. What was he like?"

"Well, he would be just perfect if . . ." Mom pauses theatrically before dropping down beside her on the daybed. "Your greatest passion is golf, which mine undoubtedly is not."

"So that was it then?"

"That most certainly was it." Mom fixes the clasp on her hoop earring.

Saskia puts on a suitably contrite face, while Mom stands up to check her reflection in the mirror. "Besides, I didn't want to miss out on all the action here. Would you like some cake or a glass of champagne to toast Naomi's special day?"

Saskia follows Mom into the kitchen, causing Naomi's guests to scoot off for the living room when they see an adult in their midst. Mom finds the champagne that she hid in the vegetable drawer in the fridge and pours two glasses while Saskia scrapes the bakery box for icing.

Manny comes in and feigns surprise when he sees Mom. "Don't tell me you turn into a pumpkin at midnight?" Manny deftly helps himself to champagne. "How was your date?"

"Suffice to say, he was no Prince Charming," Mom replies.

"He must have been some toad."

"Takes one to know one," Saskia blurts, as she refills her glass. She waits for her comment to land but her words slip past them.

Mom catches Manny's eye and flushes slightly as she sips

her drink. "Shouldn't you get back to the young ones?"

"It's early yet."

"For you, maybe. But it's getting late for me." Mom puts down her half-finished drink.

"Nonsense," Manny says, handing the glass back to her. "There's still time for you to go to the ball."

"If only. My dancing days are behind me."

"Far from it. You look young enough to be Naomi's sister," Manny says.

"For crying out loud, that's impossible!" Saskia exclaims, emboldened by the champagne that she's downed. "She's our mom."

"Lordy!" Mom's smile zips tightly. "Would somebody please tell me that I'm someone besides a mom?"

"I'd be the first to tell you," Manny says. "If you'd only listen."

Saskia would like to fold back the evening. Words are slanting around her. Her head feels slippery as she tries to configure these angles that keep on multiplying.

The champagne and icing start roiling in her stomach and she feels the urge to lie down. She stumbles back to the maid's room to find that the reception is gone and the TV is skipping. The scattershot images make her queasy so she curls up and closes her eyes to steady her brain.

Mom comes in, with her coat on. "Seeing as I'm back before my 'curfew,' Manny and I are just stepping out for a stroll."

Saskia tries to attach that thought to something familiar, and can't. So she lets it slide. Then she smacks the TV repeatedly and fiddles with the antenna until the picture returns.

When *The Honeymooners* is finishing, Naomi prances in

clutching a cigarette holder, looking a treat in her diamanté choker and flapper costume. "Where's Manny?" Naomi asks. "It's time for my toast."

"He went out with Mom."

Naomi gives her a withering look. "What, she took him walkies?"

"I don't know. Maybe they went to the store to get something. I'm just saying what I heard." The words taste odd in her mouth. "Or think I heard."

Naomi seems nonplussed by what she heard. So she disconnects the thought. "The champagne's calling my name," she announces brightly as she tosses the boa over her shoulder, and with a whoosh of sequins and feathers, bustles off.

* * *

Saskia is thrown for a loop when she awakens fully dressed in the maid's room. The TV is still on, her teeth are covered in fur, the waist of her jeans is digging into her stomach, and she's thirsty as all hell.

Mom's not in the kitchen, making sense of the post-party chaos while making coffee. Saskia wades through the mess to down some water, then pick at the remains of the cake, but when she sees that a cigarette has been extinguished in it she starts in on the leftover cookies instead.

A blobby noise that she can't place comes from the front of the house. It doesn't sound quite right so she follows it. There's no one in the dining room and the living room stereo system has been turned off. She listens harder and thinks it's a radio from outside. But it's not coming from the street, it's coming from somewhere in the apartment. Spongy silence greets her when she presses her ear to Mom's closed bedroom door. Then she hears what sounds like sobbing and follows the sound down the hall.

Her knees feel uncertain as she opens the door to her room.

Toby is sitting on the bed comforting Naomi, whose tear-stained face is smudged with last night's makeup. A stray boa feather, stuck to Naomi's wet cheek like a molted reminder of last night's giddiness, seems to say it all. A raptor has singled them out to prey on them once more.

"What's wrong?" Saskia shrieks.

Toby starts to say something, then stops.

"What is it? Is Mom okay?"

"Mom's fine," Toby says, without meeting her eye.

"What's the matter then?" Her question provokes a fresh flood of tears from Naomi, who just shakes her head. Saskia looks to Toby for an answer, but he motions for her to leave.

She goes in search of Mom and an explanation and knocks repeatedly on the master bedroom door. How Mom can sleep through this she doesn't know, so she goes in to wake her.

The sun slices the air, stabbing the smooth satin bedspread on the neatly made bed. The indentation is still there from where she sat watching Mom get dressed the night before. She checks under the plumped pillow. Mom's nightdress is still there.

The bathroom is empty, save for lipstick-blotted tissues and Mom's crumpled nylons.

Saskia sniffs the bottle of Charlie on the makeup-strewn dressing table as though the scent could lead her to her mother.

She checks every room of their trashed apartment, but Mom isn't there. She checks the service entrance and even goes down to the laundry room, but Mom isn't there. But Mom couldn't have gotten very far without her pocketbook, which is still in its customary spot on the hope chest.

Finally, Saskia hears the key in the lock and dashes to the door. Mom comes in empty-handed and dressed in last night's clothes, her silver shoes shining like a fifty-cent piece in the daylight.

"Toby and me didn't know where you were," Saskia exclaims, sloppy with relief.

"You mean Toby and I," Mom corrects her, in the voice of decorum.

Saskia hugs Mom as if she could fix her to the foyer floor forevermore. "Where were you?"

"I already told you." Mom strokes Saskia's forehead. "I just stepped out."

"What happened to your face?" She touches Mom's chin, which looks like a scoured turnip. "Are you okay?"

"I got it while I was out walking." Mom unbuttons her coat with a secret smile.

"You're done up all wrong," Saskia says when she sees that the buttons on Mom's cocktail dress are awry. "How'd that happen?"

"I wouldn't know," Mom replies coyly.

"Wait. Did you fall down?" Saskia inspects the palms of Mom's hands to see if they got hurt in the fall. She can't understand why Toby, who is watching them from the bedroom doorway, isn't happy to see that she's back. "Stop joking, Mom. What happened?"

"I went out for some fresh air."

"You were out 'walking'?" Toby says, in a tone that tells Saskia this isn't funny anymore.

"Indeed, and the time just slipped away," Mom replies,

smoothing her tousled hair.

"Is that so?" Toby leers.

"Don't get fresh. When you want me to look the other way, I look the other way. When you want a free rein, I give you a free rein."

"But this is different," Toby says adamantly.

"To continue along this line of argument would be ill-advised," Mom says with scratchy innocence. "You wouldn't want me putting the spotlight on you now, would you? I'm going to lie down and by the time I get up I want this place looking shipshape again."

Naomi joins Toby, clutching her robe tightly to her chest. "What happened to you?"

"Why the tragic face? You made it perfectly clear you didn't want me here last night, so I made myself scarce." Mom daintily steps out of her silver shoes and with that, their trust in her is forever tarnished.

* * *

From the window seat in the living room, Saskia can tell that it's one of those brisk autumn days, crispy like a candy apple. Some kids from the building are playing handball in the park, but love or money couldn't get her to go downstairs. Not after what happened this morning. Not with the thought of what Mom did last night still banging in her head.

"You don't want to know what's going on here," she whispers to Daddy's framed photo, his eyes punching through the glossy image on the mantelpiece. No one has left his or her room since Mom got back and it's now late afternoon. Naomi hasn't taken any phone calls and Mom's bedroom is clearly a no-fly zone.

A door slams and Toby comes into the foyer in his pajamas. Either he doesn't see her in the living room or he pretends not to.

She follows him to the kitchen to find him eating cold soup from a tin can. "What's going on?"

"I don't know. You tell me." He flinches as he cuts himself on the lid.

"Was Mom really out walking?" The mere thought blisters her brain. "That doesn't make an ounce of sense."

Toby runs his bleeding finger under the tap. "Truer words were never spoken."

Saskia gives up and turns to leave.

"Wait a minute." Toby chucks the soup in the overflowing garbage and gets a beer from the fridge. "Sit down."

Saskia pulls up a chair, feeling as though she's been summoned to the principal's office.

Toby pulls the tab and takes a bracing gulp. "Mom left last night with Manny and came back this morning. You do the math."

It's like a pop algebra test. "No, that's nuts. Think about it; she's way too old for him."

"Think again," replies Toby grimly.

"But that doesn't explain her chin."

Toby sighs. "Hello? He has a beard."

It's not algebra. It's advanced calculus. "You're not saying what I think you're saying."

"Oh, I'm saying." Toby takes another swig.

The image of Manny's hairy ass bumping up and down on Mom makes Saskia want to blind her mind's eye. "That doesn't mean she was there."

"Where else would she go at midnight? Besides, Naomi

tried calling him all night and the phone was always off the hook."

"How could he do that to Naomi?"

"Beats me. Mom's guilty of a lot of things right now, but at least she didn't know about Naomi and Manny." Toby shakes his head in disbelief. "How Manny has the brass balls to pull this one off is beyond me."

"Have you asked Mom about it?"

"Yeah, right. Like I'm really gonna do that."

"But shouldn't we tell her?"

"Naomi feels lousy enough as it is. That would finish her off."

Saskia and Toby sit in silence at the kitchen table, until the sky outside the window darkens and the aircraft warning light on the Chrysler Building starts winking in the distance. When the grandfather clock strikes seven, Saskia gets up to marinate the hamburger meat while Toby rouses Naomi from her room and persuades her to come and eat with them.

They tuck into their sloppy joes until the patter of approaching high heels alerts them. Naomi's chewing halts when Mom comes into the kitchen, wearing one of her new outfits.

"Is this some kind of mutiny? I thought the place would be tidied up by now." Mom finds a clean glass among the dozens of discarded ones and pours herself some water.

"I'll get started after dinner." Saskia can't bring herself to look at Mom's chin, which is now covered in powder.

"Aren't you going to offer me any food?" Mom asks.

Saskia plows into the messy silence. "I thought you were still sleeping."

"I'll have it later when I get back from my walk," Mom

says, the picture of rude health.

Naomi looks at her imploringly. "Please don't go out again."

Mom hums brightly while she rinses her glass off in the sink.

"I really don't think it's a good idea," Toby interjects.

"Last night, you didn't want me here. Tonight, you want me here." Mom throws her hands up in pretend confusion. "Make up your mind."

Saskia jumps in. "We have. We want you to stay with us."

"You kids have each other. I need a night off."

"But you had one last night," Toby says.

"So? There's nothing wrong with that. I'm the adult here after all, which means I can walk when I want, where I want, and with whom I want." And with that edict, Mom collects her coat and pocketbook and leaves her clusterfucked children behind.

* * *

The past becomes more past to Saskia that night, as she drifts through the empty apartment with its sour-sweet stench of day-old alcohol and the gloomy tang of food abandoned in haste.

Time has ceased to fulfill its function ever since Toby and Naomi left for Arthur's in what could have been a day or a decade ago, but was probably only a matter of hours.

After the door slamming and decision-making that happened right after Mom left, there was silence, or what she thinks was silence because all she was conscious of was the ocean in her head. Then there was a void where she must have dropped off, exhausted by the weight of water, whereupon she woke to an apartment as dusty and deserted as Pompeii.

After eating the cold remainders of everyone's dinner, Saskia puts on Naomi's purple high heels and tries on her best dress, the Biba one that Oma got for Naomi when she visited London, the one she never even lets her touch. But it was too intimate, like wearing her sister's used underwear, so she changes into Naomi's nylon green slip instead.

Then she goes through Toby's room, idly examining the roach clip, the "Nixon Knew" button, the chewy-looking thing wrapped in paper, and the old Valentine's Day cards in the cigar box by his bed. She's never done this before, but the skein of protocol is now ruptured. That much she knows.

Having the place all to herself is like being in quarantine, or what she imagines jet lag to feel like. She eats ice cream straight from the tub right there on the couch, with her feet on the table, shoes and all, among the lipstick-smudged glasses and birthday bouquets, now shedding their petals.

Then she goes to Mom's room to solemnly study the items on her dressing table like she was reading Sanskrit, before falling asleep on Mom's bed, wearing Mom's pearl necklace, with all the lamps on.

She must have dozed off again, because she wakes up on a moist cushion of spittle. At first, she thinks Mom has come back, but it's only the chatter of her brain, spinning impossible dreams.

The bedside clock says 3:13 but that can't be right, so she goes to the window to check the time against the illuminated Con Ed clock tower. She's never been up at this late hour, not even on New Year's Eve, and feels like a mere firefly in comparison to the dense grid of phosphorous light.

She puts on Mom's silk bathrobe and returns to the living

room to watch TV, but there's only crap and more crap on at this time of the morning, so she turns it off and plugs the silence with music. The records are still a mess from the party, so she starts putting them back in their sleeves, until she comes across John Coltrane's "My One and Only Love," which was once, and not so long ago, Daddy's favorite song.

Clutching the disk as if it could steer her to him, she puts the album on, then switches off the lamps one by one. She starts by sitting in front of the mantelpiece, but it feels as though she's waiting for Santa so she moves back to the couch and lies down, smoothing the silken folds of the robe around her.

With hands clasped in prayer, she squeezes her eyes shut and pleads for her father's spirit to return. Nothing happens, so she frowns and calls out again to the heavens, more intently this time. She scans her surroundings for a sign, but all she can make out is the distant wail of a siren above the muted traffic. She holds her breath and summons every cell in her body to claw his silent soul back into being. All she wants is to suspend the relentless nothingness of death for just a minute, or even two.

When the song ends she swings the needle to the beginning to start it over again. She repeats this, twice more, then switches the record player off.

She reaches into the air, as though she could shape Daddy with her bare hands. A creaking floorboard heralds her surge of hope, but it fades as the silence returns, noiselessly echoing throughout the empty apartment.

Drained by the effort of trying to conjure him, she opens her dry eyes and surrenders herself to the knowledge that has accompanied her throughout this restless night. She will spend the night alone. Mom will spend the night with Manny. Naomi and Toby will spend the night with Arthur. And Daddy will spend the rest of time away from her.

6.

The Three Stooges

November becomes a month Saskia would like to forget. Confusion and its partner, denial, are now her constant companions when Marathon Mom, as she is dubbed for her after-dinner "walks," starts spending nights at Manny's more frequently.

At first, it freaks Saskia out to wake up and find Mom gone, but she gets used to that. She gets used to Mom arriving back home as the three of them are leaving for the day. She gets used to the smell of Manny's cigarettes in Mom's hair. She gets used to the complicated silence that comes when she helps Odessa change Mom's still-made bed. She gets used to bullshitting about Mom's whereabouts when Oma calls. She gets used to practicing a speech in her head in which she tells Mom why she has to stop what she's doing, now. She gets used to losing the nerve to actually say it when they're together.

Now that Mom has been released from nine months of pounding sorrow, she is unrecognizable. She may as well have a new face, or have gone blond with lust. She buys an Afghan kaftan and starts using Manny-words and drinking Manny-margaritas. She stops seeing Libby and Tom when she decides they're square.

Manny is never mentioned by name, but he is the invisible ink drawn in the curve of Mom's hips and the high notes of her laugh. Saskia doesn't understand how Mom can't see that Manny is also scribbled all over Naomi, so shapeless and distant, or Toby, who starts looking into transferring to colleges out of state.

The nights when it's just the three siblings, they are clumsy but considerate. They seek to listen to each other's mood. Toby and Saskia do their best to bring Naomi back to herself, but she is everywhere but with them. Naomi is still a passenger to rejection and is in a place they can't reach.

That is bad, but December is worse. Mom is home every night now, but the secret that's not a secret is that's due to Manny getting a hotel gig in Florida.

But Christmas won't be Christmas. There will be no tree. It may as well start raining oranges when the snow globe that is Saskia's world is turned upside down by the news that they're moving to a cheaper place on the Upper West Side. *The change will do us good,* Mom insists. *It's meant to be.*

Saskia feels as if she's losing her bones. Not living here will be like living without any muscles. She doesn't know how she will be able to stand not calling this place her home.

* * *

"This isn't the Upper West Side, this is Harlem," Saskia declares in disbelief when the cab passes a single-room occupancy hotel on West End Avenue with laundry hanging from its windows, then draws up next to a torn mattress on the curbside in front of their new building.

The doorman, whose red jacket is liberally trimmed with cheap gold braid, comes out to help them carry their bags inside the lobby. Saskia can detect the scent of roast kasha while the three of them wait for Mom to get the keys from the super.

The super arrives to take them to the second floor in the service elevator and helps them negotiate the sticky lock while Mom reapplies her lipstick. How on earth Mom found the time to put on her face before the moving men arrived this morning is beyond Saskia, who's still wearing the clothes she slept in.

"Ta-da!" Mom trills and throws open the front door. The kids traipse into the foyer, which reeks of cigarettes and is in need of a paint job, and exchange skeptical looks.

To the right, there's a galley kitchen overlooking the garbage cans in the back alley and an adjacent maid's room. The swing door connects the kitchen to an interior-facing dining room with peeling plaster rosettes, and off to the other side of the foyer, the living room tenders a distant glimpse of the Hudson River through the bare treetops of Riverside Park.

So far, not so good.

They then find a bedroom and a bathroom with a rust-stained tub, before ending up in the master bedroom. "What's this doing here?" Saskia says, pointing at some boxes, a TV set, and an empty beer bottle. "It's not ours."

Toby thumps his forehead with the heel of his hand. "Don't tell me the maid's room is my new bedroom. It's too small to even change my mind in."

"This place is like *The Twilight Zone*," Naomi adds and picks up an ashtray from a nondescript dresser set to examine a cigarette's dying embers. "I think we just stumbled into another dimension."

"Mom?" Saskia hurries back down the hall with Toby and Naomi. "The super gave us the key to the wrong place."

"I don't believe that's so," Mom says, adding the new set of keys to her Tiffany key ring.

"But someone else's stuff is already here," Toby says with strained patience.

"That may be, but this is the correct apartment." Mom busies herself with hanging her coat up in the front hall closet.

"Would you just listen to us for once?" Naomi snaps. "There's been a mistake."

Mom sucks in her breath. Just as she's about to speak, Manny comes through the front door struggling with a pair of speakers and a shopping bag. "I need a hand here," he barks.

Mom grabs one of the speakers and disappears down the hall, leaving her kids to stare at the owner of the boxes, the beer bottle, and the early-nothing dresser set.

"I thought you were in Florida?" Saskia splutters.

"I was. Then I took what's called an airplane and now I'm back in New York. It's also known as twentieth-century travel." Manny passes the remaining speaker to Naomi, who flushes when his hand brushes against hers.

"What am I supposed to do now?" Naomi asks softly.

"For a kid who goes to private school, you're not too swift, are you?" Manny smirks. "Go put it in the bedroom."

Toby takes the speaker from Naomi and shoves it back to Manny. "You can't talk to her like that."

"Hey, I was just spelling it out. I don't want there to be any confusion about where my things belong." Manny puts the speaker down and takes off his coat.

"Your *things*?" Toby looks to Mom, who has just rejoined them. "Earth to Mom. What's going on here?"

"Manny's our new roommate." Mom is so poised, so pretty, so ruthless. It should have been obvious that her red lipstick signaled danger.

"What?" Naomi manages, sounding as if her soul has been winded.

"You heard me." Mom hangs up Manny's coat next to hers in the closet. So, they've been her Three Stooges.

"How many Soyers does it take to get a job done?" Manny

hands the speaker to Saskia, who fumbles with it and starts toward the maid's room.

"Where are you going?" Mom asks.

"I thought you said he was our new roommate?" Saskia replies numbly.

"Darling, he's my new roommate."

Saskia blushes. Curly was always the slow-witted one of the three.

"Hopefully, by the time I get back upstairs, one of you will have succeeded in completing this simple task," Manny jibes as he goes out the front door.

The quality of silence thickens as Naomi runs down the hall to the bedroom, leaving Toby and Saskia alone with Mom.

In the crowded seconds that follow, there seems to be two Moms, moving in two directions; one, in her entirety and the other who is jazzed and jagged. There's a hum to her skin and the air feels noisy as Toby tries to find a way to say what needs to be said.

"Mom," Toby starts firmly. "There's something you should know—"

"Uh-oh. Here comes a lecture in bringing up mother," Mom interrupts tartly.

"No joke." Toby is now sharper in tone. "We need to talk."

Something in Toby's voice gives Mom pause, but then she jumps ahead again. "Maybe we've done enough talking. Maybe you need to listen to me, for once."

"Hear him out," Saskia pleads. "This is different."

"I'll tell you what's different. After feeling like I woke up in the wrong life, Manny's helped me find myself again."

"But *how*?" Saskia beseeches. "You're practically old enough to be his mother."

"Oh, I didn't realize Libby was in the room too," Mom shoots back, and then her manner softens. "I didn't expect you to understand right away, but I did expect you to want for me. And it would appear our wants are different now."

Hate hits Saskia's heart and she deliberately drops the speaker. She doesn't care that her display ends up costing her a month's allowance. For in choosing Manny, Mom has chosen her happiness over theirs. They will never be as they had been.

* * *

Saskia wakes up the next morning in the same bed and in the same clothes. But nothing else is the same. Closing her eyes, she imagines that she's back in Gramercy Park, a day and a lifetime ago. Opening her eyes she is met with the sunlight, spotlight sharp, highlighting Naomi's bare mattress, which is shoved in the corner as though it reached a dead end. A bag of shoes is spilled across the floor, as if Naomi abandoned them in her haste to leave for Arthur's with Toby the night before.

The air yelps as a car hits its brakes one floor down and the motor of a truck shudders like a hound. The sound of a male voice from the other room gives her a spurt of hope. She opens the door to call for Toby, then stops.

It's not him, it's Manny.

She closes the door and her mind, overcome by the sheer distance of it all.

Mom strides in, efficiency in motion, purse in hand. "Manny and I have decided to forgive your little blunder, and reinstate your allowance."

Saskia rolls over to look at the alligated wall.

"Thanks guys," Mom taunts in a falsetto tone. "That's big of you."

Saskia puts the pillow over her head.

"Say something at least, or we might have to reconsider."

Saskia ignores her.

Mom manages her impatience and says, "Just to show there's no hard feelings, I've come to see if you want breakfast."

Saskia doesn't budge.

"Do you want to go out to eat?"

Silence. And then Saskia cautiously asks, "You mean you and me?"

"No, I'm inviting Mayor Beame as well. It's a simple yes/no question. Are you joining us?"

Us kind of weeps with strangeness.

"*Us* us, or Manny and us?"

"I doubt he's planning on having the remains of last night's pizza for breakfast, so yes, us. I'm taking the entire household out for breakfast."

"So Naomi and Toby got back?" Saskia eagerly asks.

"The correct English is came back and the answer is no, they didn't. They certainly chose a fine time to shirk off. Now are you with me or not?" Hands on hips, eyes daring.

Saskia caves.

After a stodgy meal of eggs, yellow rice, and black beans at a Cuban diner, the lopsided trio return to this new situation called home.

Saskia knows that she should start unpacking, but that would be an admission that this is home. It is not, nor can it be. That's impossible, with Manny here. It may be where they happen to now live, but to her, home will forever be the one they just left.

She makes a space to curl up on the bed, and starts sinking into something she can't get out of. Her body feels like a sandbag. The effort to think, to plan, to move, exhausts her. Life has weighed her down again. Whatever kind of happiness that comes along after unhappiness has now moved further from reach.

* * *

In the weeks that follow, a flatness engulfs the siblings while an artificial propriety settles over the household, like still water covering broken glass. Saskia urges Naomi to come clean with Mom, but Naomi refuses, saying she doesn't want to give her the satisfaction of knowing that Manny chose Mom over her.

As for the apartment, it's funky. Every time they light the oven, hordes of cockroaches stream down the sides, like droplets of rusty water. Toby's four-poster bed doesn't fit in the maid's room, so a foldout takes its place. The edges of the Oriental rug curl up against the living room wall like a splayed sock. The bathroom sink permanently drips. Gusts of winter wind make the windowpanes rattle. The pipes clang at odd hours of the night. Mournful sirens can be heard from the Hudson river traffic.

Arthur's return to Northwestern forces Toby and Naomi to spend more time uptown, whereupon they become a two-tier family, living separate lives and eating at separate sittings, like magnets that repel.

Mom invites Toby and Naomi to join them for meals, but at Manny's insistence stops pandering to them, seeming to prefer a wide berth over the critical scrutiny of her eldest kids.

Saskia becomes the fifth wheel, the spare tire rolling back and forth between the polar pairs. She hates even being in the same room as Manny, but loves her mother too much to relinquish her to hairy him. Manny seemed so playful when

Saskia met him, but he now uses Mom to call the shots. Like a bearded cockroach, he appears when she least expects it, never ceasing to spook her.

Mom and Manny's clocks seem to meet. Every day is a day in which they sleep late, and every day is a day in which, over warm gin and tonics, they endlessly discuss the broken mechanics of their lives. How she could have acted, how he could have been a world-class pianist, and how they'll prove to all the naysayers that time doesn't matter. They can still have what's coming to them. But it's talk that doesn't come cheap, now that Mom's supporting Manny who quit the shoe store to focus on his music.

By the end of January, Saskia has learned a lot of new things. That the headless chickens deposited at the tree on the corner of her block are part of a Santa Sangre ritual. That she has to wait by the token booth in the subway station to avoid the winos who live on the platform. That she has to wrap her arms around the platform post when the train comes in, in case some mental defect pushes her in front of the oncoming local like they did to that poor Barnard student just two stops away.

She always believed in her heart of hearts that Manny would be history by the time they reached the first anniversary of Daddy's death-day. But now that February is upon them, she's having second, third, and fourth thoughts.

7.

Not Just Peanuts

With eavesdropping as her new pastime, Saskia learns that despite their savings in rent the family is still living beyond its means—and that Oma has agreed to start footing the bill for the kids' tuition and Odessa's weekly shift on the condition that Mom gets a job.

The morning after she hears this, Saskia awakens to find Mom drinking coffee while circling help wanted ads in the *New York Times* and says, "It's okay, Mom. When they see you went to Sarah Lawrence they'll want to hire you."

Toby emerges from the maid's room and blearily reaches for a cup of coffee and a cigarette to jump-start his day. He took up smoking when they moved uptown and since Saskia won't let Naomi smoke in their room, she can smell when the two of them are in Toby's room, talking in hushed tones with the music turned up for privacy.

"Aren't you going to wish Mom luck?" Saskia asks him.

"Luck," Toby says lackadaisically while he investigates what's in the refrigerator.

Saskia leaves for school. Monday is bowling day and she hates it with a vengeance. She seems to be the only person in the school who doesn't want to get high and since she has yet to make friends, she always ends up walking to University Place with Emerson.

She made a play for Ethan, but it was obvious he had a thing for Becky and never gave her a second look. She tried hanging out with Becky after school but they didn't quite click since Becky turned out to be a total pothead. Andy was too popular for the likes of her so then she attempted to buddy up to Tabitha and Florence, but that went nowhere. The two of them are everything she isn't. They can talk to Ethan without getting tongue-tied. They always have a snappy answer for everything. They know what they want. They are a unit of one.

And then there was *that* incident, when she walked into the darkroom while Florence was developing negatives, and Florence cursed her out for ruining her shot. Tabitha comforted Saskia when she found her crying in the bathroom, and explained that Florence was upset because she was entering the print in a citywide competition, but it definitely set them back even further.

Saskia would do anything to be friends with Tabitha, who has a kind of glow about her. Judging from the stuff she writes in English, Saskia would bet good money that she'll write a bestseller one day. Whereas Florence can get spiky quickly and vent at the drop of a hat, Tabitha is more gracious. But it doesn't matter, since they're just fine without her.

After an abstinent day at school, she returns home to find Manny watching TV in his robe, eating an Entenmann's coffee cake with his fingers, straight from the box. His perpetual pajama party weirds her out. She's in the kitchen getting some Chips Ahoy cookies, when Mom comes in carrying a shopping bag and the day's mail.

"You can congratulate me," Mom announces. "I got a job. I'm going to work part-time at Charivari."

"What's that?"

"It's a boutique right here on Broadway. But that's not all. I also signed up to volunteer for Jimmy Carter, just to get back at my mother for telling me what to do."

Saskia thought Mom would be something cool, like an

interior decorator, and wonders if Oma figured on her blue-blooded daughter getting a salesclerk kind of job.

Mom pulls a bottle of wine from a paper bag and starts sifting through the drawers for the corkscrew. "And I get a discount so we can go shopping there."

Saskia wonders what, if anything, will be left from her paycheck if they fall into that habit but smiles, hoping she'll be proved way wrong.

* * *

When Mom goes to Jimmy Carter's campaign headquarters the following Saturday, Saskia tags along for the ride.

The disused storefront on Columbus Avenue is still buzzing with excitement after Carter's thumping win in the Iowa caucuses. Signs proclaiming "A Leader, for a Change" adorn the walls and a basket of "Not Just Peanuts" campaign buttons are on the front desk, being overseen by a glamorous thirtysomething blond in tight jeans and a tangle of necklaces.

"Good afternoon, I'm Mrs. Soyer. I signed up last week." Mom extends her gloved hand.

The woman sizes her up and laughs abruptly. "This ain't the PTA, lady. We go by first names here. I'm Morgan. And you?"

"Meredith," Mom replies. "And this is my daughter Saskia."

Saskia settles on the bench by the door with her textbook, but is soon distracted by the phone's constant ringing and the blast of cold air every time someone comes in. She puts the textbook down and clocks Mom taking notes while Morgan shows her how to use the Xerox and franking machine.

Morgan puts Mom's cup of coffee at an empty desk and says, "You can start by typing these addresses. We need to get the mailing out today. Don't forget to make two copies. The carbon paper is in the top drawer."

Mom places her pocketbook by her feet and squints as she lines the carbon up with the paper, then loads it onto the platen after several attempts. She sucks her bottom lip while she slowly taps the keys, flinching when the bell signals the carriage return. Then she brushes aside a fallen strand of hair, leaving a warpaint-like trail of blue carbon ink on her cheekbone.

"Mom," Saskia hisses. "Mom!" She points to her face and makes a brushing motion.

Mom starts when she hears her name and turns, knocking over her mug and splashing her silk scarf with coffee.

"Now look what you've gone and made me do," Mom exclaims and rises from her chair only to trip over her pocketbook and stumble, scattering a neighboring tray of unopened mail onto the floor. Mom looks at the mess in dismay, then darts to the ladies' room, flush-faced.

Saskia avoids the volunteers' curious looks and hurries to the bathroom, to find Mom's leather boots peeping out from under the closed stall.

"Mom? I'm so sorry. I didn't mean to make you do that. I'm such a spaz."

The bolt slides and she pushes the door open to find Mom sitting on the closed toilet seat, head in hand. Saskia moistens a hand towel in the sink and gently rubs the blue stain off her mother's wet cheek, kissing it dry. The only thing she hates more than seeing Mom cry is being the one who makes her cry.

"Did Oma pay you to do that?" Mom jokes weakly and takes off her silk scarf for Saskia to rinse in the sink.

Morgan strides in and hands a purple Sherman cigarette to Mom. "You smoke?"

"I do now." Mom's hand shakes when she accepts a light. "I'm sorry to be a drag on the campaign."

"Lighten up. It's not the end of the world."

"It's just that sometimes . . ." Mom stifles a cough when she inhales. "Never mind."

"What were you going to say?" Morgan presses.

"No, it's unbecoming to complain, especially in front of strangers."

"Hey, I'm no stranger. We're working together. What is it?"

Mom pauses to compose herself. "Nowadays, I feel like everyone is waiting for me to fail."

"Like who?" Morgan lights herself a green Sherman.

"My kids, my mother, you name it," Mom confesses. "It's been like that ever since my husband died."

"You look too young to be a widow," Morgan says, dropping her match to the floor. "When did this take place?"

"Eleven months ago," Mom says forlornly. "In those early days, there were nights when I wished I'd never wake up. It's different now that I'm with someone who gets me, but now my two eldest act as though they expected me to wear sackcloth and ashes for the rest of my life. If it weren't for Saskia, I wouldn't have any family on my side."

Saskia rubs the stained scarf with liquid soap, her conscience as cold as the water coming from the tap.

"Family," Morgan snorts. "That's an institution as moribund as marriage. I was married too, but I divorced years ago. Wedlock is a padlock."

"Well, that's one way of putting it." Mom tosses the unfinished cigarette into the toilet. "I gladly served nineteen years in my marriage."

"So if you're such a big fan of 'holy matrimony,' then where's your ring?"

"Larry would have wanted me to find my feet, and wearing it around my boyfriend made me feel like I was having an affair, so I took it off." Mom regards her bare fingers as if they weren't hers. "My mother can't stand the fact that I'm seeing someone younger. I keep on telling her that he makes me happy, but she's not ready to hear that."

"Typical," Morgan scoffs. "That's parents for you."

Mom pulls a lipstick from her bag. "If she had her way, I'd be back home in Philly dating eligible men from the Social Register."

Morgan takes the lipstick from Mom. "Allow me. The light's lousy in here," she says as Mom turns to her, lips pursed obligingly. "You remind me of all the reasons why I sent my girls to boarding school after my divorce. Everyone gave me a hard time, but I knew it was best."

Mom lets Morgan apply the lipstick, then says, "They must be very mature young ladies."

"Oh, they are," Morgan enthuses. "To change the world you have to change the individual, and to change the individual you have to change their upbringing."

"Don't you miss them?" Saskia asks. Morgan is like some exotic scent she can't tell if she likes or not.

Morgan looks at Saskia as though she didn't notice that she was standing there all along. "I don't have time to miss them. Besides, it's not like we don't talk."

"But that's not the same, is it?" Saskia asks.

Morgan speaks slowly, as though she's the Anne Sullivan to Saskia's Helen Keller. "Precisely. I'm showing them a new way of life to help make them better people."

Saskia's mouth mutely chews the air.

"They don't go to Miss Porter's, by any chance?" Mom asks. "I almost went there, but ended up at Germantown Friends instead."

"God no. That place is too white-bread," Morgan vaunts. "I sent them to New Mexico. I'm sure your kid here would dig it. I'll bring a brochure so you can see for yourself."

Saskia visualizes the states ticking by one by one, miles tumbling into more miles, the Great Plains stretching like oceans of grass with herself alone on some butte, and ever so accidentally splashes Morgan as she wrings the scarf. She'd rather be left back than be shipped out west.

"Boarding school?" Mom demurs. "I'm not sure about that."

"You don't know what you're missing. I'll tell you, it sure freed me up for my work."

"What do you do?" Mom asks.

"I'm an actress."

"Have I seen you in anything?"

"Oh, I'm in all the soaps and I do theater. You're very attractive, did you ever act?"

"Well, funny you should ask. Someone from William Morris approached me after they saw me in summer stock, but I didn't follow up on it."

"Are you crazy? Why the hell not?"

"One second I was having some fun, then the next second I was married. Everything happened so fast."

"And you never gave it a shot?"

"Well . . ." Mom falters. "I always meant to, but before I knew it I was pregnant. Then that put an end to that."

"We don't have to live the way our mothers did," Morgan

bellows above the roar of the hand dryer, which Saskia is now using to dry the scarf. "You have to move with the times. You should come to an encounter group with me. It'll blow your mind." Morgan fishes for a piece of paper in her bag to write her number on.

Saskia goes outside to wait by the piles of nicotine-colored snow while Morgan makes Mom promise to give the campaign a second chance.

"Mom?" Saskia reaches for her gloved hand when she finally emerges. "Are you really going to call her?"

"As a matter of fact, I am. I found her perspective very refreshing." Mom clutches Saskia's arm as her foot encounters a patch of ice. "Manny always reminds me I have the right to go with the flow, too."

"Does this mean I'm going to boarding school?" Saskia asks as they turn right on Broadway.

"I'd sooner dye my hair orange than send you away," Mom replies.

"Does this mean that Naomi is going to instead?"

"Heavens no. What makes you say that?"

"Mom?" Saskia hurries past a one-armed Vietnam vet panhandling in front of the Metro Theater. "There's something I want to say about Manny."

"Then say it."

The truth weighs like a stone on her conscious. "But I'm afraid it'll make you mad."

"Then don't say it." Mom waits for the light to turn green. "Why ruin a pleasant day?"

* * *

The next morning, Morgan calls to invite Mom out to brunch and she comes home midafternoon brimming with Beaujolais and bonhomie. Then that Monday the two women go to a lecture at the Ms. Foundation where Mom buys Saskia a copy of the record album *Free to Be . . . You and Me.* On Wednesday, Morgan calls to invite Mom to an off-Broadway show in which she's starring. When Manny gets a last-minute restaurant engagement, Mom ends up taking Saskia on what turns out to be an uber-weird night.

Saskia thought off-Broadway literally meant off-Broadway in Times Square, but this disused warehouse on East Fourth Street is god-awful Broadway. The East Village looks like downtown Beirut. Saskia could swear she heard a distant gunshot, when the cab dropped them off right by a group of winos huddled around a burning garbage can.

The play is a political satire in which Morgan has a solo—sung to the theme tune from *All in the Family*—with an antinuclear message. The man sitting beside Saskia falls asleep and she would happily join him, but the place is too cold.

After the show Mom mingles in the foyer with the other theatergoers, all of them drinking sangria with their coats on.

"What are you doing?" Saskia asks when Mom helps herself to seconds and starts toward the stage door.

"We can't leave without congratulating Morgan."

"You mean *moron*?" Saskia retorts.

"Don't be rude," Mom says and waves to get Morgan's attention. "And for goodness' sake, say something nice."

"Well, hello ladies," Morgan breezily greets them.

"You were terrific," Mom says. "That was just super."

"Well done," Saskia mutters, embarrassed by Mom's girl-crush.

"And what a turnout," Mom continues, giddy with praise.

"I know. Isn't it great? Too bad Gray wasn't here tonight, to introduce you."

"Gray?" Mom queries.

"My therapist. You know, the one I want you to meet. I have him to thank for my career. He was the one who encouraged me to get serious about my life."

"You weren't working before you met him?" Mom holds Morgan's drink while she lights a cigarette.

"God no. I was just at home, climbing the walls looking after my kids by myself, until Gray showed me that there are other ways to parent and other ways to live."

Saskia yawns and picks up Mom's hand to see what time her wristwatch says.

"You know full well that motherhood can be as restricting as monogamy. Gray doesn't believe in exclusivity. He thinks sex is about playing and having fun, *n'est-ce pas*?" Morgan says. "He also says that—"

"Can we go now?" Saskia interrupts their mutual-admiration society. "It's pushing ten and I have a math test tomorrow."

Mom gives her the iron eyebrow, so Saskia goes to sit by the radiator until, two or three decades later, she and Mom clamber into the back of a cab.

"That was a fun evening," Mom says. "I'm glad we went."

"The show stunk, and Morgan stunk the most of all. She's a legend in her own mind who can't act to save her life," Saskia blurts in exasperation.

"Who are you to say?" Mom's voice is shot with contempt. "She's doing what she set out to do. She didn't give up."

The air in the cab sours as a bitterness seems to take seed

within Mom.

"Motherhood and marriage," Mom chants in sarcastic singsong. "Were supposedly the be-all and end-all for my generation. I bought into all that apple pie baloney, and look where it got me."

Her words are a bruising reminder that Saskia is one of the apples that Mom blames for her blight. It's like the seasons between them have changed. Spring doesn't follow what used to be winter. They are in a permanent state of fall. "Just drop it, Mom. Forget I said anything."

"I'm tired of tiptoeing around, being everything to everyone. I'm finally answering to myself," Mom declares loudly. "I've the right to want more out of life without seeking your approval."

"I said okay," Saskia intones glumly as she watches a squeegee man at a red light hustle for change.

"I've known Morgan for all of five days, but she's already shown me more respect than Libby or any other of my so-called friends, who judge my choices from their well-feathered little lives."

"Okay then."

"Okay," Mom mimics. "Is that the only word you know?"

"What do you want me to say?" Saskia shoots back. "It's not my fault."

"I never said it was."

"Then why are you shouting at me?" Saskia exclaims as the cab turns onto Broadway.

"I'm not shouting," Mom yells, before continuing in a clipped voice. "I'm just expressing myself as I see fit."

* * *

On the morning of Daddy's first death-day Saskia opens her eyes expecting to see pale-yellow walls and the matching bedspreads that Oma purchased from Liberty of London. Instead, she is met with the sight of a cracked ceiling and paint swatches and the sound of two drivers arguing over a parking spot on the street below.

I miss you, Daddy, she mouths, not wanting to wake Naomi, whose matted hair looks moss-like on the pillow. She wonders if Daddy can hear her thoughts or look down on her like a sputnik in the sky. But if death is an infinite void, then he's as far away as the galaxies combined.

She rolls on her stomach and pulls the blanket over her head, feeling here, there, not quite anywhere. Now she exists in a parallel abyss, not fully present, not much of anything except an aching, arid mess.

Time was different before. It was once a geyser, a wellspring from which all good things flourished. She used to see growing up as a series of exclamation points. She'd go to Rome! Get her first job! Fall in love! But she is no longer a citizen of that self.

Saskia gets dressed and goes to make breakfast, the tap of her loafers breaking the morning stillness. She plans on ticking both God-boxes by lighting a memorial candle in a church and a Yahrzeit candle in a synagogue, like two ship-to-shore distress flares. She puts the coffee on to hurry things along and gets out the Raisin Bran.

Mom comes in, donned in a negligee. "Why aren't you dressed yet?" Saskia asks crossly.

"What's the rush? It's Sunday."

"Don't you know what today is?" Saskia wills the water to boil faster.

Mom pours two glasses of Tropicana and says, "Tilly

– 118 –

called to invite us to the cemetery for some Matzi-something or other, but I told her that's not where we're at right now."

"I'll go." Saskia pushes away her cereal and springs up. "I haven't seen Tilly for ages."

"There's no way I'm letting you take the subway to the back end of Brooklyn by yourself, and I'm certainly not accompanying you. Anyway, I'm not sure wallowing in the past is best for us right now. As Morgan says, we need to follow our bliss and learn to—"

"Yeah, yeah. Find our whatever," Saskia snaps.

"Don't take that tone with me."

"But we need to do *something*." Saskia stamps her foot. "It's not just another day. We can't just act like he never existed."

"You're not the only one who loved him."

"If you loved him so much, then what's Manny doing here?"

"You have no idea what it took me to get to this point. When I lost Larry, I thought I could never put one foot in front of another again," Mom says, eyes blazing. "I should be congratulated for not giving up."

"I'm sorry," Saskia says, as cowed as she was angry just moments ago.

"Manny will be wondering where his juice is. Now stop acting like a teenager and remember every day is a gift," Mom says, balancing the glasses while opening the swing door.

Saskia runs back to her room and climbs into bed, fully dressed, to cry. Maybe she has it all wrong. Maybe she has to jettison the past. Either that, or she's living in cloud cuckoo land.

8.

A Hostile Integration

Every Wednesday after school, Saskia returns to an encounter group meeting in the living room. Her house now resembles some skewed version of the Statue of Liberty. Instead of the poor, tired, and huddled masses, she finds the empowered, enlightened, and self-actualized women of the Upper West Side talking loudly over warm bottles of Ernest and Julio white wine. But on this particular Wednesday the meeting was canceled since they had to go shopping for a new outfit for Mom to meet Morgan's agent in.

"It never occurred to me what a sacrifice I made, forsaking everything I worked for to juggle having three kids in six years," Mom explains to Morgan as they sift through the clothes racks in Loehmann's Backroom.

Saskia hates the way these encounter group sessions make Mom carry on so. She hates the way Mom makes her children call her Meredith now. She also hates the way Mom shines the spotlight on their past, which is clear to Saskia in a way that the present is not.

"How about this?" Saskia holds up a corduroy suit.

"I'm trying to help Meredith *get* work." Morgan selects an orange shirtdress instead. "Don't listen to her."

"But Mom, you look good in navy," Saskia says.

"You mean Meredith," Mom corrects her.

"What's wrong with 'Mom'?" Saskia grumbles.

"The term is limiting," Mom says tartly. "I have an identity outside of motherhood."

"Whatever you do, don't mention you have kids. Let Lenny

think what he wants to think," Morgan says.

Mom holds up the dress that Morgan chose in front of the mirror and touches the softening under her chin. "Do you think I'm too old to be doing this?"

"Nonsense. If I can get work in soaps, Lenny can get you work in soaps. You don't look a day over thirty."

"What's your secret then?" Saskia asks, sugar-sweet.

"Saskia, don't be rude," Mom says. "I'm sorry, Morgan."

"Your daughter's quite the comedian," Morgan retorts. "But I've got news for you, little sister. I'm thirty-five and that doesn't stop me from getting hired."

"As what?" Saskia rejoins.

"If you're going to act like a child, I'm going to have to treat you like one," Mom says in no uncertain terms. "You wait out here while I try this on."

"My kids are just the same," Morgan says. "Here, let me help you." Morgan thrusts her moccasin pocketbook at Saskia, like she's a hotel chambermaid, and follows Mom into the cubicle.

Morgan's bag is unzipped with her wallet right on the top. With her heart going like a jumping bean, Saskia flicks the wallet open to examine her driver's license. Morgan is forty-one. And her real name is Megan McBride. And she was once a brunette.

"I sometimes forget you're a mother," Mom says from inside the dressing room.

"I take that as a compliment," Morgan replies. "Spin around and I'll zip you up."

Saskia turns the leaf to a spanking-new school photo of two elementary school-aged girls. Inscribed in tipsy letters it reads, "To Mom. Love Marit and Rene."

Morgan never let on that her daughters were so young. They couldn't be older than seven and nine, tops. Saskia shoves the photo back in the plastic sleeve and helps herself to a few dollars, as though Morgan owes her for making her feel sorry for her kids who are stuck in some desert town two thousand miles away.

Mom comes out of the changing room to examine herself in the full-length mirror. "Well?" she asks.

"I don't like the color," Saskia says. "It makes you look sallow."

"No, it highlights your skin tone beautifully," Morgan says. "You're positively glowing."

Mom frowns at her reflection and sucks her lower lip.

"Lenny will sign you right away," Morgan says, and in so doing, seals the deal.

* * *

The following Tuesday afternoon, Saskia finds herself waiting in a window booth at Charles' Coffee Shop on the corner of Fifty-Eighth while Mom is off meeting Morgan's agent. They're supposed to be downtown in twenty minutes for parent-teacher night at the Collective, but that doesn't look like it's going to happen.

Mom had downplayed the appointment when she'd sworn Saskia to secrecy the week before. "I don't want Naomi and Toby getting ahold of this one," Mom had said. "I'm not mentioning it to Manny until there's something to tell. I can't wait to surprise him."

Mom had prepared for the meeting meticulously by brushing up on her elocution and deportment. She'd spent the previous week practicing tongue twisters in the bath and vacuuming the apartment with a book balanced on her head. She'd also thrown herself on a crash diet of pink grapefruit, cottage cheese, and black coffee while Saskia forewent Entenmann's and English muffins to help keep up her morale. It was a small price to pay, given that Mom could land a commercial, quit her dumb job, and move them back to Gramercy Park.

Saskia just loves the idea of Mom becoming an actress. Everyone always says Mom looks like Natalie Wood, so why shouldn't she cash in on that? Saskia's so busy thinking about how they'll spend her first paycheck that she starts when Mom taps on the window of Charles'.

Saskia hurries outside to join her. "Well?"

"Well what?" Mom has her sunglasses on even though it's dusk. "You're so monosyllabic. Can't you string a sentence together?"

"How'd it go?"

"How many times do I have to tell you to enunciate when you speak?" Mom fumbles for a subway token in her change purse when they reach the station at Columbus Circle. "I don't think it's going to work out."

"But why not? Did you tell him you did summer stock?"

"That's hardly relevant. He's not what I had in mind."

"Why's that?"

Mom waits until they're on the downtown platform before she answers. "It's because he handles background players."

"What's that?" Saskia asks, with a sinking ache.

"He hires extras to appear in TV shows." Mom peers down the dark tunnel to see if the local is approaching. "Morgan is on the soaps, but in the background."

Saskia's hope flattens like a penny beneath a wheel. "So she lied to you."

"Don't exaggerate. Morgan is on TV," Mom says. "It just happens to be in a nonspeaking capacity."

"That's lying."

"It's easy for you to sit there and pass judgment on us working mothers," Mom retorts. "She's a theater actress who is doing what needs to be done in order to make a living."

"But she said she's in all the soaps!"

"And she is." Mom wipes her lipstick off with a hankie. "But if it's a choice between waiting on people in a store or waiting around like some hungry cattle on set for twelve hours, then I'd rather stick with what I know."

"Maybe you'll get discovered."

"Darling, ingénues get discovered. Not widows who are the mother of three." Mom takes off her hoop earrings and slips them inside her pocketbook. "I may pass for thirty on a good day, but at times like this I feel about a hundred."

"What are you going to say to Morgan?"

"I'm going to thank her for getting me through the door, and tell her that it's not for me. At least I got to tread the boards that summer," Mom says wistfully. "And I'm going to make an appointment to meet her therapist, Gray, to see if he can help me as much as he helped her."

"But why?"

"Because there're no second acts in life, and it's too soon to call it curtains on mine."

* * *

It's one of those rare dinners where all of them are actually seated around the same table. But just because it's rare doesn't make it special.

Manny, who is at the head of the table carving the chicken,

tut-tuts when Saskia helps herself to seconds on bread. "You're going to get fat if you continue eating starch like that."

She returns it to the basket.

"No one's going to want to eat it now that you've touched it," Mom adds.

"Can you pass it over when you've finished your game of hot potato?" Naomi says.

Saskia hands Naomi the breadbasket and finds the appetite to push back. "It's not fair. How come you never get on her case?"

"You know full well she takes after my side of the family," Mom replies. "While you take after your father's."

"I'll translate," Toby says. "She's saying you're more shtetl than Philadelphia Main Line and that you might get fat."

"I'm not fat," Saskia declares sullenly, wishing for the thousandth time that she had her sister's effortless figure.

"Of course not. You just have to outgrow your puppy fat," Mom says, before hurrying into the kitchen when the timer rings.

"If I were you, I'd start watching what you eat," last-word Manny adds.

Saskia gives Manny the death stare and stabs the peas on her plate.

Toby winks at Saskia from across the table.

"Do you like breast?" Manny asks, offering the plate of carved meat to Toby.

"No, I'm a leg man myself." Toby is the picture of earnestness. "Do you like breast? My guess is that you prefer a mature bird to a young chick."

Saskia chokes on her peas, trying not to laugh. Naomi suppresses a smile.

Manny scowls and serves himself. "Everything is always a big joke with you. Don't you take anything seriously?"

"I'm not laughing," Toby replies. "Does anyone hear me laughing?"

"I didn't hear a thing." Naomi tries to keep a straight face as she reaches for the butter.

Mom comes back in carrying a steaming bowl of broccoli. "What's so funny?"

"I was just asking Manny if he likes breast," Toby replies.

"Really, Toby," Mom says with a frown. "Don't be fresh. It's unseemly."

"I think it's a perfectly legitimate question. I would place good money on him selecting a premium cut over wings, and I bet he's very particular about his choice of bird."

Manny stops carving and lets the utensils fall with a clatter.

"You're not a Perdue man. You're after quality white meat, am I right?" Toby asks.

Manny glares at Toby and bails from the table.

"Are you happy now?" Mom says to Toby, as she takes off her apron to follow Manny from the room.

Naomi shoves aside her plate of uneaten food as soon as Mom goes. "Another enjoyable meal. I'm out of here."

Seconds later, Mom ushers Naomi back in. Saskia detects a lecture coming on when she sees Mom's flinty expression and springs up to bring her dish into the kitchen.

"Sit down." Mom refills her wineglass and glares at her kids, daring them to defy her. "Do you know how long it took me to prepare that meal?"

No one moves.

"I was in the kitchen for an hour. We were at the table for no more than ten minutes."

The siblings stare straight ahead.

"What do you have to say for yourself, Toby?" Mom says, voice barbed.

"I was just making small talk," Toby retorts.

"No, you were making trouble. And I've had enough trouble to last me a lifetime, thank you very much," Mom says.

They digest that statement for a moment. Naomi starts to say something and stops.

Mom tries a new tack. "I want you to be okay with where I'm at and equally, I want to be okay with you."

Naomi nudges Saskia, cheeks puffed like she's going to be sick.

"Your point being?" Toby says.

"Manny isn't about to go anywhere, and I can't be the referee all the time," Mom says evenly. "So it's time for you to move on."

"I see." Toby holds her gaze. "And how do you suggest I go about doing all this moving and shaking?"

"Morgan has a fantastic shrink who happens to be local," Mom says. "I was thinking of seeing him myself, but the money might be better spent on you."

"Who, me?" Toby bitterly scoffs. "*I'm* not the one around here who needs their head examined."

"It's your responsibility as the eldest to set the right tone."

Toby sighs and gazes at a point above Mom's head.

"I'm only asking you to try it, is that so much to ask?" Mom cajoles.

Toby exchanges a look with Naomi, who shakes her head no behind Mom's back.

"If not for me, then for us."

"Which us?" Toby replies tersely.

Mom gathers her words. "The us that communicates, has conversations, eats together. Not the boarding house I've been running."

It's like a game of statues, Saskia thinks. No one moves when the others are looking.

"It's ironic," Toby says. "Every time I've tried to talk to you for real, you won't listen, and now you want to pass me off to a complete stranger."

"Is it wrong to want a different conversation?" Mom asks.

"It's just that—" Toby starts to say.

"I'm the one who's offering a solution," Mom interrupts.

"That may be, but—"

"I can't do this without you."

Toby looks at Naomi who rolls her eyes and shrugs.

"This is the deal then," Toby says. "If I go, will you promise to hear us out? And by us, I mean all three of your kids."

"I promise," Mom replies. "What's the worst thing that could happen? You have everything to gain and nothing to lose."

* * *

Mom and Manny go out that Friday night and with that, there's a feeling of more air. Saskia and Naomi spend the evening putting up posters in their room while listening to the Grateful Dead. They make each other laugh by "losing" Manny's toothbrush out the bathroom window. They've long finished eating their Kraft macaroni and cheese dinner and are watching *The Sonny & Cher Show* in bed by the time Toby returns from his first session.

"What took you so long?" Naomi asks. "You've been gone forever."

"We had a lot to talk about so we ran over the hour."

"Ouch. That's going to cost." Saskia moves over to make room for Toby, but he settles on the radiator cover instead.

"No, it isn't. He did that as a friend."

"Since when are doctors friends?" Saskia asks.

"Since when are you the expert?" Toby says, with an edge to his voice.

Saskia checks his expression to see if he's kidding. He's not.

"Did he have a fancy-schmancy office?" Naomi asks.

"Not at all. He lives in Morgan's building. In fact, they sort of live together."

"They?" Naomi asks. "Are they a couple?"

"No. It's not like that. They're more like a community of friends."

"How many are you talking here?" Naomi says.

"I didn't exactly conduct a head count, but maybe eighty or so."

"How on earth do they manage that?" Saskia is baffled.

"It's not an ant colony. They all room together in different apartments in the same building, but Gray kind of runs the show," Toby explains.

"You called the doctor by his first name?" Saskia asks.

"He's not a doctor, he's a therapist. A supercool one at that." Toby seems to warm up. "It's hard to describe. I consider myself to be a hip, downtown kind of guy, but I felt like a country rube in big-city company around them. They're all involved with the bigger picture, like politics and self-awareness and stuff." He looks at his slack-jawed sisters and sighs. "Let me put it in a way you'll understand. It's like they live in some super-elite Gotham City and Gray is their Batman."

None of these terms seem to go together. Saskia tries to picture what this Gray might look like, and draws a blank. He doesn't even sound like a person. He sounds like a place, or something that could happen.

"So, did Bruce Wayne make you lie down on a couch?" Naomi says.

"I'm not going to tell you anything if you're going to make fun of it," Toby warns her.

"Kidding. What did the Caped Crusader have to say?" Naomi asks.

Toby's expression darkens. "He said my relationship with Mom is a hostile integration."

Saskia tries to package his statement. "Is this what the doctor said?"

"For the tenth time, Gray's a therapist, not a doctor. But more than that, he's an ally and a friend. He *listened*, which is more than Mom is capable of," Toby says, then proudly adds, "And he identified me as a seeker."

Saskia and Naomi exchange looks, and then Naomi asks, "What's that?"

"It's someone who actively seeks to fulfill their potential. Which I can't, because Mom keeps holding me back." Toby becomes increasingly incensed as he elaborates. "He said the first step's the hardest, and then it becomes surprisingly easy. He said once you begin to question your conditioning, then everything else falls away. He said it's obvious Mom doesn't give a rusty fuck about us, and the sooner I accept that, the better off I'll be."

"My, my. By the sounds of it you've had quite a cheerful evening," Naomi says.

"Don't be flippant. It's about you as much as it's about

me." Toby gets up to leave. "You weren't the only one who was betrayed."

"No shit. Difference is, I don't need someone to tell me that," Naomi shoots back.

"What's with him?" Saskia grumbles after he slams the door. "I've never seen him like that before."

"Don't worry, we'll be one big, unhappy family again in the morning." Naomi turns up the volume on the TV and adjusts her pillows. "What else did you expect? Morgan's a nut job and Mom set up Toby for this. It was bound to fail."

* * *

Over the next couple of months, the Toby who Saskia knows fades like a print that has been left too long in solution. She can't explain it, she can't quite place it. But that doesn't mean it isn't happening.

Toby looks the same, but he's not the same. He's in therapy three times a week. He loses his humor. He locates his anger. He gets in touch with his inner child. He appoints blame. He finds his wounded self. He talks about the process.

And then one blustery April afternoon, on her way home from school, she sees him standing on the corner of West End Avenue, surrounded by suitcases. He doesn't know she's there, waiting for the moment that's been a long time coming to pull focus.

A cab pulls up and pops the trunk. And then she knows what this moment means. It means he's moving out for good. It means he's doing this for his own good. It means he's doing this for as long as it takes, or forever.

She calls for him to wait but he doesn't hear her. Or chooses not to. She can't stop what's already in motion.

Hello to another goodbye, another ending, another thing for her to get over.

There's a letter from him to Mom waiting on the dining room table when she gets home. Saskia already knows what it says, but that doesn't stop her from reading it anyway.

He is moving in with the Sullivanians. He is ceasing contact with the family while he undergoes intensive therapy. He is dropping out of Columbia. He has no regrets about his present, only his past. He has come to this decision independently. He is legally an adult now. He would be a hypocrite if he continued to live with one. He needs to find himself. He can't be a part of something that he doesn't believe in anymore.

And just like that, with a click, he's out of the shutter, changing the family picture forevermore.

9.

Doing History

Saskia is sitting on Toby's folding bed, alone in the funk of his new bedroom. She's not allowed to be here, really. It's against the Sullivanians' rules. She thought Toby was kidding when he said that, but he couldn't have been more serious. That's what he's been like ever since moving here. Stern with change and angry with those who don't share his vision.

In the days that became weeks after Toby left home, she felt as if she were waiting for a boomerang that didn't return. It defied logic. *How* could he be seven blocks near, yet seem so afar? *Did* he mean what he wrote to Mom? *Was* Mom right in maintaining that he just needed some space to cool down in?

Mom stopped saying that, after she got the call. It was late, and the ringing had woken Saskia up. Mom's voice had risen so sharply she thought someone had died so she'd snuck down the hall to listen in. *He hates me.* Mom wept while recounting the conversation to Manny. *He said he's permanently ceasing communication at his therapist's advice.* So, this is how it works, Saskia thought at the time.

It doesn't.

The phone call had changed things, or so Mom thought. Together with Manny, they started hauling ass and setting curfews, but it was already too late. By that point, Naomi had lost seven pounds, was cutting classes at school and had started doing History with Gray.

Saskia knew all this, because she had been coopted into being Naomi's alibi. So as long as she maintains that they're swimming together at the Sixty-Third Street Y, then Naomi can keep coming to these meetings.

Lying to Mom makes Saskia feel like a word whore, but it's all part of trying to right the yin and yang of her broken family and keep in with her siblings. So that's why she's here, for the third Tuesday running, sitting once again in Toby's room.

Everyone from the eleven or so shared apartments in the same building is assembled in what is supposed to be the living room but has been set up like a lecture hall. But she's never sat in on a session or set eyes on Gray, so she couldn't say for sure.

Saskia doesn't know what History is, but she can see what it's doing to her sister. *Try me* or *why don't you ask Toby,* Naomi taunts Mom with brittle insouciance. *It's complicated* and *I'll tell you one day,* is all Saskia gets when she broaches the subject on their weekly walks to and from Ninety-Seventh Street. When pressed, she'll elaborate. *Gray's the first person to help me make sense of myself.*

It seems funny to Saskia that having gone through his entire life with his very own room, Toby is now sharing one with three other guys—one from Milwaukee and the others from Lincoln and Wichita, random cities in distant states she's never set foot in, now joined in the name of community, or is it counterculture, or some such fancy word that they like to bandy about so freely.

But Toby evidently likes his new setup and acts as though his recent roommates are the best friends he ever had. *Arthur?* He tolerates the question the same way he tolerates her. *I've moved on.* Relationships become interchangeable. *My therapist is also my roommate. My roommates are my new family.* Words become flexible. *I'm learning to get off my focus. She's my alternate validator.* Theirs is a togetherness that excludes.

Toby seems oddly happy nowadays, except when it comes

to the topic of Mom. Then, as fast as heat conducting in a silver spoon, he goes moody and even tearful and shouts at Saskia to leave.

Saskia scans Toby's bedside table. In place of his Columbia textbooks, there are secondhand volumes on Marx and nutrition and one of those shiny books—the kind you'd see at train stations or drugstores—about government conspiracy theories. She riffles through his datebook to find that his weeks are now a complicated jigsaw of therapy appointments, Group meetings and something called FD. Scribbled notations run down the margins. *Our ways are not for others to judge. Sex is playing. Don't seek validation, just the truth.*

She promises Toby she'll stay in his room, but she's sick of keeping promises when everyone around her is breaking theirs. To the sound of applause from the front of the apartment, she sneaks into the room next door, which has another four cots, and then the final bedroom, which sleeps three. These rooms, with their bare walls and empty suitcases and fruit crates doubling as drawers, speak of decisions made hastily at best.

She ventures down the hall and sees a bra hanging on a partially open door. Knowing she shouldn't but that she will, she peers inside. There's an unmade mattress and a purple chiffon scarf draped on a lamp. There's a condom wrapper and a lipstick-covered cigarette butt in the bedside ashtray. There's a list of names taped to the back of the door. There's a dirty-sweet smell to the air.

The list falls down when she closes the door, so she hurriedly reattaches it. It's then that she sees it. *Fuck dates* is scrawled in pencil above the couples' names, which include Toby's. *FD.* Just like she saw in the datebook.

Footsteps alert her that someone is approaching, so she

dashes back to Toby's room just as he comes to get her to join in the History.

"Do I have to?" She balks when they reach the corridor outside the living room, which is decorated with posters that read "The Personal Is Political!" and "No More War."

"It's nothing to be scared of. We just share our memories and reflections."

"I won't have anything to say," Saskia protests.

"You don't know that yet. And anyway, my roommate told Gray you're here, so you have to attend. House rules."

"But—"

"But nothing. Gray wants you to take part," Toby says earnestly. "He's so insightful. One session with him puts everything into perspective."

Saskia wants to know *whose* perspective, but it's too late.

The room feels eggy with anticipation.

A reedy man is rocking a grown woman who is crying, while others sit together holding hands. Some stare at her, others seem not to take notice.

Toby leads her to a dais, where a burly man is seated on a director's chair. At first glance, he looks like an out-of-work Macy's Santa. Only this one has food in his beard and her sister by his side.

"Here she is, Gray."

"Ah. The little interloper." Gray turns to Toby and asks, "What do you have to say for yourself?"

Toby sounds apologetic. "We're only as strong as our weakest link?"

Gray waves him off and beckons Saskia to come closer. "Do you know what we do here?"

Saskia presses her hands together to stop them from

shaking. "Not really."

"We tell the truth and process trauma. That's the work."

His scent of tobacco and spittle makes her stomach float.

"I see. And I help others to see. It's what I do. It's only when we externalize what's suppressed that we can begin to process." Gray seems to lose interest and motions for her to sit beside Toby. "Naomi was in the middle of telling us about her background."

Her knees welcome the chair.

"How would you describe your childhood?" Gray asks.

"It was nice." Naomi checks herself and then adds, "I mean it was passable. It was certainly bourgeois. I wanted for nothing materially."

"Let me guess. I bet you took European vacations?" says a woman with Cleopatra hair.

"No, never. Just summer rentals and the occasional Christmas break."

"It sounds like you were spoiled rotten," a mustached man sniggers.

"Too right. I've seen her apartment. They have furniture that looks like it belongs in a museum," Morgan says, from her perch in the corner.

"Go on. Admit it. You're just another rich kid," the mustached man taunts.

"I guess you could say we were, but then when Daddy died on us—"

Gray interrupts her. "Correction. Didn't we agree that his death was a form of suicide?"

"Sorry. When Daddy *chose* to die, that's when things started going downhill," Naomi explains in a choked voice.

"Another correction," Gray interjects. "That's when you

became aware of your mother's psychosis."

"You're right. I was blind before that." Naomi's eyes fill with tears.

"Blind and. . .?" Gray urges her. "Come on, get off your focus."

"Catatonic with depression." Naomi finishes his sentence and wipes her eyes.

Gray nods astutely.

"Needy, anxious, and filled with buried hatred," Naomi recites.

"Was your mother ever violent?" a red-haired woman asks.

"I was spanked a few times."

Toby leans forward, hand raised. "Remember that croup attack?"

"I was really young then," Naomi murmurs, avoiding Saskia's bewildered gaze.

"Mom fell asleep when you were sick and you almost died," Toby says. "Mom had a death wish and wanted you to die."

"Do you have anything to add to the History?" Gray addresses Saskia.

The room seems to billow like a sheet. "Mom was probably tired," Saskia says weakly.

"Tired?" Gray bursts into laughter. "You're a disapprover who wants to approve. Why do you think they call it a 'nuclear family'?"

The room knows what Gray wants. "Because it's toxic," the room answers.

"Family is the root cause of social anxiety. And I'm the gardener trying to get rid of the weeds so you, the flowers, can grow. How many of you were endangered by your parents?"

"My mother fed me peanut butter before my allergy was diagnosed, and almost killed me," a woman in overalls offers.

"I almost choked once, when mine made me finish a sandwich against my will," adds the woman with Cleopatra hair.

"My father made me swim in the deep end before I was ready, so I almost drowned," a ponytailed man adds with an air of incensed excitement.

"The average parents are corrupters." Gray's words cut like a blade. "The sooner you own that thought, then the sooner you can embrace your individualism."

Applause erupts. A woman seated next to Saskia breaks down in tears and confesses, "Every single time I hear Gray speak, it reminds me of why I had to disown my entire family."

Gray makes a gesture and the clapping ceases abruptly. "What else do you have to share with us?"

Naomi takes out a letter she's prepared and clears her throat. "If anyone had told me fifteen-odd months ago that this was my future, I would've laughed out loud," she reads. "I always viewed private school and a comfortable home as my birthright. Yet I've found it necessary to renounce these privileges because they come at such a cost. I can't live a minute more in my mom's crowded love nest, so I'd rather fly right out of her life. Therefore, I'm asking you, as my new true family, to let me make a fresh start. Let me become a stronger and more focused individual, through what I'm learning with the Sullivanians."

Whispers whoosh throughout the room as the members confer among each other.

"Let's have a house vote then." Gray says. "All in favor of Naomi joining us?"

Toby is the first to raise his hand, then everyone follows suit. Gray asks, "That's decided then. Do we have any Adepts in our midst?"

Saskia's mind collapses under the burden of yes, it's happening again. That thought propels her out of the meeting, down the hall to where she left her coat. *Double-fuck them for using me*, she thinks. *If they don't want me, I don't want them* is what carries her to the lobby, where she finds Naomi and Toby waiting for her.

"I know it's hard for you to get it." Naomi is the first to break the ice. "But if I don't leave home, I'm going to end up jumping in front of a bus or checking myself into a funny farm."

"If you're going to lecture her about finishing high school, then save your breath," Toby interjects. "She's going to be in our theatre productions."

Saskia stews in silence, then asks, "What about college?"

"You think that's the only path, but I'm clear it isn't," Naomi explains. "There's a world of possibilities, once you open your mind to the process."

"For someone who is so clear, you seem to have forgotten you're a minor," Saskia says vehemently. "You can't just run away and drop out of school. Mom will call the police."

"So, let her," Naomi says with cold contempt. "I'm not a runaway from the boondocks living on a bench in Port Authority. They'll see that I have a place to live and a job."

"Job?" Saskia is mystified. "You've never worked a day in your life."

"Gray's offered her a babysitting job for his children, in exchange for room and board," Toby announces proudly.

They all stop talking when the elevator shudders to a halt

and an elderly lady with a shopping cart slowly makes her way from the elevator to the front door. Saskia is the first to continue. "So the great hater is a parent?"

"He's not a hater." Naomi looks at her in disbelief. "He's a forward thinker who believes the archetypal family model is limiting."

"He's creepy and controlling," Saskia insists.

"Not understanding doesn't give you the right to invalidate his methods." Toby jumps to Gray's defense. "He wants all kids, not just his, to be raised by babysitters until they're old enough to go to boarding school."

Boarding school. Of course, Saskia thinks, remembering the photo of Morgan's daughters. "That sounds awful."

"It's pure genius. By not exposing children to parental hostilities, they're able to form their true self amongst a community of friends," Toby explains.

"So, we had friends at school. You don't need to go to boarding school for that."

"Yeah, but think of the mess we returned to every night," Naomi adds.

Family dinners? Watching TV together? Who's the stupid one here? "What are you talking about?" Saskia exclaims.

"The constant drinking, the tension, their obsession with materialism," Toby lists with grim pleasure.

Did they? Were they? Saskia's mind rabbits. "I don't remember any of that."

"What house did you grow up in?" Naomi is askance. "Daddy wanted out so badly, he died."

And took us with him, is Saskia's first thought. *I wonder where this will end,* is her second. "We were happy."

Toby shakes his head sympathetically. "It was never like

you thought it was. I know that's hard to accept, but you need to hear us out."

"It's easy to put this all on Manny, when it's really about Mom," Naomi explains patiently. "She had a choice. She could have had any man in Manhattan, but she chose Manny. She chose to invite him to move in with us, she chose not to even tell us, and then she chose to overlook how that made us feel. And now I choose not to live with a bully and a liar."

"But Mom never knew about you two—" Saskia can't finish her sentence, for there it is. The dark mirror in Mom's being that gives nothing back.

"You're not ready to accept it yet, but it's there," Naomi says plainly. "And we'll be here, once you stop resisting the obvious."

"You know the truth," Toby adds. "And we know the way. You're never too young to join us, and start the process."

There is only one truth. Saskia loves Mom above all others. She believes that Mom's Manny-malfunction is a fault of circumstance, not character, and that her true mother will come back.

The lines are drawn in the silence that follows.

Goodnights become goodbyes.

Then she sees what this will be, stretched ahead of her.

Like cinnamon and sequins, her siblings have always been a source of dash and hue. Not having them around will be like not having blue. They will grow distant and the memory of them will fade. The sky will become beige, her heart sallow. She will look back and wonder if it ever was as bright as she remembered, or if she was always color blind.

* * *

And so, her sister goes, along with Mom's pearls, her diamond studs, and thirty dollars from her sock drawer. Mom and Manny go to report the theft to the police, but then it all goes belly-up when the cops go to Naomi's apartment share and Gray tells them to go to hell. By that time, Toby has also called Mom to say that he will go to the cops and testify that Manny used to supply him with pot if she presses charges, so unless Mom wants Manny to go to jail under the Rockefeller Drug Law, she should just go blow.

And then it all goes quiet.

Mom tells Saskia, just you wait, Naomi's guilt will soon get the better of her. But Naomi doesn't come back.

Mom writes to Naomi, but the letter is returned unopened. As is Oma's, who writes as soon as she hears the news.

Mom declares that the sooner she gets the freedom she wants, the sooner she'll come to her senses, but Naomi still doesn't come back.

At school, Emerson keeps asking Saskia why she looks so sad, but she can't find it in her to explain how everything got so messed up. Maybe it was all her fault for not spelling things out to Mom, and it's too late now that both her siblings are Sullivanians. She always wanted her own room but never in this way. This proves that something is wrong with her. She must be unlovable, because she keeps on losing everyone she loves.

10.

714

Like a fish looking for a school to attach itself to, Saskia starts getting off the subway a stop early every day to meander past the Sullivanians' building on her way home from the Collective. She even takes up smoking, to have an excuse to loiter on the corner like a toothless shark.

Her heart flip-flops every time the building door swings open, in case it's Naomi or Toby. But it never is. On one occasion, she catches what sounds like Toby's piano playing coming from an open window. She struggles to hear it above the uneven chorus of traffic, but the harder she listens the more the sound evaporates.

Her empty cigarette pack marks twenty days, twenty nervous hours, twenty more bedtimes with no one to talk to in the dark, twenty more times she sets the table for three, and another twenty solitary mornings. When her fifteenth birthday comes and goes without a word from them, she knows that Toby and Naomi aren't coming back anytime soon.

To make matters worse, Manny is always on her case now about everything from homework to her table manners. It's as though he senses her unspoken blame of him, so he's quick to find fault in her instead. She hates being alone in the house with him while Mom is at work, so she starts going to the library every day after school, except for the days when Odessa is there to watch her back. Saskia can tell by the set of her mouth that Odessa holds Manny in quiet disdain, and just loves the way she holds her ground around him.

When Saskia learns that they've enrolled her in summer camp, she knows that she has to come clean with Mom before she's shipped off to the back end of nowhere for seven long weeks.

But it's not so easy. Ever since Mom abandoned her encounter group meetings and campaign volunteering, they've become like John and Yoko, spending days in bed, curtailed only by Mom's part-time shift at Charivari and Manny's occasional gig or the few piano lessons he's managed to pick up.

One stiflingly humid Saturday afternoon, Mom takes Saskia shopping for her camp uniform. The heat of the sidewalk bores through the soles of her flip-flops as they walk down Broadway to Morris Brothers, searching for scraps of shade to protect them from the boiling June sun. Even the traffic seems listless. The cars are slow to accelerate and the buses fail to gather speed.

A little girl rocks desultorily on a mechanical horse in front of the barbershop while they wait for the light to change and, just as they're about to cross, Saskia spies Morgan in a tube top and a pair of cutoffs in a phone booth on the opposite corner and yanks Mom's hand to stop her.

"Easy there, Rocky," Mom jokes. "You don't know your own strength."

"Let's go have a Baskin-Robbins ice cream," Saskia stalls. "I'm starving."

"How can you be hungry in this—" Mom trails off and stiffens when she catches sight of Morgan.

"Leave it," Saskia implores.

But Mom marches through the flashing yellow light and positions herself outside the phone booth, glaring at Morgan like she's a cat in the henhouse.

Morgan finishes her call and taps the door, motioning for Mom to move aside.

Mom shakes her head no, hands on hips, perspiration stains under her arms.

Saskia feels like a kitten caught in a catfight.

Morgan pounds the door until Mom steps aside, claws at the ready. "Well?" Mom says.

"Well what?" Morgan adjusts her tube top and starts walking.

"What do you have to say for yourself?"

"I don't know what you're talking about." Morgan picks up her pace.

"You betrayed me. You had no business brainwashing my kids with your so-called therapy." Mom trots alongside Morgan to keep up with her. "What kind of person goes about breaking up families?"

"Oh, come off it," Morgan retorts. "Don't be such a hypocrite."

"What do you mean?"

"You've conveniently overlooked that you were the one who asked me to introduce your son to Gray in the first place." Morgan walks off, top cat once again.

"Just forget about her," Saskia pleads as Mom stands there dumbfounded, oblivious to the pedestrians streaming past.

Mom fumbles for her sunglasses in her pocketbook and then staggers, sending them plunging to the pavement. "I don't understand," she says vacantly.

Saskia picks up the glasses and pulls Mom into Morris Brothers, where she parks her in a chair next to a fan in the shoe department.

Mom puts her cracked sunglasses back on and sits, clutching her purse amid the bustle of the other mothers going through their carefully annotated lists as they kit their children out for camp.

A harried clerk with a pencil behind his ear approaches. "Can I get you anything, ladies?"

Mom doesn't seem to hear him, so Saskia extracts the photocopied inventory from Mom's pocketbook and sends him to the stockroom to find a pair of Dr. Scholl's in her size.

They sit like strangers on the IRT, while a toddler chases a balloon around the maze of empty shoeboxes and discarded tissue paper strewn across the floor.

"I wish I never met that hateful woman. This nonsense is all her fault," Mom finally says.

Saskia is lacing up her boot. "I hate her, too. What do you think, Meredith?" She holds out her foot to demonstrate how it fits.

"I think she's trying to pin the blame on me, and I—" Mom says indignantly.

"No, I mean—" Saskia butts in.

"Don't interrupt me while I'm talking!" Mom shouts, slamming her hand against the armrest so hard that a child in a nearby stroller starts to cry.

"I wasn't. I was just saying." Saskia's eyes smart with tears.

"Oh, don't you start too," Mom continues. "I'm tired of listening to everyone else's beef. I may not be perfect, but I'm doing my best."

Saskia goes to wait outside while Mom pays. She is running out of time. It's only three weeks until she goes away through August. She has to work fast. As they trudge home with their shopping bags, she vows to set Mom straight before she leaves for camp.

* * *

The next Saturday morning when Manny is out giving a piano lesson Saskia decides to go have that talk with Mom, that talk they should have had months ago.

She finds Mom airing her bed and tidying up the room.

Saskia closes her eyes and plunges in. "Did you ever ask yourself why Toby and Naomi left home?"

"Is that any way to start a conversation? Pull the sheet up, please."

Saskia straightens it and waits. She folds the blanket back and waits. She even plumps the pillow and waits. Until she can wait no more. "Well, did you?"

"Did I what?"

"Did you ever ask yourself why Toby and Naomi became Sullivanians?"

Mom looks at her as though she's grown a third head. "It's because they lost their father."

"Is that what you think?"

"It's what I know." Mom pairs the stray shoes scattered around the room and places them beneath the bed. "They were never like this before Daddy died."

"I bet you didn't realize that Manny was close to Naomi once." Saskia's hands start to shake. Will she have to draw an anatomically correct diagram to illustrate what she's talking about?

"That's teenagers for you. You're friends with them one minute, then you're on the outs with them the next. Now, go hang this up." Mom hands her a wet towel that was left on the floor.

Saskia places it on the rack in the adjoining bathroom. "No, I mean close-close. You know what I mean?"

There's silence. Saskia counts to ten, waiting for Mom to

explode. But nothing happens. She peers out of the bathroom to see the bedroom's empty and follows the sound of running water to the kitchen where Mom's clearing the brunch dishes.

"Did you hear what I said?" Saskia asks.

"What are you talking about?" Mom sponges down the table. "I don't have time for guessing games."

"The part about Manny and Naomi?"

"What part?"

"You know. The part why Naomi and Toby don't like him anymore?"

"I thought you were talking about Naomi. Now you're bringing Toby into it? You're not making any sense. Go fetch the dustpan and brush."

Saskia retrieves them from the hall closet and comes back to find that Mom is now watering the plants in the living room.

"What's with you today?" Mom asks as she plucks dead leaves off the begonia. "Don't you have any homework to do?"

"Yeah, but we were in the middle of a conversation."

"Is that what you'd call it? I'd say it was more like Twenty Questions, and you know how I hate playing games."

Saskia has passed the point of no return. "I was just asking why you think Naomi and Toby don't like Manny anymore."

"Saskia, if I stood around trying to figure out who cared for whom and who didn't, then I never would have had the courage of my convictions to marry Larry in the first place. You have no idea how hard I fought my parents on that one."

"Didn't you ever wonder why they got so pissed off when he moved in?"

"Those two wouldn't have liked it if I'd brought Aristotle Onassis home with a suitcase full of hundred-dollar bills. I'm not some stick-in-the-mud who waits around for the approval of others. What am I supposed to do, run alongside their lives for the rest of mine?"

The slam of the front door means that Manny has returned.

"Manny?" Mom calls. "Saskia was in the middle of some long-winded theory about why Naomi and Toby cooled on you. Do you know what on earth she's talking about?"

"You mean all the times I was there for them before they started acting like they never knew me?" Manny scoops back Mom's hair and starts kissing her neck. "Or when I set them straight when they were being fresh to you? Or the time when your daughter's imagination started running overtime?"

Saskia's mind roars. She always thought the truth was a simple thing, a fact that could not be altered or denied. But like a dance, it takes two. One to say it, and the other to be willing to listen.

*　*　*

As Saskia's freshman year draws to an end, Ariel, a graduating senior who is going to study modern dance at Bennington, asks her to her leaving party on Central Park West. This being Saskia's first and only invite of the year, she snaps it up.

Saskia thinks everything about Ariel is cool. Ariel's hair is so long she can sit on it. Ariel always wears a beaded choker. Ariel is a vegetarian, as well as being the only girl she knows who openly lives with her boyfriend under her parents' roof. Ariel asked her to join the United Farm Workers Union, so Saskia now spends many an afternoon handing out leaflets in Washington Square Park, jostling for the attention of pedestrians more interested in scoring pot than reading about economically exploited migrants.

Saskia changes four times before settling on cutoffs and

an embroidered button-down top that Naomi left behind. She goes to say good night to Mom, who is giving Manny a massage in the middle of the living room floor. Mom gives her taxi money and makes her promise to come home at a decent hour, before losing interest in wearing the mommy-mantle.

"Don't do anything I wouldn't do," Manny says as he makes himself comfortable with some pillows.

Grossed out, Saskia clears out, and reminds herself that she better be sure to make a lot of noise when she comes home in case they get carried away and get it on right there in plain view.

She bids good night to the block guard, who was hired after a student from Teachers College was raped on the adjacent avenue, and goes to the nearest bodega to stock up on Parliaments. She's tempted to pocket her cab money, but the crosstown bus is as infrequent as Halley's comet and there's no way she's walking through East Harlem. So she hails a taxi and soon finds herself on the landing outside of Ariel's fourth floor apartment, where, from inside, a Doobie Brothers record can be heard playing.

Saskia considers ditching the party and sneaking off to a double feature at the Regency instead, but when she pictures what might be going down uptown she presses the front door buzzer.

Ariel greets her with a Heineken-soaked hug and leads her to the kilim-strewn dining room with its table full of food before hurrying off to answer the door again. Saskia helps herself to orange juice and tries to blend in with the walls while everyone else drinks and yucks it up.

She examines a bronze horse statuette, as if it could start talking to her like Mister Ed.

She smiles at Becky, who waves as she goes into another room.

The bottle of vodka on the table whispers, *Take me to your lips. You know you want to.*

She slips into the kitchen. Thank god for the service entrance, she thinks. She could always disappear down the fire stairs.

The vodka calls out to her again, louder. *Try me. I won't let you down.*

But alcohol is bad for you. It's even worse than smoking, her conscience bickers, like Punch and Judy. *Yeah, but it's fun. Don't you want to have fun for once?*

When Ethan comes into the dining room, she answers the vodka's call and adds it to her juice. The first sip makes her splutter; the second goes down a treat. She knocks back the remainder of her drink and feels the commotion in her head start to untangle.

Ethan, who is trying to fill his plate with potato chips while juggling a cigarette and a can of beer, spills the chips. He points to the mess he made and says to her with a winning smile, "Be a doll."

Hello booze, goodbye shyness. Alcohol has made her visible again.

She picks up the chips and clambers to her feet. Ethan rewards her with a fresh can of beer and says, "I never thought I'd live to see the day when you'd be drinking."

"There's a first time for everything." The booze knows which strings to pull to make her as jaunty as a marionette. "And I mean, everything."

"Grab an ashtray and come with me. There's something I've been wanting to ask you."

Beside herself with excitement, she follows him to the living room to perch on his chair, ashtray in hand. "Well, what is it then?"

"Has Becky ever said anything about me?" Ethan asks hopefully.

The cords instantly tighten. "Not that I know of."

"But you'd let me know if she did, wouldn't you?"

She nods.

Ethan brightens when he sees that Becky is selecting a record on her own, and grabs Saskia's beer. "Just think of this as good karma," he says, then goes to offer her can to Becky.

Now her brain feels like a cat's cradle.

Andy, who has been watching them from the couch, shakes his head in disgust. "A fetus in utero has better manners than Ethan." He brandishes a plastic baggie of pills as though it's a packet of Shake 'n Bake. "Do you want a disco donut?"

She looks around to make sure he's talking to her.

"Yeah, you, Cinders. Come here."

She is all too happy to join Andy, who extracts a tablet from the bag and hands it to her. The pill looks like a Bayer aspirin with 714 stamped on its side.

"What is it?" she asks.

"It's a Quaalude. They're just like getting drunk, but less fattening."

"Do you think I'll like it?"

"No. I think you'll love it, and you'll love me for giving you this." Andy places it on her tongue, Communion-like. "Do you promise to renounce sobriety?"

She swallows the pill with the remains of his beer and waits. A tingling sensation blankets her. She struggles to extract a cigarette from her pack. Her lips go fuzzy and her body softens. Then a laugh rises up like a fart. This isn't a good party, it's a great party, and what's greatest is that she's fitting in.

"My god. She walks. She talks. She even laughs," Florence quips, when she saunters over with Tabitha, who turns Saskia's cigarette around when she sees that she's trying to light the wrong end.

When a rumor spreads that Ariel is doing coke in the bathroom, Tabitha, Andy, and Florence leave a blitzed Saskia on the couch to go join in on the act.

A blond boy in a Pink Floyd T-shirt catches her eye from across the room.

I'll show Ethan, she thinks hopefully. She takes a drag of her cigarette and extends her arm, almost burning a hole in the cushion.

The boy leaves his friends and makes his way over to her.

She oh-so-casually tries to blow a smoke ring and lets her hand drop to the space between them.

He puts out her cigarette, and then picks up her hand to admire her amethyst ring. The touch of his skin gives her bubbles down below.

"Hey," he says.

"Hi there." It feels like she's talking under water. "Where do you go to school?"

"Dwight," he says, stroking her wrist with his finger. "Or as we like to call it, Dumb White Idiots Getting High Together."

"You're funny," Saskia giggles.

"And you're pretty."

"Pretty what?" She flirt-slaps his arm.

"Pretty foxy. I'm Ben."

"I'm Saskia."

"I like your eyes." Ben leans closer, smelling of Noxzema

and Heineken.

"I go to the Collective." She can't stop grinning like a dork.

"I kind of figured," Ben says with a smile. "Ariel goes there and this is her party."

"I'll never remember . . ." Saskia starts to hiccup. "I mean I'll never forget . . . I don't know what I mean. I'm a little fucked up."

"Do you want to come with me to get another drink?"

Ben hooks pinkies with Saskia and leads her down the hallway to a darkened bedroom with a dressmaker's dummy.

Saskia giggles when she stumbles into an ironing board. "You goon. The kitchen's back there."

"No shit, Sherlock." Ben pulls her down next to him on the batik bedspread. "But at least it's quieter in here and we can get to know each other a little better."

They kiss, and his tongue turns her inside out. In a hot second she becomes his pleasure sack—a rippling bag of skin and sweat and the sweetest heat imaginable. Every cell of hers billows with the oneness of him touching her *there*. Blissed out and higher than the Twin Towers combined, she moans and whispers, "I think I love you."

"That's nice." Ben pulls away and reaches for the near empty beer can. "I need a slash. I'll grab us another Bud while I'm at it."

"Promise you'll come right back?" She bites his finger lightly. "Promise now?"

He traces the shape of her mouth with his thumb and leaves the door slightly ajar.

She luxuriates in her blurred, sensual state as she listens to "Hotel California" and the laughter coming from down the hall. Lulled by the music, the warmth of the bed, and her chemical cocktail, she closes her eyes to rest up for just a minute.

* * *

Saskia's eyelids flutter, then snap open when she sees light seeping in from behind the drawn curtains. She listens for music but the apartment is quiet, save for the distant scream of an ambulance on the street below. She scrambles to sit up when Ariel, who has changed from her party clothes into a bathrobe and braided her hair for sleeping, comes in and briskly opens the curtains.

"Hey, Rip Van Winkle. Wake up," Ariel says. "I thought you'd left already. The last people went home about twenty minutes ago."

Saskia's throat has turned to sandpaper and her tongue is cleaved to the roof of her mouth. "Where's Ben?"

"Your knight in shining armor galloped off. He went on a stogie run at midnight and never came back."

"Did he leave me a message?" It feels like there's a molting cat where her brain should be.

"No, but he left you a monster hickey."

Saskia covers the love bite on her neck with one hand while straightening the covers with the other. "Did he leave a number?"

"No, but he did make off with the cigarette money," Ariel says disparagingly.

"Did he say anything about me?" Saskia discreetly hooks her bra and buttons up her shirt.

"Wait. Don't tell me you went all the way?" Ariel asks.

Saskia blushes and shakes her head no.

"That's just as well. I hate to break it to you, but that guy screws anything that has a pulse. I mean if you were simply out to lose your cherry, then Ben is your man. But judging from what I know of you, you want something memorable, something that feeds into your Mills and Boon fantasy of what you think sex is about," Ariel says. "Am I right or am I right? I was fifteen, too, once upon a time."

Saskia gropes under the bed for her clogs and misplaced dignity.

"There's no need to be ashamed of what you did. Fumbled, drunken encounters are just classic stages of any teenager's sexual awakening. You can ask my mom if you like. She's a Gestalt therapist."

"No, it's fine. I'll take your word for it." Saskia scoots to the door and says, "Thanks anyway, it was a swell party."

Saskia takes the fire stairs two at a time down to the lobby. The doorman is asleep in his armchair and she doesn't have the heart to wake him. She steps outside and mercifully hails a taxi to take her home to Mom, who must be apoplectic with worry by now.

"It'll be a long hot summer." The cabdriver shakes his head when his transistor radio reports a triple homicide in Alphabet City. "Mark my words. We'll be lucky if the city survives."

She instructs the driver to wait until she's safely inside the building. It feels like her heart is about to hop skip and jump out of her chest as she opens her front door.

The hall lamp is off and there's pure silence.

"Meredith?" she whispers to no one as she takes off her clogs and creeps toward her room.

Poor Mom must have fallen asleep waiting for her. She opens the door, apology at the ready, but there's no Mom, no note from Mom on her pillow instructing her to let her know she's arrived home in one piece, no nothing, except the early morning daylight tipping through the windowpanes.

She gets undressed and slips into bed, telling herself that this is a good thing, really.

But it stings.

She thought that Naomi and Toby's departure would provoke Mom into acting like her real mother again, but she's starting to suspect that a part of her mother went AWOL with them too.

* * *

It's like Ben turned her tap on and left it running. She can't stop thinking about him and fantasizes about him constantly as she gets to know herself in the bathtub. She spends her allowance on a bottle of Revlon's Moon Drops eau de toilette in romantic readiness for their first date.

She pictures how it will happen: he'll get her number from Ariel and call to explain that his parents are very strict so he had to make curfew that night. He'll invite her out on a horse-and-carriage ride around Central Park. He'll confess that he's never felt this way about a girl while they neck in front of the carousel. She'll change schools to be with him. They'll go steady, then go to college with an understanding.

By the time she leaves for camp the following week, it's clear that she won't ever see him again. Yet she's still grateful that he gave her a taster of promise. The promise that she is somebody who someone could like someday. There is hope. She's discovered that she isn't allergic to men, and that they aren't allergic to her.

11.

Fuck You Very Much

When Saskia's bunkmates at camp find out that she's from Manhattan and ask her how many times she's been mugged, she takes it as a sign that she doesn't belong there. But by the second week, she finds that she does indeed belong. Mornings that commence briskly, communal meals, and the placid routine of activities and chores restore her sense of order. She writes weekly to Oma, Odessa, and Tilly. She receives a prize for her arts and crafts project. She swims before breakfast and perfects making her bed with hospital corners.

Here, she is free to whitewash her past. She highlights some truths, and colors over the bits that are too messy. By day, she is Saskia of Gramercy Park whose siblings are off at college, but, come night, her thoughts become smudged with worry about the impending Parents' Day, which marks the halfway point for the summer.

She can't blend Manny into this mix. She hasn't breathed a word about him to anyone and explicitly instructed Mom that only immediate family members are allowed to visit. If Manny were to tag along, then she would feign sickness and check herself into the infirmary. If anyone asked, she would say that he was a distant cousin.

On the morning of Parents' Day, she gets to the parking lot early and waits with her friends by the hospitality table, which bears plates of star-shaped cookies and pitchers of lemonade. There are noisy family reunions when the cars start to arrive. Dogs that have been cooped up for the ride race around in circles barking excitedly, while the campers embrace their parents.

Saskia is scanning the road for their station wagon when she spies a distant figure approaching on foot in the midday sun.

Squinting, she sees that it's Mom.

She starts running toward her, prickly with the awareness that she's left any chance of blending in with her tent mates who stayed in rank to serve refreshments, back down the road.

Mom limps to a halt and puts her Channel Thirteen tote bag down to throw open her arms in greeting.

Mom. In all her her-ness, comprised of that nameless element that forever joins them, are together once again.

"What happened?" Love and anxiety are never very far apart. "Did you break down?"

"I came up on the bus, but it dropped me off at the junction a mile back." Mom's sunglasses keep slipping down her nose, now slick from the heat.

"Why didn't you just drive here?"

"I sold the car. You have no idea how much it costs to keep one in the city."

Saskia's mood stumbles. Even the day workers at the camp arrive by car.

The pressurized desire to conform starts building in Saskia's head as she becomes conscious that Mom's sweat-stained wrap dress and espadrilles contrast sharply with the other mothers' suede loafers and kelly-green ensembles. At least Mom came by herself, she tells herself, but even that doesn't dispel the sense that they are moving in an alternate step to those around them.

She'd planned on taking Mom on a tour of the camp and showing her the macramé she won an arts and crafts prize for, but Mom confesses to having developed a blister from her walk so they claim a picnic table beneath a shaded oak tree, near a family who are playing Frisbee.

Mom produces a tub of coleslaw, chicken sandwiches, potato chips, and a bottle of 7Up from the tote bag. Saskia regales her with stories about what she's done and who she's met, looking for the formula to put them back in sync.

"You're not the only one with news," Mom announces as she unties the laces on her espadrille to ease her foot. "I got another job."

"What happened to the other one?" Saskia peels the chicken from the mayonnaise that has congealed in the heat.

"They wouldn't give me a raise, so I quit. You'll never guess what I'm going to be doing next."

Saskia casts her mind around hopefully. "Becoming an air stewardess?"

"Good god, no. Whatever gave you that idea?" Mom wipes her mouth with her hand. "Far, far from it, in fact. I'm going to make pasta."

The words clog in her throat. "What do you mean?"

"I'm going to be working for an establishment where one can procure fresh noodles."

"So, you're going to be selling it?" Her choice of verbs feels uncertain.

"No. I'm actually going to be in the kitchen, preparing it with my own two hands," Mom says with ersatz cheer. "I'm sure it will be quite amusing."

Saskia struggles to picture Mom in a chef's cap and apron. "But why?"

"Because someone has to pay the rent, and someone has to keep the show on the road, and that someone around here is me." Mom's mouth hardens. "I asked Oma, but she won't give me a penny more as long as I'm living with Manny."

"Can't he at least get a real job and chip in?"

"Manny's doing his best, but that's not how we operate."

"But that's not fair to you."

"Don't you go jumping on the bandwagon too," Mom says querulously.

There are a thousand things Saskia could say to that, but instead she asks, "Did you look around first for something else?"

"I filled innumerable applications and was offered something at Saks, but I didn't want to run into my old crowd in my old haunt, on the wrong side of the counter," Mom says with unalloyed candor. "Being a cook wasn't high on my list of preferred jobs, but needs must."

"Couldn't we cut another corner or sell another one of our prints, until you find something else?"

"At the pace we've been going there's not much left to sell. I've even had to part with some of my jewelry. That is, what your sister didn't make off with," Mom says with weary despondency. "None of this was on the curriculum at Sarah Lawrence. I'm realizing now that I would've been better off learning shorthand than getting my BA."

And with that, another piece of what Saskia held to be true collapses. All the things she'll never have, and the chances that'll never come to be, are ever growing. And all of this makes her feel smaller in a world that is so endlessly good at being complicated.

"I knew you would understand. Money doesn't grow on trees and besides, I wanted you to have all of this." Mom gestures toward the distant tennis court and archery range.

"You deserve it."

Looking at her verdant surroundings makes her conscious of how much camp really costs Mom. The other girls are here because they belong, but she's here because Mom made a sacrifice. And that thought makes her want to take the whole summer back. Money follows them like a trail of coins for the rest of the day, a persistent jingle that reminds her that if only for Mom's sake, she must make this experience count.

And much later that afternoon, when Saskia dons her Martha Washington costume to take part in the Bicentennial Parade, she knows that her worn out-ish and poor-ish Mom will have to slip off at dusk to limp down the road and wait at the highway junction for the bus back to New York, with her tote bag as empty as her bravado.

* * *

Saskia could kiss the piss-stained sidewalk when the chartered bus deposits the campers in front of Grand Central that mid-August afternoon. The bus ride, with the constant singing, chatter, and falsity has left her frazzled. She exchanged addresses with girls she'll never set eyes on again because she gave them her old details.

Saskia's first down the steps, welcoming the smack of heat, hot enough to make your eyeballs blister, melded with the scent of Sabrett's hot dogs. Waiting beneath the Tiffany clock, she eagerly searches the group of parents for Mom. When the crowd starts thinning, she sits on her trunk, while families load their station wagons and lock their car doors before heading back to the suburbs. By the time it reaches the hour, Saskia is one of a handful of campers left in the care of a chipper counselor. She wonders how she will get home if Mom doesn't show and keeps willing her to emerge, like Venus de Milo, from the sweaty sea of commuters.

Mom finally appears, hair damp with humidity, face smudged with fatigue.

"You're late-late-late," the counselor trills, as she checks Saskia's name off her list. "Some of us have places to go."

"Please," Mom says. "It's not as though I didn't try. I had to leave work early."

"Then you should have made arrangements with your husband," the counselor tuts, ponytail wagging. "That's what they're there for."

Saskia would like to stick the counselor's pencil where the sun don't shine and hurries Mom into a cab.

"How's the new job?" Saskia snuggles up next to Mom.

"Not so shiny new anymore," Mom admits with a sigh. "Let's just say I'm broken in."

"What happened here?" Saskia examines a cut on Mom's palm.

"I got acquainted with a paring knife." Mom regards her hands as if she's never seen them before. "Remember how I used to have manicures every week? It looks like I take in laundry now."

"Those days will come back."

Mom smiles feebly. "Let's hope so."

Their conversation stalls along with their cab in midtown traffic. Saskia gazes at a family wedged in an adjacent Beetle and feels like she's remembering another person's life when she recalls all the times she sat between Toby and Naomi in the back seat.

"Have you heard from anybody?" Saskia ventures.

"Oh, I've heard from plenty. The taxman, our landlord,

Ma Bell, you name it."

Saskia can't avoid the inevitable. "Have you heard from them?"

"Not a peep. You have no idea what it's like telling people that your own kids don't want to know you." Mom shakes her head in disbelief. "They look at me like I'm a monster, like I've done something wrong."

Their cab runs a red light and nearly collides with a Pontiac and a crosstown bus. A three-car pileup is preferable to what's waiting for me at home, Saskia thinks. "Don't worry, Meredith. I'm back."

"I've tried calling, but neither of them ever speak to me," Mom continues. "I write, and the letters are returned unopened. The only time they contact me is when they want money. How much more of this can I take?"

Saskia watches some kids frolicking in the open fire hydrant while Mom pays the driver and the doorman carries in her trunk. Mom turning up alone and not mentioning Manny has infused her with the hope that he's good and gone. She promises to be good if God delivers his end of the bargain and puts in a silent 911 to heaven while Mom unlocks their front door.

But the lines to heaven are down. Empty Chinese food containers, brimming ashtrays, and the *New York Times* crossword puzzle spread across the living room floor are all the evidence she needs. Saskia grabs Manny's pack, snaps his last cigarette in two and buries it in the leftover food. "Where's Manny?"

"He's at a gig," Mom shouts from the kitchen. "He's playing at a dinner dance at an old-age home in the Catskills." Mom comes into the living room, bearing a William Greenberg chocolate cake with "Welcome Home" etched in icing across the vanilla outline of the New York skyline.

Saskia wants to wrap herself in the moment. Time calms, as she absorbs the blessedness of her mother's love. "It's magic."

"I missed you terribly, angel child," Mom says, cutting two large slices. "I've missed not having you around."

Starved of TV and sugar for seven long weeks, Saskia pigs out on cake, *Hogan's Heroes*, *Sanford and Son*, and *Rhoda*, and is snuggled in Mom's bed watching coverage of Gerald Ford's presidential nomination when Manny gets back at eleven.

"Let her stay with me, just for tonight," Mom coaxes.

"Don't you think she's too old for this?" Manny grumbles.

"You can sleep in the maid's room," Mom adds. "I won't make a habit out of it, I promise."

"All right then," Manny says. "But I still think she's too old for this."

Saskia throws Manny a saccharine smile and mutters, "Fuck you very much." Nestled up in the four-poster bed, she gives her inner worrywart the night off. At last she's home and at last she's with her Mom, who loves her best of all again.

* * *

It dawns on Saskia that there are chips in the loving cup when Manny starts spending more nights in the maid's room. At first, she puts it down to his occasional gigs, or Mom having to get up early to go to work, but she gradually clocks a growing testiness where love and libido once reigned.

Slammed doors, hushed arguments, and Mom's red-rimmed eyes fill her with giddy promise. The more withdrawn Mom becomes the more Saskia blossoms, as she pictures the moment when Manny leaves and her campaign to get Toby and Naomi to come home begins. It won't be easy, but it's possible. What's impossible is this drift continuing, like a horizon with no end.

She gathers that Manny's been giving more than lessons to an aspiring pianist on Sutton Place when he comes home with a T. Anthony briefcase. Mom starts sleeping by herself and the house goes to pot. There's a surge of cockroaches in the kitchen and grimy rings sprout in the bathtub, but thankfully, Odessa still comes every week to clean and offer Saskia counsel.

The miracle on 104th Street occurs just days before Saskia starts her sophomore year, when Manny bunks out for the East River's high-end shores. Saskia is thrilled to see the last of him. Although she puts on a sympathetic act for Mom, she's a twenty-one-gun salute inside. At last, hairy him, his Hush Puppies and cheap dresser set, are gone for good.

* * *

The Friday after Manny moves out, Saskia cuts her last class to go drop the news on her siblings. She doesn't know how she'll say it, but say it she must. Now that Manny's no more, they can be as they were again.

It was spring when they left and it's autumn now, but her blood is running winter-cold with nerves by the time she reaches the Sullivanians' apartment building.

She enters the lobby by slipping past the A&P delivery boy, then takes the stairs to Toby's floor where she rings the buzzer. There are footsteps, then the door gives slightly, as though someone is leaning against the other side of it.

"Hello? It's me, Saskia. Toby's sister."

Even breathing can be heard from the reverse side of the

metal frame.

"Remember I used to come here to do History with Naomi?" She doesn't know if she's talking to Toby or to one of his hundred-and-one roommates.

"Toby, is that you?" She presses her ear against the crack. "Just say something. Say cheese." She waits. "Say anything, please."

There's a sigh and then the sound of receding footsteps.

It wasn't Toby, she convinces herself. It couldn't have been. I'll have a better shot with Naomi, because she hasn't been here for so long, she tells herself. She remembers from Naomi's forwarding address that her apartment is on the fifth floor. Arriving there, she finds four doors. One with a buggy outside, another with a mezuzah, the third has a walker alongside it, and the fourth with a "Nuclear Power? No Thanks" poster that she figures must be Naomi's.

She hears voices coming from inside the apartment and kicks herself for thinking she would actually catch either of them by themselves in the middle of the afternoon. She knocks until a drop of light spills through the peephole. "Please let me in. I'm Naomi's sister."

There are hushed murmurs and the sound of rapid footsteps. Then Naomi opens the door, leaving its security chain fastened.

"Hey, long time no see." Her words crumble under the pressure of Naomi's gaze. "Don't make me stand out here like a lemon."

Naomi grudgingly unfastens the chain and lets her in. "Take off your shoes then." Saskia slips off her sandals while sneaking a look around the foyer. There is a labeled cubbyhole for mail, and baskets for shoes and umbrellas. A mop is propped in a bucket by the door. A radio is playing in one bedroom; guitar practice is coming from another, blended in with the sound of someone showering.

Their hesitant kiss hello doesn't land. Their greeting buckles under strain. Something has been removed from their familiarity. Something has been taken from Naomi too. She's been rearranged, and gone from curves to a series of sharp angles.

"I've never seen you so thin."

Naomi registers her remark with a brisk shrug. "I've been working." She wrings the mop and motions for her to step aside so she can continue cleaning. "On one of our productions, that is. Today just happens to be my turn on the Rota."

Saskia struggles to fill the silence.

"It's been a while." She finds herself talking to her sister's back. "I bet you didn't know I went to camp this summer."

"How would I have?" Naomi seems to be doing what she is doing from a great distance.

"It was neat. I learned to sail and everything."

Their conversation evaporates as fast as their wet footprints on the floor.

"I turned fifteen. The three of us should go and celebrate sometime."

"What are you after?" Naomi replies, in a tone, the meaning of which she finds hard to grasp. "A cake or something else?"

"There's a lot to celebrate, in fact." Before she knows it, the words leave her mouth. "Manny's left. He's gone and shacked up with someone else."

Saskia's big news is reduced to a mere pebble.

"That doesn't mean a thing to me." Naomi's tone factual now. "I've already processed what happened there in my treatment. Manny was the contaminant, but Mom is the cancer."

That statement carries Saskia to a place she doesn't want to go. The space occupied by hope becomes clogged with the awareness of her expendability. "If Mom's the cancer, then what does that make me?"

"You're still at the symptomatic stage where you want to play the victim. Truth is, you're the one who rejected our ways." Naomi starts putting away the cleaning materials. "You have a choice, same as anyone. Toby and I were clear about that from the start."

Something inside Saskia gives away and threatens to come pouring out. There is too much of me and too little of them, she thinks. "So Manny or no Manny, neither of you are coming home?"

"We *are* home. You think you are, but you'll soon realize that you're not."

12.

The Next Best Thing

During the following month, Saskia perfects her culinary skills so Mom can relax when she comes home from another long hot day in the pasta shop kitchen. Although Mom is positively aching for Manny, Saskia takes guilty pleasure in seeing her wings clipped. She prefers Mom docile and dazed with depression, rather than the empowerment that comes when she's plugged into Manny's prick. At least she can recognize her old mother when she's sad.

However, one Saturday when she refuses to get out of bed, Saskia fears that she'll never be able to right her listing Mom. So she cajoles her into going to the Met, thinking that the Indian summer sunshine will set her straight again.

Mom, looking Jackie-like in her navy headscarf and sunglasses, stares blankly out the window as the taxi drives through Central Park, psychedelic in its autumnal glory. Saskia regales Mom with what she learned in school about Frederick Law Olmsted, but her words seem to bounce off her.

The Metropolitan Museum is a piece of bygone New York that still beats in the heart of fear city. Saskia loves its calm splendor and plans on rounding off the afternoon with tea across the street at the Stanhope, for old time's sake. The Met's grand staircase usually makes every entrance seem regal, but today she feels like Sisyphus as she gently steers Mom up to the main galleries, where they silently drift from room to room.

When they come across Camille Corot's *Hagar in the Wilderness*, Mom catches her breath.

"What is it?" Saskia asks, tight with nerves.

Mom sinks onto the wooden bench as though punctured, buries her head in her hands, and starts to weep. "I can't bear to look at that hateful painting. All I see is myself."

Saskia puts her arm around Mom and gives the hairy eyeball to a pair of curious blue-rinse matrons. She hates to admit it but the exiled woman, with her anguished eyes wailing over a prone child, who could be Saskia, does look like Mom. It's freaky, but the picture is the spitting image of the two of them, alone in a barren wasteland with only a distant angel to bear witness to their suffering.

With that creepy vision in mind, she hurries Mom back into a cab to return to the uneasy calm of their disbanded household.

* * *

It's the Christine Valmy facials and Bergdorf shopping bags that signal that Mom has emerged from her man drought and is drinking again from the fountain of love.

"What's he like?" Saskia is getting ready to join them for dinner on the East Side.

"Well, he's a professor—"

"How old is he?" Saskia interrupts.

"Heavens, how would I know? Somewhere in my ballpark, I suppose."

Thank goodness. Mrs. Robinson has turned a new leaf, Saskia thinks. "Where does he live?"

"He has a place on the Upper East Side."

"Does he have a beard?" Saskia is warming to this mystery date already.

"Why no. He's quite European in his manner. Now please, make an effort for me. I want to make a good impression."

"Aren't you going to tell me what his name is?"

"It's Stefan. Now scoot."

Saskia is buzzing at the prospect of Mom going out with an honest-to-god European. She pictures him as someone like Mr. French from *Family Affair*, who lives in a sprawling apartment on the right side of town.

She dresses for dinner, then lies down like a snow angel on her mother's bed. Seeing Mom blot her lipstick and slip into a silk dress is as soothing as a forgotten lullaby. "Can I pick out your earrings?" she asks.

"Yes please." Mom reaches for the bottle of Charlie. "I almost forgot how good you are at that."

Saskia swaps the Charlie for Chanel perfume and then chooses a pair of pearl studs for Mom. "How about these for a change? They go so well together."

"You're quite right," Mom says. "You always know how to look after me."

Saskia brushes Mom's hair, then steps back to survey their reflections in the mirror.

At last, this looks like the future she wants. A classy woman who looks like her real mother again, alongside her own orderly reflection. Saskia hugs Mom as though she could climb back into her skin, overwhelmed by her sumptuousness. "Do I look nice?"

Mom kisses her on the forehead. "Nice? No. Beautiful? Yes."

Saskia holds Mom's hand as they walk down the street, with the distant trees in Riverside Park caught on the cusp of golden brown, to hail a cab. "The Heidelberg Restaurant, please," Mom says and rolls the *berg* elegantly, as though she's already European. The cab crosses through Central Park, but

– 173 –

instead of turning down Fifth it continues east on Eighty-Sixth Street and pulls up on Second Avenue in the heart of Yorkville.

Saskia follows Mom through the narrow restaurant closely hung with paintings to a table in the back.

"We're first," Mom says. "How do I look?"

"Gorgeous." Saskia is crisp with nerves and smiling hopefully at the arriving customers who look like they might be European.

"There he is now." Mom waves and hurries over to greet Stefan with a kiss.

Taking him in all at once would be like staring straight into the sun, so Saskia narrows her eyes pinhole-like and starts with his feet. He's wearing brogues. She likes that. She also likes his wool slacks and tweed jacket. He has hazel eyes and his dark hair is mercifully short, and better yet, tinged with gray.

"Stefan, this is my daughter Saskia. Now if you'll both excuse me, I need to use the ladies room."

"Pleased to meet you." Saskia bobs, as though meeting royalty.

"And you, Sofia." Stefan puts his cigarettes on the table, then slings his jacket over the back of the chair next to Mom's.

Her ears ting. "Actually, it's Saskia."

"Pardon me. I'll try and get my mind around that." Stefan takes his seat, then motions for the waitress to bring him a beer.

Saskia expects those famous European manners to appear, so she waits until he's seated before she sits back down, hands folded neatly on the table.

"Here you go." She hands him the ashtray. And waits for him to see right through to her famished heart.

"Have you ever had Kraut food before?" Stefan finds a

match and lights his cigarette.

"Oh, yes, we used to go to Luchow's all the time. They do the best schnitzel." She waits for the calm exchange, the smoke rings that spell out, *I will never be your father, but I will be the next best thing.*

But no such smoke ring exists. Only the scent of cabbage that's drifting across the table.

"Have you been here before?" Saskia tries again.

"Sure, I'm the one who made the reservation, remember?"

"Silly me." She doesn't like the way she feels. A hungry soul draped on a smile. "Do you live around here?"

"My place is right over on Madison."

"I bet it's nice."

"It is, if you like the smell of onions," Stefan says with a chuckle.

"Onions?"

"I have a rent-controlled walk-up above the Jackson Hole burger joint."

Saskia falters. "I'm sure it's lovely."

"It's the perfect size for me," Stefan says, as Mom sits back down with a radiant smile and moves her chair closer to his.

Saskia tucks the napkin over her dress when their food arrives and minds her manners as she eats. At first, she tries to follow their conversation. Then it all slides off the table. His indifference to her is as palpable at the mustard pot in front of her. He's just a regular Joe; he's no father-in-waiting. He's not going to *cure* her life. She was wrong to think he could.

"Meredith?" Saskia says when Stefan goes to the bar to get change for the cigarette machine. "Let's just skip dessert and go now."

Mom gets out her compact to touch up her lipstick. "Do I

have anything on my teeth?"

"What difference does it make? You can brush when we get home."

"You're going home," Mom says, closing the compact. "I'm going home with Stefan."

"What do you mean?" Saskia feels as though she's been Anschlussed.

"I'm out on a date, not at some tea dance." Mom tests the scent of her own breath by blowing on her hand. "I told you that before."

"But I thought you said he was European . . ." Saskia's sentence trickles out when Mom suppresses a smile.

"Whether he be European, Armenian, or American, you'll find when you grow up that things are always more exciting when there's a man on the horizon."

And then, Saskia sees it. She is the Pluto in her Mom's world. Mom is her Earth, her source of life, the one to which she will always gravitate, but Stefan has knocked against her orbit and is now the rising star in Mom's universe.

"Please, don't be so glum. Be happy for me." Mom burrows in her pocketbook for a ten-dollar bill. "I'll be back after lunch tomorrow, I promise."

Saskia grabs the note and blazes out of the restaurant, bumping into customers in her haste. The traffic is backed up on Second so she starts walking west on Eighty-Sixth Street. She passes the old-timers at the Paprika Weiss deli and the drunks spilling out of the Berlin Bar before hailing a cab on Park.

She asks the cabdriver to change stations when "My One and Only Love" starts playing on the radio, but he tells her to take a flying fuck so she stiffs him for a tip when he drops her off at her building. When she gets upstairs, she triple-locks the front door and turns on every single light.

She doesn't want to be home alone, in a roach motel of an apartment that creaks like an old ship, with the refrigerator's electronic sighs, the occasional drone from the elevator shaft, and the uneven drip from the bathroom tap reverberating throughout the household.

She opens the door to Toby's old room, once home to her brother, the firstborn, senior-year class valedictorian, now home to the shopping cart, the dry cleaning, the spent seltzer bottles.

Naomi's discarded Bonne Bell lip-gloss is in their bedroom, along with her high school yearbook, her empty twin bed marking the abrupt juncture where one future ceased and another began.

Then finally, she sits at Mom's dressing table, studying her surroundings as though she's come to say goodbye to that girl who looked to her mother for answers, only to find more questions.

She wants what she doesn't have. Her family. A social life. Boyfriends. Fun.

I've given everything for nothing, she thinks. I'm tired of grabbing air.

She hears a siren and thinks, if something happened to me right now, nobody would know.

It's not supposed to be like this. I'm not supposed to be like this. I *won't* be like this anymore.

"I'm sick of everyone changing except me," Saskia declares loudly to no one. She grabs Mom's Erno Laszlo lipstick and uses it to write, "Today is the first day of the rest of my life," on the mirror of her closet door.

No more being a good girl, she vows. No more waiting around for my family to snap out of it. It's time for me to grow up, and *fast*.

13.

You Ignorant Slut

Mom starts spending nights at Stefan's since he lives near her job, so Saskia toughens up by going to sleep with the lights off and with the front door on only one lock. She squirrels away the food money that Mom leaves and throws herself on a crash diet of Carnation Instant Breakfast and caffeine pills and blows the surplus on makeup. She shoplifts a bottle of nail polish. She gives her Laura Ashley pinafore to the Salvation Army and buys her first pair of high-heeled shoes, which she practices walking in at home.

She ramps up her efforts to get Ethan's attention, by keeping him in cigarettes. She lends him money that she has no hope of seeing again and even does his history essay for him. He tolerates her sitting next to him in class, so long as she brings him coffee and donuts for breakfast. It doesn't matter that he's not interested in her, just yet. What matters is that eventually, he just might be.

Her day is made when, in late October, Andy invites her out to lunch. Over Famous Ray's pizza, she learns that he lives in a hotel suite since his parents work in TV and split their time between New York and LA, that he left his last school when he started getting bullied for being gay, that he believes in astrology, and that his favorite color is turquoise. He learns that she misses her old neighborhood, that she stopped fitting in at her old school, that she's not sure about astrology, and that her favorite color is purple.

They window-shop at Bigelow before returning to school, where they come across Florence and Tabitha sharing a cigarette on the stoop. Saskia motions to them for a drag and then blows a perfect smoke ring. All told, it is her best day ever at the Collective.

* * *

Saskia is overjoyed when Andy invites her to a Halloween party at his hotel suite and decides to redefine her goody-two-shoes persona by going as a Quaalude. The night before, she cuts out two giant white cardboard circles, pencils "714" on the side, and straps them together like a sandwich board. On the day itself, she gets dressed in a pair of white tights and an oversized Hanes T-shirt that Toby left behind, and watches her face disappear with each coat of mascara, eye shadow, and frosted pink Maybelline lipstick that she applies.

She takes a swig of Mom's vodka, then heads to Broadway to get a cab. It takes several attempts to get into the back seat and when she manages it, she has to sit on her knees and hike up the costume to prevent it from bending. She grips the straps for balance while the cab speeds downtown. The white cardboard blocks her view, so she feels like Zeus riding on a bumpy cloud as the wind streams through the open window.

When the taxi pulls up in front of the Essex House the doorman throws her a Hades-like look while he opens the side entrance since she can't enter through the revolving doors. Then the tight-lipped Russian concierge sends her up to the ninth floor where the noise seeping from Andy's suite confirms that the party is in full swing.

Outside in the wallpapered hallway, decorum and sobriety reign. But once she crosses the threshold, she will be checking her brain cells and liver function at the door. This thought would have scared her once upon a time, but now she's up for it. So she knocks.

Andy, decked out as one of the Village People, hoots with laughter when he sees her and announces, "You get the door prize." He leads her through the foyer of the teeming suite to the gold-tapped bathroom and opens the medicine cabinet to reveal a hand mirror bearing neatly chopped rows of cocaine.

She hesitates when he hands her a rolled-up twenty. "Houston, is there a problem?" Andy asks.

She grabs the rolled note and snorts a line. And with that first, delicious kick, a unicorn seems to prance through her brain. The roof of her mind lifts, and she is filled with a munificence that keeps on multiplying. She is where she wants to be, with the person she wants to be with. The crystals reveal their magic. *You can be happy. You can have friends. You can be.*

* * *

When Saskia rocks up to school on Monday, Florence and Tabitha corner her in the hall before she has time to go upstairs. "Well, well. Just when we were getting tired of watching you flail around like a bug on its back, you learned to crawl," Florence says in a deadpan manner while she snaps Saskia's photo.

"Are you calling me an *insect*?" Saskia says indignantly. "And what's with the photo?"

"Let's just call it field research for my science project," Florence says, brushing her hair out of her eyes while winding the film on her camera.

Saskia tries to pass them, but Tabitha, with arms akimbo, blocks her. "You've always seemed nice enough, just green as corn." Her pursed lips melt into a smile. "But that's okay. I like corn."

"Seeing as we can't step on you, or poison you, we're going

to teach you how to walk," Florence drawls.

"What are you saying?" Saskia asks.

"She's just messing with you," Tabitha says. "What she's really saying is would you like to be our friend?"

There's a second when Saskia doesn't believe them, then in the next second she wants to slam them for all the times they made her feel left out, but then it's as though she puts on a pair of glasses and sees them for who they are. Their swagger and sass is just their way.

She recalls bits of gossip she overheard. That Florence was kicked out of Catholic school when she started acting up after her parents split. That Tabitha's father is no longer on the scene. That their banter is just that. They do it to shine a light on each other. And that's when it all begins to brighten.

And just like that, it's land ho. After a year of drifting solo, she finds her New World. And what a place it is. Andy, Florence, and Tabitha become the points on her compass, orientating her to a side of the city she never knew.

The four of them nickname themselves Charlie's Angels and start hanging out in Andy's suite while his parents are out of town. Weekends become about scoring pot at the bandshell in Central Park, buying munch-out material from the Carnegie Deli and then getting completely wasted while watching *Saturday Night Live*.

They teach Saskia to mind-flip and to laugh at the shit that bugs her. They take her to a place where she feels lighter. They find commonality within their differences. They defuse her at those times when her head feels like it could explode. They have an encyclopedic knowledge of sex, so when they find out that Saskia is the sole illiterate among them they nickname her 'ignorant slut' and tease her mercilessly about Ethan.

"What do you see in him? He bread-crumbs you all the time, and you continue to eat it up," Andy asks, one night when Saskia is doing a Tarot reading about Ethan.

"I don't know. I just have a feeling he's really sweet underneath it all." Saskia chooses a card. "What does this one mean?"

Florence pretends to consult the deck and says knowledgeably, "Oh, Four of Wands. That means you're gonna get gang banged."

"Stop! You're awful." Saskia gathers the cards in embarrassment.

"It's not the Wand, it's the Magician." Tabitha giggles when Saskia tries to slap her. "I'll bet good money that Ethan is no wizard."

"Say something," Saskia implores Andy.

"I'm with them on this one. You can do way better," Andy concurs.

"I, for one, am not wasting time on any of those limp dicks at school," Florence boasts. "I'm moving to Paris the second I graduate; then I'm going to fuck my way through France and become a famous photographer."

"I'm going to LA to become a director," Andy says. "With or without my parents' help."

"I'm right behind you." Tabitha shuffles the deck. "First college, then Europe, then I'm going to publish my first book, and after that I'll—"

"Contract full-blown herpes," Florence jumps in.

"What do you want to do?" Tabitha asks Saskia, when they finish refilling their glasses with the remains of a bottle of Bacardi.

College. Careers. The exclamation points she once envisaged in her future have become question marks. *Paris. L.A. Europe.* They might as well be talking Mars. "I don't know," she says dejectedly. "I used to think that I did, but that seems forever ago."

Tabitha senses her mood plummeting and asks, "A month ago, did you ever imagine us being here like this?

Saskia shakes her head no.

"Go big. What do you want to be?"

The answer is so simple, it's almost stupid. "Happy," Saskia declares.

"You can be happy anywhere," Andy says. "Where then?"

Saskia sips her drink and deliberates. "Maybe London. I've always loved *Upstairs, Downstairs.*"

"Depends who's upstairs," Florence jokes. "I like it better when they go downstairs."

* * *

In the coming weeks, she plays chicken with Mom to see who will blink first and call the other on her new behavior. But Mom is too Stefan-struck to notice that they're playing, or that Saskia's lost five pounds and that her liquor supply is shrinking. When Mom comes home every few days to drop off groceries, pick up the mail, and collect clean clothes, she's a dazzling ball of energy that dispenses money, kisses, and compliments before flying out the door to meet Stefan for dinner. Those encounters squish Saskia's spirits to pulp. It's so obvious that she can never make Mom as happy as a man can. Mom's enough for her, but she's not enough for Mom.

One weekend when Mom and Stefan are away in the Poconos and Andy's parents are in town, she invites Tabitha and Florence to spend the night at her place.

Florence arrives first, waving a wrap of cocaine. "Ho-ho-ho. Christmas has come early."

Saskia prepares vodka and orange juice when Tabitha shows up, and carefully tops up the Stolichnaya with water so Mom won't notice it's been depleted. Then she returns to her room to find the girls sifting through her clothes to find themselves better outfits.

They are going to try to get into an after-hours party at The Loft, but will have to pass for eighteen to be allowed in the club. It takes them one hour, two cocktails, and three lines to get ready. After a frenzied round of changing, Saskia aims for the Diane Keaton look in a vintage dress, which she sluts up with rhinestone earrings, spandex leggings, and a tiny silver star from Capezio pasted to her cheekbone. Florence opts for fishnets and a mini, while Tabitha goes for all-out glamour in a wrap dress and stilettos.

"We're fifteen, we're coked up, we're horny," they chant as they teeter to the elevator, the clatter of their heels echoing in the marble hall.

"I think the doorman was checking you out," Tabitha whispers to Saskia as they parade through the lobby.

"Oh, shut the fuck up. As if." Saskia is hiding behind her outfit, her wobbly confidence lurking dangerously close to the surface. Ben was her first and last sexual experience, and even though they constantly joke about getting laid, having guys go down on them and giving head, the only Latin she knows is what she learned at school.

Their breath mists in the November night air as they hug themselves to keep warm while waiting for a cab. They heard that the bouncer would be more likely to let them in the club if he saw their outfits, so they went coatless.

By the time the cab turns on lower Broadway, the crowd outside The Loft is already spilling onto the street. They touch up their lip-gloss before leaving the warmth of the taxi to enter the melee.

"Remember, we're hot and they're not," Florence says, hoisting her bra strap to create more cleavage.

They spend the next twenty minutes trying to eye-fuck the bouncer, stamping their feet to fight the chill and jostling with the ever-growing crowd. When the clouds start to spit rain, Tabitha is the first to admit defeat. "Maybe we should bail and do a bar instead."

"Don't you think we'll get proofed?" Saskia says, now shivering in her flimsy dress.

"Oh, god. What a pair of crybabies," Florence snaps. "Is our playdate over already? Is it time to pack away our toys and go night-night?"

They pick their way to the curb in their high heels, carefully avoiding the freeze-dried lumps of dog shit as the rain gathers force. A passenger gets out of a taxi and a shouting match ensues when multiple parties scramble to claim the cab as their own.

"Hey, ladies. Yeah, you girls," a corpulent chauffeur with an ebullient manner calls from the window of a double-parked Rolls Royce. "Do you want to come in and get dry?"

The rain overcomes their reservations so the girls clamber in, avoiding the gray South America-shaped stain in the middle of the back seat.

"Have a drink, help yourself to the minibar." The chauffeur generously offers what's not his. "I just dropped my passengers off, so it will be daylight before they stumble outta there."

"I bet you anything they think we're famous," Saskia says

and sips her glass of Asti Spumante, feeling as though she's swapped places with Caroline Kennedy for the evening.

"Do you want a chaser?" The chauffeur hands them a lit joint.

"This is more like it." Tabitha takes a hit and passes it to Saskia. "We're having our very own VIP party."

Saskia stares through the rain-streaked window at the jet-set crowd. What would that Mennonite girl think if she could see her, now that she's one of the beautiful people? She downs her sparkling wine, then mixes a miniature of vodka with a can of Tab.

"Oh, what the hell," the chauffeur says, removing his cap to scratch his head. "I'll take you home. It will be my good deed for the week."

Florence gives him Saskia's address and the girls share excited looks as the Rolls pulls out and heads toward the Village, then northward until they find themselves on Eighth, driving past the hookers and transvestites seeking refuge from the rain under the scaffolding by the General Post Office. When they stop alongside a fire truck at a red, they start throwing kisses at New York's Bravest.

"I'd blow him any day as part of my civic duty," Florence murmurs when one of the firemen winks at her.

"Fuck, *yeah*." Tabitha pouts at the captain. "He's fit to serve."

"I'd do him right here, right now," Saskia says, striking a pose.

"I'd do him in front of your mother, if that was part of the bargain," Florence adds.

"My mother?" Saskia says. "Hell, she'd charge admission."

"Your mother?" Tabitha teases. "Shit, she'd try to cut a

deal with the city for a group rate."

"To us and our fucking mothers. Neither snow nor rain nor cold nor gloom of night can prevent us from having fun!" Saskia toasts, proud as punch for having hitched a ride home on a wet Saturday night in a Rolls, no less.

14.

Dr. Dip-It-In

Saskia leans her head against the window while the Greyhound bus idles in traffic in the Lincoln Tunnel, feeling queasy from the exhaust fumes. It's been 1977 for three whole days now. It's been five days since she went to Oma's, and four days since she tried calling Toby and Naomi to wish them a happy New Year. It will be two more days before Andy gets back from vacationing with his parents in Aruba and another six until school starts, but just a matter of hours until she meets Tabitha and Florence at the Papaya King on Eighth Street so they can go and shoot her Christmas wad on retro-chic clothing at Reminiscence.

It's too dark to even look at the *Cosmopolitan* she purchased for the ride and besides, reading on buses gives her a headache. But her bigger headache is that she's sitting next to some creepy Christian girl, who started oohing and aahing when she saw the Empire State Building on the approach to the tunnel, as though the mere sight of it was enough to get her off. Now Saskia's stuck in the tunnel with the Hudson River sloshing above them, honking cars all around them, and Miss Jesus Fish is trying to make conversation.

"I'm so excited," the girl says, offering Saskia a cherry Lifesaver. "I've never been to New York."

"I could tell." Saskia accepts the candy with a flicker of a smile.

"Are you from the city?"

"Yup." Saskia stifles a yawn. "Bred and buttered."

"I imagine it's a hoot living here."

"Yup again."

"I'm joining up with some other girls from my church at the Barbizon Hotel for Women to go hear Billy Graham at Madison Square Garden."

"Really," Saskia says flatly.

"It's the only way my parents would let me make the trip. It's very strict at the Barbizon. No men are allowed past the ground floor."

"Is that so."

"Since you're a native New Yorker, maybe you can tell me where I should go shopping for clothes?"

"The Pleasure Chest has some great things." Saskia imagines the girl viewing a pair of crotchless underwear and titty tassels and closes her eyes to fake-sleep.

She doesn't know what made her want to bitch up on Miss Jesus Fish. Maybe it's because she pictures the Christmas the girl had with her cozy family and compares it to the one she had with what's left of her crazy family. She wants to pull time backward or rush it forward, away from this place that has been deflated by the absence of so many.

Saskia woke at seven on Christmas Day, not because she meant to, but because she was too keyed up about Stefan coming over to spend the night on the West Side for the first time since he'd met Mom. Even though she knew it was a long shot, she'd set the table for five. Then Mom pointedly put back two settings and told her to get real, Toby and Naomi weren't coming home.

Mom went back to bed after breakfast, tuckered out from having worked late at the pasta shop, filling all the last-minute orders on Christmas Eve, but rallied in time to make a roast dinner for Stefan just the way he liked it. And even though

Saskia didn't want him there, she white-knuckled her way through the day to make nice for Mom.

That's why they had duck instead of beef. And Stefan was the reason why they stayed in the city for Christmas instead of going to Philadelphia, which is why she's here, on a bus, having taken a vacation from her life. Even though there wasn't a lot to do at Oma's, there was something soothing about eating too much and going to bed at a time that she would generally be getting dressed to go out. It was familiar, which her home is not. Oma wants what she wants; soft edges and no hard questions—just the fuzzy cushion of contentment that comes with love.

She could have come back for New Year's Eve and gone out with the girls to watch the ball drop in Times Square. If so, she would have got shit-faced and probably barfed on some windy street corner. Instead, she'd pillaged the liquor cabinet after Oma went to bed and made the mistake of drunk-dialing Toby, then Naomi, to wish them a happy whatever. But she hadn't reached them. Either they were pretending not to be there, or they were out drinking Kool-Aid, selling flowers, having three-ways, or doing whatever else it is that brainwashed people do during the holiday season.

The bus nudges past the faded turquoise-tiled state line that separates New Jersey from New York. It slowly picks up speed and they finally emerge from the tunnel. The sunlight chimes against the Manhattan skyline, which sings crescendo-like against the cobalt heavens. The mosaic of skyscrapers is sacred to her and more beautiful than any Michelangelo. This girl might have Jesus but Saskia also has a covenant. She has a covenant to serve her city with pride.

She follows the girl down the stairs at Port Authority and

stops her. "On second thought, forget the Pleasure Chest and try Gimbels or Altman's instead," Saskia tells her. "I think they'd be more to your liking."

* * *

Enticed by the promise of cocaine on tap, Saskia arranges to meet Andy at the white-brick Lexington Avenue high-rise where Dr. Harry Something-or-other-stein lives with his partner.

Andy refers to Harry as Dr. Dip-It-In because he has a waterbed and likes to swing every weekend at the sex club Plato's Retreat. Harry is Andy's conduit for Quaaludes, top-drawer cocaine, and unread EST literature. Andy became Harry's pharmaceutical foot soldier after running up a sizeable tab and is now working off his drug debt by delivering repeat prescriptions to the doctor's Upper East Side clientele.

Given his reputation, Saskia is expecting Harry's girlfriend to be a nubile beauty and is surprised when a middle-aged woman opens the door to greet her.

"You must be Saskia. I'm Nadine. Please, come in," she says as she ushers her into their duplex. "The men have been tied up."

Tied up? Given the doctor's reputation, that could mean any number of things. Saskia follows Nadine to the living room, which is decorated in beige, save for one bright orange wall. She perches on the couch while Nadine goes to fetch refreshments, willing herself not to look at the cover of the *Playboy* on the coffee table.

"Tell me about yourself," Nadine shouts from the kitchen. "Are you a junior like Andy?"

Saskia turns the magazine upside down. "No, I'm just a

sophomore."

"Where do you live?" Nadine comes in with a tray of soft drinks and snacks and sits down next to her.

"On the Upper West Side, with my mom." Saskia reaches for her soda, wishing Nadine had offered her some of the hard stuff.

"Are your parents divorced?"

"No, my dad died almost two years ago." Saskia coughs as the Pepsi goes up her nose.

"How awful," Nadine says.

"You can say that again." Saskia can't begin to describe how his death put the kibosh on everything.

Nadine helps herself to crudités and passes a dish of hummus to Saskia. "Have some of this. I just made it."

Saskia reaches for the serving platter.

"So, have you got it yet?"

"Yes, thanks," Saskia says, grabbing another carrot stick. "The hummus is very good."

"No, I mean have you got *it* yet." Nadine looks at her with dripping sincerity.

Saskia pauses, carrot stick in hand. "You mean the food?"

"I mean *it*; *it* is realizing that you chose what, when and how you got what's going on in your life." Nadine sounds like a Jewish Confucius. "The first step is accepting what *it* is. After that, the rest follows. I know this because I'm an EST trainer."

"Really?" Saskia replies with a gritted smile.

"Once you get *it*, everything begins to shift," Nadine enthuses. "You should come to a seminar and check it out sometime. I could offer you a discounted rate."

Saskia is saved from dodging her invite when the key goes in the lock and Andy and Harry, who looks as unassuming as the math tutor she had in sixth grade, come in.

"How're we doing here?" Harry greets Saskia warmly and then kisses Nadine. "Are we ready for a pick-me-up?"

"Sure thing, hon," Nadine says and turns on the TV to where *Roots* is playing.

Andy and Saskia share an excited look, while they wait to get toasted. Harry soon returns, bearing a mirror engraved with "It's the Real Thing," and starts passing it around.

The industrial amount of cocaine reduces Saskia's bowels to mush. She excuses herself. Her pupils look like flying saucers in the bathroom mirror so she searches the medicine cabinet for Valium, but finds only K-Y Jelly, dental floss, and Dentyne.

"We have school tomorrow," Saskia announces when she returns to the living room, where *The Tonight Show* is now playing. "We better make a move."

"All in good time, my pretty." Andy artfully appraises the lines that Harry is chopping out.

By the time they leave, it's approaching 3:00 a.m.

"My nose belongs in a sling. I couldn't find any Valium, so I'm going to be up all night at this rate." Saskia wiggles impatiently as the elevator descends.

"Was I right or was I right?" Andy says and windscreen-wipes his nose. "Didn't I tell you he has good stuff?"

The doors open and they pile out, practically tripping over a pair of poodles being held on a leash by a suntanned blond in a floor-length fur coat, before tumbling into the smudged early hours of their white night.

* * *

High school is now all about getting high at school. Saskia is determined to make up for all the time she wasted being straight. Her new tack doesn't go unnoticed; Tracy is on her ass all the time about being late and Emerson makes her read textbook passages out loud in class if she suspects that she's stoned. Saskia soon gets the hang of it, and takes perverse pride in Emerson's exasperation as evidence that she's changed.

Emerson then goes all good cop on her, and tries to get her to talk about what's *really* going on by inviting her out for lunch, but Saskia tells her she's *really* fine and then blows her off on the appointed day.

Saskia gets her ears double-pierced at a tattoo parlor on Astor Place, just to get back at Mom for ditching her for Stefan. Odessa clocks it right away but it takes Mom a week to even notice—and when she does, she compliments her on her new look instead of scolding her for not waiting until she is sixteen. Saskia doesn't know what pisses her off more: the fact that her ears get infected and the holes close up, or her inability to make anything stick to her Teflon Mom.

So when Mom goes off with Stefan to the Caribbean, Saskia doesn't have to try too hard to convince her to let her stay in New York instead of going to Oma's, arguing that it's her midwinter vacation, too, and that there's nothing for her to do in Philly. On the Friday that Mom leaves, Saskia steals one of her Christine Valmy vouchers and cuts her last class to go and get high in Central Park before having a Fifth Avenue facial in celebration of Mom's weeklong departure.

She's decided to blast Daddy's anniversary out of her brain by going to a Valentine's Day costume party at Dr. Dip-It-In's, since cocaine has proved to be too strong a siren song for her to resist.

By eleven that very night, Saskia is doing a line with Andy in the doctor's study while someone pounds incessantly on the door. "Give us a minute," she shouts as she adjusts the wedgie in her fishnet tights.

She leaves Andy and flounces back to the living room to check out the crowd for a suitable guy. Despite her frequent forays, she hasn't met anyone since Ben. Going to a pint-sized school certainly has its downside when it comes to fishing in the man-pool, so she's testing the oceans of the Upper East Side by dressing as a Catholic schoolgirl, in a minute plaid pleated skirt, stilettos, and a cheap gold cross.

She pushes through the crowd to find Florence—who has come as Roseanne Roseannadanna—sitting on the kitchen counter and in conversation with a rakish twenty something guy in a bloodstained button-down shirt.

"Patrick, I'd like you to meet Saskia, my partner in crime," Florence says and hands her a warm bottle of Rolling Rock.

"Just call us the Caped Crusaders." Saskia thrusts her tits forward as she swigs her beer. "Always at the ready to swoop down and save the day."

"The pleasure's mine," Patrick says. "I like your little-lost-lapsed look."

"Do you now?" Saskia lights up. "Flattery will get you everywhere."

"I was just trying to guess what Patrick's come as. Any ideas?" Florence giggles.

"JFK?" Saskia wagers, but Patrick shakes his head no.

"I know! RFK," Florence offers.

"Wrong again." Patrick looks at the girls expectantly. "It's Gary Gilmore. But A+ for effort." He produces a vial from his pocket. "Do you want some party favors?"

"The way to my heart is through my nostril." Saskia helps herself to firsts, seconds, and thirds, before passing the cocaine o Florence. "Where's Catwoman?" she asks, searching the oom for Tabitha.

"She just left. She's been on a short lead ever since her mom found that roach clip in her book bag." Florence tilts her ose up for inspection. "All clear?"

"Good to go," Saskia says. "Gee, thanks, Patrick."

"Anytime. It's always good to help a fellow Catholic." Patrick winks and helps himself to his supply. "Ever been to he club Infinity? I could get us in later."

Saskia starts rattling away, like she's at a cocaine confessional, alking loudly over the music. When she needs the bathroom, he finds a woman in a skewed sequined mask passed out in he tub so she has to wait for the one upstairs. By the time she eturns, Patrick and Florence are making out by the fridge. The ight of them kissing leaves her spent and soulless.

She slips out to the balcony where Andy, who is dressed s Hugh Hefner in a pair of silk pajamas and a velveteen athrobe, is having a smoke.

"What is it?" Andy drapes a discarded jacket over her houlders.

"How come Florence always gets some, but I never do?"

"That's not true. Besides, we all know Florence could flirt or the entire Tri-State Area."

Everything she's tried to blanket with booze and blow omes to a boil. "I thought I'd hit it off with Patrick, but now ie's taking her to Infinity later."

"You just haven't met the right guy yet. One day, you will," Andy says. "I promise."

"When? When I've hit menopause or joined the Shakers?"

"Oh, *puh-lease.*"

"Seriously," Saskia continues. "Something's wrong with

me. I just know it."

"There's nothing wrong with you."

"Bullshit. It's like guys look right past me. Something about me puts them off."

"You're fabulously foxy." Andy lights a cigarette and hands it to her. "The stars haven't matched up yet; but mark my words, your Jupiter will align with some nice guy's Venus soon enough."

Saskia sucks at the cigarette, her mood now blackened to a crisp. "I don't know why I bothered coming here tonight. I hate Valentine's, and not for the reasons you think."

"What then?"

She grips the rail and looks at the city below. "Today is Daddy's second death-day. His un-birthday, so to speak."

"That explains it," Andy says sympathetically.

Her pain digs into her like a bone spur. "I'm going to tell you something I've never told anyone. Promise not to laugh?"

Andy nods.

"The night before he died, I saw a stupid limo and stupidly wished that I could ride in one." Her words follow, hard and fast. "And then abracadabra, what do you know? Days later, my pumpkin arrived to take me to his funeral."

Andy reaches for her hand, but she pulls away and accidentally knocks the head off her cigarette. "I jinxed him. I know it doesn't make sense, but I feel like I put something on him just the same and hate myself for having ever thought that."

Andy relights the cigarette and hands it back to her. "What happened to him had nothing to do with you."

"For all I know, it did." She hungrily puffs away at the remains of her smoke. "I'm toxic."

Andy draws his velveteen robe around him as the wind picks up. "You've just perfected a way of punishing yourself for something you had no control over."

She sighs petulantly and gazes at the partygoers inside the apartment who are dancing to Earth, Wind and Fire. "You say that, but what do you really know?"

The line of his mouth tells her that she's hurt his feelings, and that realization cuts right through her shitstorm. In her mind, Andy has a soul like sunshine. He's the clement one and she tends to bring the clouds. She's greedy for his warmth, forgetting that he too knows the shade of self-doubt. It's time for me to listen, not to vent, she thinks, flushed with shame.

She spies a half-full bottle of champagne on the table, dumps the contents of two abandoned glasses into the potted plants and then pours the bubbly. "I'm so, so sorry. Told you I'm toxic."

For a febrile moment, she thinks that Andy's going to stay mad at her, but then he takes the drink and says, "You should come with a yellow hazard sign." He pulls her down on the seat beside him and confides, "I created my own mind-fuck too before I came out. I convinced myself my parents do what they do in order to spend as much time away from me as possible."

"How'd you turn that off?"

"Now it's my turn to share my deepest and darkest. When my head's exploding, I write a list of everything that's getting to me and send it out the window."

"Are you for real?" Saskia asks disbelievingly

"I shit you not. It's an advantage of living on the ninth floor. Just watching it disappear clears my mind." Andy removes a handkerchief from his bathrobe pocket and hands it to her. "Now it's your turn."

"To what?

"Just wad all of that crap in this. Then let it go."

Saskia downs her drink. "But how? I don't have anything to write on, or with."

Andy sighs in exasperation and says, "Be pedantic. Or don't. It's your choice."

She takes the handkerchief from him and checks to make sure that no one can see them from inside, then closes her eyes to scrunch the swell of her thoughts into the white square.

She pictures herself on the corner of Seventeenth Street, foolish with dreams, an epoch ago.

I didn't know. I couldn't have known.

Then she lets go.

Together they watch the handkerchief bob briefly in the wind before wafting to the street below. Her mind stops free-falling and she finds the floor in her thinking, once again. She snuggles up to Andy and says, "Love you. Mean it."

"And I love you too, you magnificently ignorant slut."

* * *

The next morning, Andy sends Saskia out on a bagel run looking like a hotel hooker, since she forgot to bring a change of clothes and is still in last night's costume. A homeless man sitting on the curb of Sixth Avenue wolf-whistles as she passes by and calls out, "Hey baby. Sit on my face."

Without breaking stride, she throws him the finger and retorts, "Fuck off, asswipe." Her head is throbbing from last night's escapades and her nose is running from the product she snorted as one day passed to the next. She'd bet good money that Florence got lucky with Patrick and wishes she'd been invited to Infinity, too.

Her heart does a two-step when she sees Arthur crossing the street. She hasn't seen him since Toby and Naomi went missing in action and screams above a departing garbage truck, "Arthur! Wait up, it's me!"

He stops to look around but doesn't appear to recognize her at first. Then he slowly grins as he clocks her outfit, which clashes with the somberly dressed Moonies passing out pamphlets in front of the Russian Tea Room.

"Top of the morning to you, Miss McSoyer. What in heaven's name are you wearing?"

"Be nice." She blushes under the remains of her pancake makeup. "It's been a long time."

"You can say that again." Arthur greets her with a kiss on the cheek. "Do you have time to grab a coffee, or are you late for Mass?"

"I can do that. I drink coffee now . . . and the rest."

The conversation skids around as they get their bearings, never having spent a moment together that didn't include Toby and Naomi. By the time they're seated over drinks in a luncheonette off Fifth, she's learned that Arthur transferred to NYU over the holidays.

"I couldn't take another Midwestern winter," he confides after the waitress clears their cups. "Or Midwesterners, to be exact. I was missing New York."

"Have you seen them since you've been back?" Saskia asks of her siblings.

"Nope. Neither hide nor hair, and not for lack of trying," Arthur admits. "It never crossed my mind that it wouldn't be like before, but they don't have the time of day for me anymore."

"Or me. I thought things would get better when Manny

left, but it hasn't made an iota of difference."

"How's your mom holding up?"

"You mean Meredith?" Saskia says mockingly. "She goes apeshit if I call her Mom nowadays. She's swanning around the Caribbean with some idiot she's seeing."

"So I take it your Oma's looking after you?"

"No. I'm looking after myself, actually." Saskia tries to sound nonchalant. "I'm fifteen and three quarters now, after all."

"Fifteen going on twenty, by the looks of it. Who would've thought?" Arthur becomes pensive. "I still expect to run into Larry every time I'm on Madison."

"I bet you a bazillion dollars we'd still be 'we' if he'd lived."

"Try not to think like that. It will only get you down."

"Easier said than done."

"Listen, I'm rooming with some friends on Fourth Avenue," Arthur says, as he scribbles his details on a napkin and then picks up the check. "Here's my number in case you ever want to get in touch. Now, make a wish." He plucks a stray eyelash from her cheekbone and then blows it over her shoulder. "I have to scoot. I'm working the weekend shift at Rizzoli's and they put you in the stockade if you're late."

Never in a million years did she think she would find Arthur remotely attractive, but as she watches him disappear down the street, it occurs to her he's the nicest guy she's come across in a long time, maybe ever. Perhaps this fellow traveler is her soulmate-to-be. She folds the napkin to add to her address book, clean forgetting to order Andy's breakfast.

Drifting back toward Central Park South, her breath frosting in the roasted chestnut-scented wind, she stops to press her forehead against Tiffany's display window as though she could burrow right through to that distant point when someone will take her there to buy a diamond as big as Shea Stadium. She pauses to let a horse and carriage drive by, then wanders toward the Plaza, cherishing her Hubble-like moment as she imagines walking hand-in-hand with Arthur.

15.

Chemical Holiday

"Fuck you, Mr. So-and-So," Mom shouts at their neighbors, her cries echoing throughout the building lobby.

"I'm sorry," Saskia mouths to the retreating couple as she follows Mom onto the elevator. She used to babysit for that family, but now that they've locked horns with Mom about her intercepting their *New York Times* delivery to read over breakfast, she suspects they won't be calling on her again.

When she and Mom—who's been back from the Caribbean two weeks now—met earlier at Seventy-Ninth Street to go to Zabar's, Saskia had been buoyant from a school trip to the Joffrey Ballet and was wearing a "The Joffrey Is a Time for Joy" button. Mom was waiting for her on the northwest corner of Broadway, looking glamorous in her purple cape and midwinter tan, but as soon as she spotted her pinched mouth, Saskia began supplicating like a tree in the wind, hoping to divert the category five storm to sunnier shores.

Saskia makes Mom a gin and tonic as soon as they get inside and puts the water on to boil. Mom slams through the kitchen, unpacking the groceries, and accidentally nudges the eggs from the table onto the floor. "Now look at what you've gone and made me do," she exclaims, cursing loudly.

Mom pours another hit of gin into her glass and stomps into the dining room to watch TV. Saskia is left to clean up the mess while Mom talks back to Jimmy Carter, who is on the evening news urging his fellow Americans to carpool.

Saskia doesn't need to ask. Mom's been home every night for five days straight. It's obvious that she's hit a wall with

Stefan and is now hitting back at anyone who dares cross her path. Saskia drains the pasta, carries their plates into the dining room and then switches on the overhead.

"What do you think I'm made of, money?" Mom barks. "Turn that light off and freshen my drink while you're at it."

Saskia wordlessly obliges. Then they sit side by side in the dark, silently eating the pasta shop's reject ravioli by the blue light of the TV, until the phone starts ringing.

Mom trips on the cord in her haste to answer it and goes to her bedroom to take the call. Saskia catches Stefan's exasperated voice when she places the receiver back in the cradle, but curbs the urge to listen in.

Saskia blows her daily calorie quota by eating the remains of Mom's dinner before sneaking her own gin and tonic. After all these months of resenting Mom's absence, the tables have been turned now that she's back. Mom begrudges being home, so it's up to Saskia to make her happy again. She used to be good at it, but it's plain as day that she's lost the knack.

When *Masterpiece Theatre* comes on, Saskia knocks on Mom's door and comes in to find her in her bathroom, soaking in a shallow bath with her body looking limp and bloodless. Saskia drains the fetid water, now cold to the touch, and coaxes Mom into a bathrobe.

She tucks Mom into bed and closes the window, which is letting in gusts of cold air from the Drive. "Do you want to watch *Upstairs, Downstairs* with me?" she asks. "I can bring the TV in here if you like."

"I'm sick of being treated like a persona non grata."

"Don't say that, it's not true." Saskia covers her up with a quilt and starts towel-drying her hair.

"I always get the scabby end of the stick," Mom says

in disbelief. "I give and give and give, but everyone ends up turning their back on me."

Saskia finds Mom an extra pillow and says, "Not me. I'm right here."

Mom tries to find her words, but tears defeat her. She covers her face with her hands and confesses, "Sometimes I think I would have killed myself by now if it weren't for you."

"Please, promise you'll never say that again." Saskia climbs into bed and hugs her, flimsy at the thought of being left in a motherless, fatherless, brotherless, and sisterless world.

Every time she hears Mom laugh, sees her being gracious, or watches her get dressed up, she thinks her real mother has returned. But these moments occur with less and less frequency. The only time she saw her mother blow her top before was with her kids, never with strangers, and certainly never in public. The very way she moves is different now; she used to hold herself like Grace Kelly, but now she walks with her fists clenched and jaw set, as though itching for a fight.

Maybe I'm the one who was an idiot to think that I could twist back time, she thinks. Maybe my future is staring at me right here, right now. When she looks in her mommy-mirror, she suspects the stuff of life will be too much for her someday, too, and that she'll grow up to be a lady who shouts and stamps to get her way, then collapses with fatigue when she doesn't. She's not like her siblings. She could never turn her back on the people who knew her first and best. If she's not like them, she must be cut from Mom's cloth, destined to snag and tangle in life's wear and tear.

* * *

For the first time since she signed up with the psycho convention, Naomi actually telephoned Saskia at school to ask her to meet for brunch. On the morning of, Saskia gets to the Olympia coffee shop early to bag a booth away from the window in case Mom is passing by.

She rearranges the salt and pepper shakers while she eyes the clock above the donut counter display. As the minute hand moves past the appointed hour, she drowns her coffee in milk and strikes a pose with her cigarette. She never usually smokes in the daytime, but is eager to show Naomi how much she's grown up since they last saw one another. *Six months.* Since she barged in on Naomi at her apartment. *Ten months.* Since Naomi left home. She won't know where to begin.

She's on her second cigarette and is beginning to suspect that Naomi's going to be a no-show when her sister finally arrives in a man's worn coat and with a keffiyeh wrapped around her head.

They kiss as though bobbing for apples in cold water.

Saskia gasps when Naomi sheds her scarf to reveal a botched pixie cut where her long and lustrous hair used to be.

"Don't you like it?" Naomi sits down but keeps her coat on.

"Yeah. It makes you look like Mia Farrow in *The Great Gatsby*." More like *Rosemary's Baby*, Saskia thinks. "I've always loved your hair. What made you cut it?"

"I didn't identify with it any longer." Naomi pours some sugar onto a spoon and begins to devour it. "It reminded me of who I used to be, so I sold it. You've no idea how much you can get for a natural piece."

Watching Naomi going for the sugar like that makes her teeth sing. "But your *hair*?"

"I did it for me. It wasn't some great sacrifice." Naomi catches Saskia's quizzical expression and puts the spoon back down. "Since when do you smoke?"

"Oh, for ages now." Tobacco and coffee on an empty stomach is giving Saskia the shakes and making her want to take a massive dump.

"Well, I'm trying to quit and would appreciate if you could put it out," Naomi says primly.

Saskia stubs out her cigarette with a sigh and beckons for the waitress. "I've been meaning to forward this." She hands Naomi some mail after they place their order. "There's a letter from Oma in there somewhere."

Naomi rips open the lilac monogrammed envelope and shakes it to see if it holds anything else. "Figures." She shoves the letter, along with the rest of the unread mail, into her canvas bag. "Oma's too cheap to have cut me a check."

"Oma's not cheap," Saskia says pointedly. "She's helped us a ton."

"Us?" Naomi sneers. "I take it you've been sucking up to her then?"

"If you mean do I treat her like a person instead of a bank teller, then yeah. I'm guilty of that."

I better curb it and turn this around or she'll leave before I ever find out what she wants, Saskia thinks. Thankfully, the food arrives before either of them can change their mind.

"Did you tell Mom you were seeing me?" Naomi asks in between bites of her grilled cheese.

"Of course I did." Saskia is all innocence. "She's meeting us here in a moment."

Naomi whips around to scan the premises.

"Kidding! I know better than that."

"Hardy har-har. Very funny."

"Well, you're the one who bought her up." Saskia tucks into her plate of thigh-forming French fries. "Guess where she's working now?"

"I don't give a shit."

"Moving on. What's life like on the red planet? What do you do now that you're not in school?"

"I'm busy learning new things all the time," Naomi intones. "Between therapy, meetings, and babysitting, I don't have a moment to stop and think."

Naomi's leftover hair makes Saskia's eyes hurt. She always thought her sister was prettier than she is, until today. That sparkle that Naomi used to wear like a crown has been dulled.

Naomi catches her sympathetic gaze, and flushes. "Why are you staring like that? Do I have something on my face?"

"No," Saskia is stuck for words. "It's just—"

"Just what?" Naomi challenges her. "Say it."

Saskia comes clean. "You don't seem very happy."

"I'm happy. I'm finding myself and doing theater," Naomi declares defensively.

"So you're going up for acting jobs?" Saskia asks.

"No. I'm working in *our* theater. Political theater. Theater that amounts to something. It's nothing bourgeois."

"What does it amount to?" Saskia asks.

Naomi blinks rapidly as her mind seems to deflate. "It's nothing bourgeois," she says mechanically. "Its purpose is to raise one's consciousness."

"Those aren't your words," Saskia says firmly. "They sound like Gray's. You always spoke about theater as something you loved, not as something it *did*."

Naomi looks dazed, as though she just heard herself for

the first time, and then shoves her plate aside. "Maybe this wasn't such a good idea. I think I should go."

"You can't just leave off like this."

"Oh yeah? Watch me." Naomi starts buttoning up her coat.

Saskia feels the moment draining away and stalls. "Then at least give me some money for your share."

Naomi checks her change purse for silver. Finding none, she pulls out a baggie full of pennies and starts placing them into piles of ten down the table.

So, this is it, Saskia thinks. This is what's left of us. Rows of crappy copper that add up to squat. She reaches over to stop Naomi from counting, and accidentally knocks the coins to the floor.

"Are you trying to humiliate me? 'Cause you're doing an ace job of it." Naomi drops to her knees to pick up the coins and Saskia hastily joins in to help. They bump heads under the table then Naomi scrambles back to her seat, looking like she wants to clock her sister.

"Wait!" Saskia takes off her amethyst ring and gives it to Naomi. "Do-over."

"What's this for?" Naomi says guardedly.

"I remember you always used to borrow it, and since I missed your birthday and Christmas, it's yours."

Naomi blinks back tears as she slips the ring onto her finger.

"Do you ever think about me?" Saskia asks timorously.

There it hangs. Her truth and her greatest fear, wrapped up in a question, molded by months of silence.

"I think about you every day, numbskull." Naomi wipes her eyes on her sleeve. "Now look at what you've gone and made me do."

Saskia hands her a tissue and chokes on her next question, "Does Toby ever mention me? It's like I don't exist for him."

"I'm not in a position to speak for Toby, except to say that he's in a place where he's very committed to his principles and the choices that he's made." Naomi pauses, selecting her words. "I'm just not sure if I want what he wants anymore."

She wants out, Saskia's mind hollers in joy. "Just come home. You can have our room all to yourself. Whatever you want, it's yours."

Naomi fidgets with the amethyst ring. "I don't think I have it in me to forgive Mom for what she did."

"I'm sure she could say the same about you stealing her stuff."

"She owed me for the shit she put me through," Naomi replies pointedly.

"Enough!" Saskia exclaims. "I'm tired of being the middleman. We both know she let it out of the box with Manny, but I'm sure we can find a way to be a different *us*."

The air between them shifts as Naomi deliberates, then says, "I'll come home for a weekend and see."

"It'll be fine. I bet anything she'll even take us shopping. No offense, but it looks like you could do with a new coat."

"Okay, Miss JAP, point taken," Naomi says. "I'll have to tell Gray where I'm going if I spend the night elsewhere. I guess I could say I got a job catering at an out-of-town wedding."

"I'll even pick you up in a cab on Friday if you like."

"Promise you'll come and get me by yourself?" Naomi asks.

"If that's what you want, that's what will happen. I promise." Saskia crosses her heart and then settles the check.

By the time they part ways at Straus Park, their plan is in place.

* * *

If Saskia tells Mom that Naomi is coming home, she'll have to confess to having seen her on the sly, so she decides to sell it like it is a happy coincidence when she breaks the news the following morning. First, she sweetens up Mom by bringing her breakfast in bed. Then she tells Mom that she ran into Naomi on the subway platform at Ninety-Sixth Street while waiting for the express.

"Did she ask about me?" Mom asks.

"Of course she did," Saskia bullshits. "To be honest, it looks like she could use a break and seems open to spending the weekend at home."

Mom weighs what she said, and then comes up short. "Why, so she can help herself to more of my jewelry? I'm not her fool."

The morning comes crashing down. "What's your problem?" Saskia snaps, in hard impatience. "Grow a heart and decide what's more important. Your dumb stuff or your daughter?"

"You don't know what I've been through," Mom says, voice bruised.

"Really?" Saskia tosses back. "This hasn't just happened to you."

Mom's face topples. "I guess that makes me the fool for forgetting."

They hug, and fold back into one.

As one, they have stumbled through months of grinding uncertainty. They have been lonely together, but would have been far lonelier apart. And now their one impossible hope has become possible again.

"I'll pick Naomi up on Friday, then we'll have dinner together when you get back from work. How does that sound?"

"That sounds heavenly, my angel child."

* * *

The week flies by in anticipation of Naomi's arrival. Saskia cleans their bedroom and buys two bunches of red gladioli to place in a vase on the windowsill. She untangles the decorations from the Christmas tree, which has morphed into a brittle mess over the past three months, and packs them away. Then she leaves a spiky trail of brown bristles from lugging the tree to the garbage. She buys so much food at D'Agostino that it takes two trips down Broadway with Mom's rusty shopping cart to get all the groceries home. She calls Odessa to see if she can swap her regular day so she can be there to greet Naomi on Friday. But Odessa has a church meeting, so she promises to come and pay a visit on Saturday, instead.

On the day of days, she scores a nickel bag of pot from an entrepreneurial senior, in case Naomi needs a little help smoothing out the rough edges. She hurries straight home from school to find Mom going through the mail.

"What are you doing here?" Saskia exclaims. "Aren't you supposed to be at work?"

"I decided to take the afternoon off so that we could go and collect her together."

"I've a better idea." Saskia places her book bag on the hope chest. "Why don't you stay here and get dinner started?"

"Why would I want to be cooped up in the kitchen when I've been cooking all week? I want to join you."

"You wait here and I'll go and get her on my own." Saskia

can feel her mother's gaze drilling into her as she hangs up her coat.

"I smell a rat. If she wants to come home, then surely she wants to see me. Why are you excluding me?"

"I'm not. It's just that we made a plan."

"Well, I want to be there too." Mom's hardened expression looks like it belongs on Mount Rushmore.

Saskia excuses herself for the bathroom. Her hands shake as she firmly tells her mirrored reflection to calm the fuck down. She returns to find Mom waiting at the dining room table with her pocketbook on her lap and vodka and tonic in hand.

"To new beginnings." Mom tips her glass and finishes the drink.

Saskia glares at the vodka as though it's Semtex.

Mom rattles the ice like a sabre. "Don't be a hypocrite. I've noticed that the spirit levels have a tendency to shrink when I'm not around."

"But, Meredith, don't you think—"

"I think a little liquid refreshment is in order after my grueling workweek, thank you very much."

"Let's just go." Saskia wants them to leave before Mom has time for a refill. "You never know how long it can take to find a cab on a Friday afternoon, and we might have to wait once we get there."

"Don't worry. I have plenty of cash." Mom turns to hide the tears that form in her eyes. "We can have it wait for as long as it takes."

It's easy to forget, she thinks, that whatever she feels as a sister must be something else again as a mother. Naomi's absence has been like a splinter, causing them pain. Mom usually lets her scar tissue do the talking, but moments like this when she peels herself back makes Saskia want to wrap her in love.

"To new beginnings." Saskia impulsively kisses Mom. "You won't have reason to cry anymore."

They gather their coats and hook arms as they walk toward West End Avenue to find a cab. The sunset spilling through the late winter branches infuses the street with a rosy glow, making their block look the way she pictures a European city to look; old, but still beautiful. She makes a wish on the full moon delicately etched against the glorious evening sky.

The taxi they hail smells like a perfume factory inside. Mom mimes holding her breath and they get the giggles as they careen down West End Avenue. As the cab turns east and pulls up in front of Naomi's apartment building, Saskia's nerves start beating like a gong. She leaves Mom to wait in the cab and hurries to the building's vestibule.

She catches Mom's eye through the glass door and taps her wrist to indicate they're early. A few minutes later, Naomi emerges from the elevator carrying a paper bag and opens the door to the vestibule. Her eyes look puffy, but she grins lopsidedly when she sees Saskia, who is hopping up and down in her excitement.

"Let's just—" Naomi goes silent when she sees Mom, smiling and waving from the parked cab.

"I'm sorry. I know I said I'd come by myself but she's nagging to see you." Saskia tugs at Naomi's arm. "Just come on home now. It will be all right, I promise."

"That's right." Naomi's face mists over in pain. "You promised. You promised to pick me up on your own."

"But you were going to have to see her sooner or later.

Believe you me, she wants you back."

Naomi fumbles with her bag and drops it, spilling letters, photos, her makeup, and the well-worn wallet that Toby made for her during junior year arts and crafts onto the floor. "I thought I was ready, until I saw her. She may want me, but I'm not sure I could have her in my life again." Naomi scoops up her belongings and darts back into the foyer, letting the door slam shut behind her.

"*Please*, don't do this," Saskia pleads.

Naomi mouths, "I'm sorry" and steps back into the waiting elevator.

"I *hate* you." Saskia stamps her foot and slides to the floor in tears. She can't bring herself to look at Mom, who is watching open-mouthed from the curb.

An elderly man carrying a Barney Greengrass shopping bag comes in from the street, with keys in hand. "What is it, my child?" He hurries over to offer Saskia his handkerchief. "Are you hurt?"

Saskia shakes her head and wipes her nose on her sleeve.

"You're young, you're beautiful, and you have the rest of your life ahead of you," he says, helping her up. "Do you have a home to go to?"

"I guess you could say so," she replies, mustering the will to stand up and go back to the cab and explain to Mom how things went so wildly, off the charts wrong.

* * *

Saskia pushes through the heaving crowd of sweaty Columbia freshmen wearing "Kiss Me, I'm Irish" buttons to order another round of beers from the bartender. She's never been to the West End Tavern before and figures they won't get ID'd in this young, born-again Irish crowd on St. Patrick's Day.

She is drinking with determination. She's going to a party on Fifth Avenue later with her pals and wants to get happy, fast. Andy and Florence, in matching cropped T-shirts and leather pants, are trading insulting remarks with Tabitha—who has done up her eyes with frosted green shadow—about the bar's *Leave It to Beaver*-type clientele.

Inwardly, she's still digesting her strange day. Mom met her at school and treated her to lunch at Elephant and Castle. When it came time to go back, Mom insisted on calling Emerson to say that Saskia had a doctor's appointment, then took her shopping on the Upper East Side, instead.

When she found a pair of leather boots she liked, Mom bought two pairs. "But they're thirty dollars each," Saskia whispered in front of the salesclerk.

"It's only money," Mom said expansively. "If it makes you happy, get them."

Saskia wouldn't have questioned her impulsive generosity back in the day, but that day has been and gone. After Mom purchased three more pairs of shoes for herself, they went to the Oak Room at the Plaza for a drink, whereupon Mom excused herself to make a phone call and returned moments later all smiles.

"You'll never guess who I'm seeing tonight. My boss Scott invited me out for the second time this week."

Saskia white-knuckled her way through her soda as Mom confided in her about her big date. It would be one thing if this were a friend talking, but it bugs her that Mom's moving on to boyfriend number three, while she's still searching for numero uno. Their outing worked hell on her spirits.

So, six hours later, she's drinking warm beer in a crowded

bar, gearing up for the evening ahead in the hope that she'll pluck a warm-blooded, four-limbed clover. When they get up to leave, she twists her ankle in her new boots and hobbles after her friends, who are already on the curb searching for a cab, which are almost nonexistent this far uptown.

They heard about the party through the grapevine; a friend of a friend of Andy's from Columbia Grammar was giving it. They figured they could work their way down to another party in Peter Cooper Village in case this one was totally nowhere.

Saskia used to identify with being an Upper East Side kind of girl, but that went south with the move. Nowadays, she fancies herself a hep urban beatnik. To her, the city has become one big chaser, just waiting to be downed.

So here she is, suited and booted in readiness for a chemical holiday. She's nervous about dropping acid for the first time, but Andy assures her that a quarter tab of LSD is enough to get her buzzed without ripping her brains out.

They each digest their minute portion of colored paper on their cab ride east, through Central Park. The doorman tries to bar them from entering the building but grudgingly allows them upstairs when they cite the hostess's name. Saskia catches sight of herself in the elevator mirror and adjusts the tiny silver star from Capezio, which is threatening to become unglued from her cheekbone. Tonight, she looks like an it-girl on acid. She's wearing tight jeans without panties and an off-the-shoulder sequin-trimmed top from Fiorucci. Instead of taming her curls, she's gone for the psychedelic wench look and let them go wild.

The elevator opens directly into the apartment foyer, which is graced by an oil painting of a woman holding a bouquet of lilies. Andy—in eyeliner, gelled hair, and with a Winston dangling from his lips—cuts through the crowd like a renegade captain leading his troops. It's obvious they've made the wrong call when they saunter into the living room. Hall and Oates is playing on the stereo, they're the only ones dressed in black and there's no scent of pot. They ignore the hostess, who comes over in a diaphanous green chiffon dress to greet them, and muscle their way into the kitchen in search of booze.

"I feel like I've died and gone to Connecticut," Florence says, and gets into a staring match with a girl in a cashmere twin set who is giving her the once-over.

"Yeah, Miss Snot-Faced over there is looking at me like I'm the lawn jockey," grumbles Tabitha.

"Yuck." Saskia spits the punch back into her glass. "This is nonalcoholic. Let's go see how the other half live." She marches into the dining room and starts rooting around the teak liquor cabinet. "Bingo!" she says triumphantly, holding up a bottle of Smirnoff.

Andy, who's followed her, grabs the vodka from her. "Next stop, party central."

Saskia keeps waiting for the drugs to send her flying but feels only buzzed, speedy, and thirsty. She goes to check her pupils in the bathroom mirror to see if they've dilated. But when no magic carpet appears, she realizes their dealer stiffed them.

She takes the wrong turn on her way back to the dining room and ends up in the foyer, where a bunch of tony girls examine her as though she's a wet stool sample. She gives them face and then opens what she thinks is the kitchen door, only to discover it's a closet.

"Saskia?" A tow-haired girl breaks away from the group. "Is that really you?"

It's Kathleen. Her heart ding-a-lings as she takes in her former best friend's velvet headband and bobbed cut. She forgets that she's angry with Kathleen for not staying in touch and throws her arms around her.

"I didn't recognize you with your hair like that!" Saskia exclaims. "What are you doing in New York?"

Kathleen giggles and pulls away from this be-sequined, be-starred, and bewildering stranger. "My dad accepted another job, so I ended up back east in boarding school."

"Thanks for letting me be the last to know. Why didn't you call?"

"I meant to, but I've been busy. You know, football season and all that."

"Since when do you give a shit about football?" Saskia asks.

"Since him. Since Eric." Kathleen proudly points at a wholesome-looking boy in a plaid jacket drinking a can of Coke. "Turns out we're at the same school. We've been going steady now for months."

It takes Saskia a second to place Eric as the neighbor boy they used to wait for. And in the next second, whatever love she once felt for her old friend evaporates. It's not that she wants Waspy-ass him anymore; she wants her version of him. She thinks back to that night before Daddy died when they made their wishes, and can't believe Kathleen got her happily ever after, while she got bupkis.

"Look what he gave me for my birthday." Kathleen proudly displays a silver heart necklace.

"Did Ken doll get that in a Cracker Jack box?" Saskia sneers.

"Very funny," Kathleen says icily, tucking the heart back

nto her blouse. "Tell me what's new in your world, then."

Kathleen may have a boyfriend, but she can out-cool her, oth hands down.

"I ended up at this hip school where I'm top of the class vhen it comes to partying. There's this nude dude we draw in rt and I get to score in Washington Square Park during lunch."

"Huh. What clubs do you do?"

"I've been to The Loft and I was invited to Infinity," askia boasts. "Oh, you mean *school* clubs? I'm beyond all that rap now."

Andy sidles up, squeezes Saskia's tit, and stage-whispers, "I hink they fucked us over. I'm not seeing anything yet."

"Kathleen, I'd like you to meet my copilot Andy."

"Miss Kathleen." Andy makes an elaborate show of issing her hand. "How very grand to meet you."

"Listen, it's been really nice seeing you but I have to go iow." Kathleen extricates herself from Andy's nail-polished grasp and wipes her hand on her dress. "Eric has an early start omorrow."

"You mustn't keep the poor jock waiting then," Saskia says.

While Andy rounds up the troops to skedaddle downtown, askia waves goodbye at Kathleen and Eric, but they blank er—so she kisses her middle finger and wags it at them nstead.

She stubs out her cigarette in the dip before Andy, Florence, nd Tabitha head out the door without saying goodbye, their oockets bulging with vodka, beer cans, and a jar of caviar from he pantry.

"Check out the wampum," Andy says and pulls out the ilver Cartier lighter he apparently helped himself to as well. "Me, Big Chief Light Fingers."

"They owed us for going there," Tabitha says. "God, tha so sucked."

"Yeah, and I swallowed," Florence concurs. "That wa: about as much fun as an obligatory blow job."

"Too right." Tabitha laughs. "My jaw hurts from just being in the same room as them."

"Whose bright idea was it anyway?" Saskia asks.

"Guilty," Andy says, and admits, "I can't resist an invitation With me it's always when, where, I'll be there."

"You're such a party slut. You'd do it with anyone," Saski: says.

"Takes one to know one," Andy replies. "Speaking of sluts, who was that creature you were talking to? She looke like Ethel Kennedy on a good day."

"Her? She's a nobody." Saskia takes a swig of vodka anc adds, "I mean, we were friends way back when, but she's jus some ass-ugly goody-gumdrop who doesn't mean anything tc me anymore."

She never thought she'd be the one to swap tribes, leavin; Kathleen and her people behind while she, like an urban squaw follows the distant tom-tom of better parties and stronge drugs as she tracks the city at night.

16.

Same Old, Same Old

It had been a bender of a week. On Wednesday, she went with everyone after school to play Pac-Man at Ethan's, who lives in the same Park Avenue building as the Shah of Iran. They raided his mom's medicine cabinet and fridge and got ripped on Valium and Rolling Rock. On Thursday, the gang saw *Annie Hall*, and on Friday, they went to the Waverly for the midnight run of *The Rocky Horror Picture Show*, and she spent the night at Tabitha's. Then on Saturday, Madeleine, the York Avenue princess, threw her Sweet Sixteen at Studio 54.

Studio, which had only been open for a month, is notoriously hard to get into, but Saskia and her posse sashay past the red velvet rope and spend the night dancing under the twinkling man-in-the-moon coke spoon. Granted, she only sees the albino-looking Andy Warhol talking with wrinkly old Truman Capote instead of Warren or Jack, but at least she gets to hobnob with the jet set, see the barmen in their silver shorts, and do bong hits on the balcony with the school's hard-core stoners.

She walks back to Essex House with Andy and the girls at dawn, giddy from pulling her first all-nighter. She's never seen her city before, at this time of day, and watches the news vendors lugging bundles of the *Sunday Times* from the curbs to their stands while steam rises from the manholes. Central Park's flinty musk blends with the scent of warm bread from the twenty-four-hour deli on Columbus Circle with the red neon coffee cup in its window.

She has a George Gershwin-moment when the ground

shudders as a subway train rumbles by beneath her and the heavens lift their skirts to reveal a blushing pink sky. Her heart swells with love for New York's shabby elegance. She smiles at a homeless man feeding pigeons from a paper bag. "Good morning, starshine," he says and winks, touching a dirty hand to the brim of his army cap.

Once back in Andy's suite, she closes the curtains and tumbles into bed while Florence, Andy, and Tabitha have a party debrief in the next room.

At 2:00 p.m. she stirs and stretches herself awake. Lying there, with her hands reeking of cigarettes, heels raw from dancing, and thirsty as all fuck, she feels criminally happy.

She wiggles her way down to the bottom of the bed so as not to wake anyone, and drags the telephone into the bathroom to call home. No reply means that Mom must be with Scott, who she's been seeing for over two months. Now she has free license to get a bowl of Froot Loops and wait for the others to wake up.

Andy is the first to stumble into the kitchenette, bleary-eyed and bed-headed. He pours himself some cereal, too, and mumbles, "Feed a hangover."

Tabitha and Florence soon join them, and they all spend the next few hours in bed watching an *I Love Lucy* marathon before Saskia heads uptown in time to do the laundry before school tomorrow.

While walking up her street abloom with May blossoms, she realizes she likes not being the family Chicken Little, always waiting for the sky to fall. It can be about her, not them.

Fumbling for her keys in the hallway, she hears the water running from inside the apartment and throws open the front door, in readiness of giving Mom a highly edited account of her weekend.

Mom is sprawled face-down on the foyer floor, looking like a dead angel in her bloodstained, white nightgown.

Time is suspended for a shrill moment. Then everything happens fast. The door slams shut. Saskia is on the floor. The rug is scraping her bare knees. She follows the blood. It's not coming from Mom's wrists. It's her nose. Saskia's crying, then praying. She's hating herself for letting this happen. Her hands are shaking. Then she's shaking Mom, who finally shows signs of scotch-scented life. "I miss Larry," she slurs, throwing her arms around Saskia's neck.

Saskia hugs Mom as tight as she dares, leaving red handprints on the back of her nightgown. She struggles to get Mom on her feet and back into her unmade bed. Then she runs back to the kitchen to turn off the water that is overflowing from the sink of dirty dishes. She uses a moistened washcloth to gently sponge away the blood and applies a cold compress to the bruise forming on Mom's forehead, from where her face made contact with the floor.

Mom moans and whispers, "I'm sorry."

"No, it's all my fault," Saskia says as she works the soiled nightgown up and over Mom's head. "I should have come home earlier."

"I'm overwhelmed by the burden of my song," Mom mutters before dropping off again.

Saskia covers her with a blanket and leaves the bedroom door ajar while she pours the remains of the Johnny Walker down the sink. Her responsibilities have returned with a vengeance. She was wrong to turn her back on Mom—even temporarily. Like it or not, she must remain vigilant or risk going from a family of five, to four, to three, to two, to one.

Being the sole gatekeeper is an eight-day-a-week job, and she vows not to put Mom in jeopardy again.

* * *

Saskia is woken the next morning by the sound of a car braking on the street below. The sun flowing through the window illuminates the dust motes, drifting aimlessly. Her bedside clock radio tells her it's past eight. Mom usually wakes her up with tea and toast on the mornings that she's working, but this morning is silent and scentless.

She hurries down the hall and finds Mom lying in bed with her back to the window, staring at the wall with fathomless eyes. Saskia hugs her as though her touch could absorb her sorrow. "Are you okay?"

"Not even close." Mom's voice catches. "I'm sorry I'm such a mess."

"Don't say that." Saskia strokes Mom's hair.

"You're too good to me," Mom says. "I don't deserve it."

"Not true." Saskia carefully checks Mom's bruise.

"I wake up every day and wonder how my life evolved from such promise and common purpose, to such pain."

"Can I get you anything?" She extracts a soiled handkerchief from her mother's grasp. "Do you want to call in sick at work today?"

Mom laughs mirthlessly. "That won't be necessary."

"But it's after eight."

Mom covers her face with her hand. Saskia notices that she's wearing her wedding ring, which is usually consigned to her velvet jewelry box.

"An unexpected visitor paid a call this weekend. I discovered I was pregnant when I miscarried," Mom says flatly.

And when I phoned Scott to tell him our news, he dumped me. So, I quit my job. I'm going to the doctor this morning by myself to finish it off."

Saskia's mind somersaults. Years ago, she used to beg her parents for a little brother or sister, thinking it would be cool to have a big old-fashioned family. It never occurred to her that Mom could still get pregnant. But then again, nothing that has happened of late ever occurred to her either.

"Do you want me to come with you?" she asks, aware of how strange it is that she, a teenage virgin, is witnessing her mother's condition, which by most measures should be her own. But Mom insists that Saskia's place is at school and hauls herself out of bed to draw a bath.

Saskia goes to get dressed. Although the day promises to be warm and sunny, she selects a black top as her silent gesture to baby no-show.

Since she's running so late, she decides to skip English completely in favor of going to Washington Square Park to pool herself back together. Mom's news has made her so inexorably tangled inside that she cries on the subway platform. She ignores the kindly inquiries of an old Greek lady and pretends to sleep on route to Christopher Street.

She walks across Bedford Street and parks herself on a bench near a pair of Italian men playing chess on one of the cement tables in the square. The sun is bright and there are cherry blossoms on the trees, yet she's gone clammy inside. Her fingers feel heavy, like silt runs through her veins. Who would have thought that on this fine May morning her mother would be uptown, having her uterus scraped, while she's downtown, trying not to picture what possibilities that zygote held.

Yesterday morning, she was so happy. But today, she feels

lashed to her mother, who isn't as seaworthy as she once was. She closes her eyes and prays for Mom's tide to turn. Then she prays for a sign, any sign, to prove that she herself won't sink before she reaches shore.

Realizing she hasn't had any breakfast, she buys an ice cream cone and is hungrily demolishing it when a man suddenly pops into her field of vision and tries to take a bite.

"Hey! What the fuck are you doing?" She gets up in a huff, promptly trips, and drops the cone. "Thanks a lot, asswipe."

Asswipe turns out to be a mustached blond, bearing a guitar case. "I'm sorry, babe. Let me buy you another."

"I'm not your babe." She picks up her book bag and marches off. "Just leave me alone."

"I only called you that since I don't know your name. I'm Rick."

He's so tall, she finds herself taking two steps for his every one. "And I'm late. Now get lost."

"Don't be this way. I didn't know how else to get your attention."

There's a burr in his voice that snags her interest.

"How many ways are there to say you made me curious from the second I saw you?" he says, as they simultaneously slow to a halt.

She surreptitiously studies the stickers on his guitar case. *Fillmore. The Greek. Liberty Hall. Sand.* She can almost hear the applause. *Maybe he's famous,* starts strumming like a riff in her mind. *He's handsome,* joins in the refrain. *He seems to like you* becomes the chorus.

She gets a cigarette from her book bag and accidentally-on-purpose can't find her matches so Rick has to light it for her. As she bends to meet his hand, she sees the hairs on his knuckles and realizes that he's probably old enough to be in college.

Rick blows out the match and asks, "So what's your name?"

"Guess."

Rick starts rattling them off. "Gloria, Janine, Marybeth, Deidre, Lois—"

"Stop!" She giggles. "You're making my ears hurt. I'm Saskia."

"Okay, Saskia." He helps himself to a drag of her cigarette and then hands it back to her. "Now it's your turn to guess. Where am I from?"

"California?" she guesses from the stickers, the rainbow charm around his neck, and the sun-kissed hue to his hair.

"Oregon, close enough. What do you think I do?"

"That's easy. You're a musician. What about me?"

"I'd say you're not in school where you should be, and by school, I mean high school. Getting warm?"

She nods, and blows a smoke ring.

"I'd also say you have something on your mind. Something you'd like to share. Am I right?"

She meets his gaze, sticky-eyed. "Getting hot."

"Well, I have something to share with you, too." They find a bench, then Rick extracts a joint from his jean pocket and lights it. "Open wide." He blows the smoke shotgun-style into Saskia's mouth, making her brain go pop.

Her head lolls, as her mind twists open like a kaleidoscope. The grass glistens and she becomes aware of a bird singing and of a bright yellow balloon climbing into the sky, as the dappled light scatters twinkle bells around them.

He picks out tunes on his guitar while they finish the joint and talk about everything and nothing. He lifts the lid on the morning. She wants to taste his every word. He's met Mick and been to Mexico. The pull of the road beckons her forward and she can hear the swell of the Pacific in the blue strings of his melodies.

"You have to come to my next gig."

"When's that then?" Saskia asks eagerly.

"We're still figuring out the details. But it'll be soon."

"What's the name of your band?"

"I'm not allowed to say until the ink's dry." He borrows her pen to jot his address on a matchbook. "But I can invite you to my birthday party next month."

"Oh, yeah? Mine's in June too."

"Ah, a fellow Gemini. Maybe we're long-lost twins." Rick lets his fingers brush against hers when he hands back the pen. "I'm the seventh. You?"

"The eleventh." His touch makes her skin tighten.

"How old are you going to be?"

She giggles when he removes a spot of ice cream from her chin and slowly licks his finger clean. "Sixteen."

"Ah, sweet sixteen. I'll be twenty."

Twenty. Won't her friends be impressed.

He puts the roach back and pats his pocket, as his face falls. "Damn."

"What is it?"

"Nothing." He starts packing his guitar away. "I'm headed uptown for a rehearsal that starts at noon. Want to walk part way?"

"But it's only ten."

"Yeah, but I left my bucks at home and need a five-spot to get me there and back, and cover expenses."

Her expression shifts as she processes the awkwardness

of his ask.

"I know what you must be thinking. I'll pay you back when I see you," Rick hastily adds.

There it is again, the prairie song of his voice. She gives him a bill.

"And just to prove it, this is my gift to you." Rick covers her eyes with one hand, then slips something over her head with the other. "Believe me now?"

He takes his hand away. She smiles when sees his rainbow charm and touches its glossy enameled stripes. "I do."

"Promise you'll come to my party?"

"I promise," she says. And by God, does she mean it.

* * *

Saskia slips into class and grabs a seat next to Tabitha and Florence, who are reviewing their English notes, when she finally makes it to second period fifteen minutes later.

"Where were you?" Tabitha asks, then recoils. "Shit, you reek. You need some gum."

Florence hands her a stick of Juicy Fruit and says, "Emerson was asking after you. Our end-of-years start after break."

"They do?"

"Hello. Don't you remember?" Tabitha gazes at her with concern. "You were supposed to come over last night to study."

"*C'est la vie*," Saskia says, stuffing the gum in her mouth. "Guess what? I met the coolest guy in the park."

"Where? At the dog run?" Florence quips.

"Go blow. *He* started talking to *me*," Saskia boasts. "And guess what else? He's almost twenty. And he's a musician."

"What does he play?" Florence asks. "The kazoo?"

"Very funny. Maybe you're jealous," Saskia retorts.

"Of you?" Florence laughs. "Please."

"Promise not to see him again?" Tabitha says sternly.

Saskia shrugs sulkily.

"Say it," Tabitha insists.

"I promise." Saskia crosses her fingers beneath the desk.

Saskia buries her head in her textbook when Emerson comes into the class and jabs her finger at the wall clock, which now reads 10:17. "Good afternoon, Miss Soyer. So glad you could join us."

Saskia pretends not to hear her.

"I know mornings are difficult for you." Emerson passes out the tests, and pointedly rights Saskia's upside down textbook when she reaches her desk. "Perhaps you'd flourish at night school."

Over the next forty-five minutes, Saskia doodles the test with flowers and rainbows while everyone else concentrates. Then Emerson collects the papers while Saskia shoves her pens into her bag and makes for the door.

"Saskia? A word?" Emerson points to a chair.

Saskia sighs theatrically and sits back down, fiddling with her new charm.

"Judging from the decorative state of this test, you might be repeating tenth grade."

Flunky. Stupid. Retard are soon drowned out in her head by *big deal. Tough shit. Whatever.* "Yeah. So?"

"So, you may have wasted my time and resources. But the one who stands to lose the most out of this is you."

* * *

Jobless now, Mom alternates between going back to bed after breakfast and embarking on projects such as cleaning out drawers—which she starts with a flourish, then takes days to complete. She begins selling banana bread to a local deli, but stops when a customer finds a hair in the product. She talks about becoming a docent at the Whitney Museum, without getting around to it. She sells another print and starts drinking wine with breakfast.

Saskia begs her to get in touch with Libby, but Mom says she doesn't need to; she has all the friends she needs. And besides, she doesn't need Libby passing judgment on her. Feeling like a big fat hypocrite, Saskia even urges her to go back to the encounter group meetings, but Mom demurs, insisting that she's moved on.

Her social life continues to be fun, but lately she can sense her worlds colliding as she bounces between Mom's dungeon-like depression and her own cutting loose. She starts adding vodka to her morning carton of Tropicana, and smoking joints between every class. She's on Emerson's watch list now, but instead of curbing her, this only eggs her on. Even her best friends can't keep up with her partying and tell her to take a chill pill unless she wants a one-way ticket to Phoenix House.

So many elements in her life have come to naught: her zilch love life, her broken family, even the boxes in the hall closet that were never unpacked. Everything draws attention to their gaping Daddy-deficit. Everything reminds Saskia that he was their gold standard who kept them going. So she keeps pushing ahead, determined not to go bust.

* * *

Saskia stubs her cigarette out in her fries and stares at the refrigerated dessert display in the Village Den coffee shop while Florence and Tabitha finish their lunch. She's depressed that she hasn't seen Rick, even though she's looked for him in the square almost daily. She certainly hasn't told anyone about the thousand and one wicked ways she's had him in her mind since they met. She could kill herself for losing the matchbook he gave her and is just about resigned to never seeing him again.

So instead, she's been pushing the Ethan repeat-button, figuring he can fill the hole in her heart, the hole between her legs, and a whole lot more. Ever since Mom's miscarriage, she's felt like a walking five-alarm fire that only a man can extinguish.

This morning, she came to school braless and in a miniskirt and sat on Ethan's lap while he was smoking on the stoop. Then she brushed his hair back and leaned over to ask if he wanted to cut school and go to the band shell with her to get high. When Ethan declined with a smirk, she scampered off to the Village Den with her friends, her dignity badly bruised.

"How come I never get lucky? There must be something wrong with me," she moans, as she plays with the ketchup on her plate.

Tabitha and Florence exchange a conspiratorial look as they finish off their burgers and motion for the check.

"Hey, dipshits. This is the part when you're supposed to say, 'Why no, Saskia, you're mistaken.'"

"Oh, excuse me, did I miss my cue?" Florence says, her voice coiled. "Why no, Saskia, I'd mistaken you for someone with half a brain."

"What do you mean by that?" Saskia bristles.

"Why do you let Ethan get to you?" Florence replies. "You've only been lusting after him like a jerk since freshman year."

"Truth? He's not worth it," Tabitha adds. "He's just another ass-ignorant stoner who doesn't know a tab of acid from his elbow."

"That's not the point," Saskia says.

"Then what is?" Tabitha demands.

Saskia rattles off her toxic troika. "My mom gets more action than me, and I'm still a virgin, while she's the one who got knocked up."

Tabitha takes the check from the waiter and says, "So you want to get humped and dumped like your mom?"

"No!" Saskia retorts. "Don't twist my words. I just want a guy to like me."

"That won't happen until you like yourself first." Tabitha examines the check. "I'm putting in $2.35 for my share."

"Stop getting on my case," Saskia says huffily. "All I'm saying is it doesn't make sense. I'm young and hot, not old and pathetic like my mom. I wish Andy was here to stick up for me."

Florence rolls her eyes at Tabitha and adds, "I can assure you that Andy would rather be with his parents in Paris for Memorial Day weekend than listening to you kvetch. Nowadays, with you it's always *moi-moi-moi*."

Saskia shoves her plate aside, boiling over in fury.

"I'm out of here." She tosses two crumpled bills on the table. "If I hear Emerson bitch and moan at me once more about not finishing my term paper, I'm going to tell her to shove it up her wrinkled ass."

"I wouldn't cut class if I were you," Tabitha says in a warning tone. "She's threatening to make you repeat a grade."

"Yeah, getting left back at the Collective would be a real

achievement. In fact, that would be a first," Florence snaps.

"Eat me," Saskia says, as she leaves the table.

"What about the tip? Or were you planning on titting the man instead?" Tabitha calls after her.

Saskia flips them the bird and steams out of the air-conditioned coffee shop to walk around the block the wrong way to avoid school. She heads down Sixth Avenue toward Washington Square Park to see if the moon is in Rick today.

A construction worker whistles as she struts past the Jefferson Market Library. So what if Ethan is more interested in his Thai stick than the chance to explore her tits. At least other guys think she looks hot to trot in her Trash & Vaudeville flirt-skirt with a fluorescent tulle bow.

While waiting by Crazy Eddie for the light, she notices a bunch of hippie-loser types passing out pamphlets and sees Naomi pressing a flyer into a stranger's hand. It's the first time she's seen Naomi since February and is still nursing a big-time grudge. She ducks for cover behind a pair of orange-clad Hare Krishna's when Naomi calls her name, then hastens east on Eighth Street. Saskia thinks she's shaken her, but by the time she turns right on MacDougal, her sister's caught up with her.

"I've been meaning to call," Naomi says breathlessly, looking rosy-cheeked and sleek-haired once again.

"Really now, is that so? It's only been three-and-a-half months since you left me high and dry."

"I knew you were angry at me for what happened."

"Or didn't happen," Saskia shoots back. "Nothing technically happened."

Naomi puts her hands up in surrender. "Okay, *Carla* Bernstein. Point taken. But I have been thinking of you, and am happy we're here now."

Thirst from the humidity drives Saskia to accept Naomi's invitation to sit on a neighboring stoop and have a drink from the corner deli.

"How's Toby?" Saskia asks as she opens her Diet Dr Pepper.

"Oh, he's just great. He's thrown himself into our latest theater project and has written an entire play himself." Naomi produces a photocopied flyer from her knapsack. "You should come along sometime. It's a spoof on Anita Bryant."

Saskia spits her gum into the flyer and tosses it on the street.

"I'll pretend I didn't see that," Naomi says dryly. "As it happens, there's something I've been wanting to share with you. I was in a bad place the last time I saw you and—"

"You said it, I didn't," Saskia interrupts.

"I was doubting my choices and struggling to keep an open mind. Gray always tells us that every experience reveals an opportunity. I realize now that I needed to do what I did so as to appreciate what I have. And I wanted to thank you for being part of that process."

"What are you blabbing on about?" Saskia says disparagingly. "I don't speak psycho."

"You did me a favor by bringing Mom along that afternoon. You know what else? I think you did that unconsciously to save me from coming home. Now I want to thank you, by inviting you to move in with us, so I can help you in the same way that Toby helped me."

Help? Her soul writhes in scorn. She can't find room for what Naomi's saying anywhere inside her. If she did, it would be like confessing to: *yes, we never worked. We never loved. We never were.* "I'm fifteen. Why would I leave home? So I can drop out of high school and become a babysitter like you?"

"You're so bourgeois. There's no shame in earning a living," Naomi retorts. "Why are you so threatened by my choices?"

"I'm not threatened. I just think they're bogus and nasty. I couldn't do what you guys did to Mom. It would finish her off."

"So, what are you, Mom's mom or her wet nurse?" Naomi shakes her head. "I think you're a willing masochist."

"And I think I'm going to see you one day on the front cover of the *Post* wearing a beret and packing a machine gun."

Naomi takes off the amethyst ring Saskia gave her, thrusts it at her, and stomps off.

"Bye, Patty, or is it Tania?" Saskia calls, as she slips the ring back on her finger. "Don't forget to give my best to the good folk at Symbionese Liberation Army." She crosses over to Washington Square to look for Rick, like he's a lost winning lottery ticket. After touring the square twice, she stops off in various liquor stores until she finds one that will sell her a half pint of vodka, which she soaks up as she sits on the base of the Cube on Astor Place, while the sky darkens.

She doesn't want to go back to school to face the hairy wrath of Emerson, and Mom's home, so she can't return there either. She has a eureka-moment when she remembers that Arthur lives close by and digs out her address book from her book bag. After finding the nearest working phone booth, she invites herself over and then drunkenly weaves up Fourth Avenue until she finds his loft, which is located above an antique store with gated windows.

She hauls herself up five, steep, dimly lit flights and gets the hiccups by the time she reaches his floor. She pauses on the top step to hold her breath but gets so dizzy that she slips, clutching the banister to prevent herself from toppling down the stairs.

Arthur opens the front door and she collapses into his arms. "Are you okay? Why aren't you in school?"

His question makes her laugh. Now her hiccups are competing with her tears, so she's half-laughing and half-crying. As if on cue, there is a clap of thunder and rain starts pelting down outside.

"You smell like a stevedore on payday." Arthur leads her into the living room. "Let's start by getting you sobered up."

She flops down on the worn velveteen couch that reeks of age and feels the room revolve.

"What's with you?" He sits down next to her with a coffee, water, and a bottle of Bayer. "Why are you getting shit-faced in the middle of the day?"

She drinks thirstily and proceeds to tell him about her encounter with Naomi. "I just hate who she's become and don't understand how she morphed into some Patty Hearst-clone who wants to brainwash me," she weeps, overwhelmed once again. "I just wanted us to learn to be happy without Larry, but it's impossible if we're all split up."

Arthur hands her a hankie. "It won't always feel this way."

"Really?" She wipes her nose and nestles up to him. "You're not just saying that?"

"Time has a way of taking care of things, I promise," he says comfortingly, putting his arm around her. "Something will give."

Her breath quiets as she savors the sensation of listening to his heartbeat.

"I'll always be there for you," he adds.

She strokes his hand, tracing the outline of his veins with

her forefinger, then moves it toward her breast.

"But not like that," Arthur says gently, moving away.

She's mortified. Her second pass in one day, roundly rejected. Feeling like an A-number-one-asshole, she stands up and accidentally sends the coffee flying across the bare floorboards. "I'm sorry, I'm such a jerk." Saskia grabs an old newspaper to mop up the mess. "I'll just fuck off now and leave you in peace."

"It's okay. You're just a little wasted now. It's no big deal." He tries to make her sit down again. "Please don't go out like this, you're in no state. Besides, you'll get drenched."

"It's the same old, same old." She shoos him away and searches for her book bag. "No one wants me the way I want them. In fact, no one wants me, period."

"That's not true."

"Bullshit. If my brother or sister really loved me, they never would've left home."

"You know I love you like a sister," Arthur cajoles. "Stay and hang out awhile. You just got here."

"That's just it. It's all back-assward and inside out. Andy loves me like a friend, you love me like a sister, and my own brother acts like I don't even exist," Saskia sobs. "I've become my mother's mother, and every time I think I like someone they never like me back in the same way."

"Don't be silly. I like you a lot. It's just that . . ." Arthur begins.

"Something is wrong with me." Saskia finds her book bag and heads for the door. "There's something ugly and horrible and broken in me that drives everyone away. I must be unlovable, because it shouldn't be this way and wouldn't be this way if anyone really cared."

She clambers down the stairs and lights a cigarette to help quiet her head. Then she starts toward the subway using an abandoned copy of the *Village Voice* as cover from the rain. She stops to finish her smoke under a shoe store awning and spies Manny inside, waiting on a customer. Her breath quickens when they lock eyes. Then she gives him the finger and stubs out her cigarette on the plate glass window.

She runs off and then pauses for shelter in the entrance of the Strand Bookstore next to a blind man, who is struggling to get his bearings. She starts to offer him her hand, but instead she crosses her arms and smirks when he steps right into a giant puddle, a mere foot from her.

17.

Sweet Young Thing

On the Tuesday after Memorial Day weekend, Emerson summons Saskia into the office during second break to tell her she has until the following Monday to hand in her term paper or risk being left back. Fed up and fucked off, Saskia cuts Spanish and heads uptown.

She opens the front door, lie at the ready, only to be met with porous silence. Mom is nowhere to be seen, but her pocketbook is on the hope chest and her bedroom door is closed. She figures that Mom's either napping or down in the laundry room doing last week's wash in time for Odessa, who is due to come later. She'll have to feign that she's home because it's the time of the month when she's flying the red flag. So she changes into her pajamas to look the part and goes to the bathroom to wash her hands.

A man, naked apart from a bandana in his tangled hair and with skin like a waxy parsnip, is sitting in a towel on the toilet, holding a necktie between his teeth while he shoots up.

Saskia's screams shred the silence. His needle rolls across the tiled floor. She flaps her hands as though he is a puff of almond-scented smoke that she could waft out through the window. Her bones go soft with fear. Then she melts in the corner as this hectic-haired stranger passes by in a flurry and ducks into the master bedroom.

She's hugging her knees and leaning against the bathroom door, shouting nonsensically for help.

Mom pushes the door open. "For heaven's sake, you scared the life out of me," she cries. "What are you doing here? You're not supposed to be back yet."

She wants to tell Mom that there's an intruder in their home. But Mom is naked under her robe. And so was he. Now he's in her bedroom. And then it all makes sick sense. He's not the stranger. Mom is.

She looks to Mom for a different answer.

Booze-diffused eyes stare back. "That's my friend, Sterling."

"Your 'friend'?" Her words feel like they're coming up the wrong way.

"I told you that I met someone new."

Saskia's heart becomes unglued. "Where did you go?"

Mom doesn't say anything.

"How could you go from Daddy to *that*?"

Mom's expression dips as she adjusts her robe. "I married a 'nice' guy and had a 'normal' marriage. And look where those 'rules' got me."

"Am I just another 'rule'? Do you even *want* to be my mother?"

"That's not an easy question," Mom says with even candor. "I could ask a similar one of you."

Her mother is no longer recognizable.

"I hate you." The words spew from a newly hewn place inside her. "In fact, I hate everything about you. I wish to God you'd died instead of Daddy."

She scrambles to her feet and runs to her room, slamming the door to stare at her severed self in the mirror. She lost her father and way of life. She lost her siblings. And even though her mother's right next door, she's lost her now too.

* * *

Saskia is aware of the light draining from her room. She's aware of voices, and of footsteps coming and going, and of Odessa arriving. She's aware that Mom comes in and stands next to her bed as though she wants to say something before hastening out again. All of this seems to be happening from a great distance. All she wants now is distance from everything and everyone she once loved.

She ignores the knock on her door. When Odessa comes in, she covers her head with her blanket while Odessa sits down and places a tuna fish sandwich and glass of milk by her bedside. "Grief is a powerful thing. There's no saying which way it will pull you."

"Did you know about Sterling?" Saskia asks, voice muffled beneath the covers.

"Yes. He's been here a few times before." Odessa tenderly rubs her back. "I just pray he doesn't die in her bed."

"How did she meet him?"

"He came with the seltzer delivery."

"How could she go from Daddy to him?" Saskia's brain feels chapped.

"You have to love and respect your mother. She's a good woman who is in a bad way."

"Can I come stay with you?" Saskia sits up.

"Heavens no. You belong here with your mother."

"I don't want to belong here anymore," Saskia frets. "I don't want to be her daughter."

"Enough of that smart mouth of yours. This is still your home and she's still your kin. Besides, I have some news."

"News?" Saskia takes a bite of the sandwich to brace herself.

"My nephew was posted to Texas. He's been inviting me

or some time now to come live with his family, so I'm moving here next month."

"I'll never get to see you again if you move to Texas," Saskia says plaintively, shoving the sandwich away. "Why do you have to go?"

"I'm not getting any younger and you're growing up right before my eyes." Odessa wipes a crumb from the corner of Saskia's mouth.

"But that's not fair." Her eyes feel like a bucket that's about to overflow. "I'm going to miss you so much."

"You can always call me, and you'll always be in my prayers."

"Please don't go. You're the only one I have left." Saskia hugs Odessa, recalling her patient counsel, the countless dinners, and those everyday moments they shared over the years.

Odessa holds Saskia's chin in her hand. "Tears don't bring anyone back. You have to look to the future and find faith."

"But the future always stinks."

Odessa tucks the covers around her and turns off her sidelight. "Child, the future is all you have. Now get a good night's sleep for once. Things always look different in the light of day."

* * *

Saskia doesn't know where she is when she wakes up next to a patch of drool on her pillow. Or what she's doing in her pajamas. Or why it's dark outside. It takes her a few seconds to remember. The clock radio tells her it's eleven; possibly the worst time ever to wake up. It's too late for dinner, too late to call anyone, too late to get up to no good.

She finishes her sandwich while rustling through her clothes for a rainy-day roach to see her through the night. As she searches her pockets, she finds the matchbook Rick gave her. She pounces on it and sees that his party is that very night.

It's a sign from the god of lust. She's going to show Mom, Arthur, Ben, Ethan, her fuckwad friends, and every other douchebag in the five boroughs of New York that she can get a guy too. She changes into pink carpenter pants, a tank top and hot-pink sandals, then slaps on some makeup and plenty of Rive Gauche perfume.

She creeps down the hall to make sure that Mom is out like a light and sneaks twenty dollars from her wallet before slipping out of the apartment. Hurrying through the lobby, she wonders if it's her imagination or if the doorman is giving her a strange look. She can only imagine what he must think about her mother, the Linda Lovelace of the second floor.

The June night air is balmy and there're cherry blossoms on the tree-lined street. A few men are playing cards on a neighboring stoop, while drinking out of brown paper bags.

She plays with Rick's rainbow charm, which she hasn't taken off once since he gave it to her, as the subway lumbers downtown. She's the only person to get off at Franklin Street. The first exit she tries is locked so she hurries to the next exit as the train pulls out of the station.

Tribeca is deserted, save for the occasional truck trundling north toward the Meatpacking District. Every other storefront has a For Rent sign. She has trouble getting her bearings and heads east instead of west. When she spies a rat rooting through the curbside litter, she starts trotting down the middle of the cobblestone street. She finally finds Rick's address at what turns out to be a warehouse, with rusted gates and broken syringes on the steps.

She rings the buzzer. She waits, then rings it again. A light comes on inside, and a tattooed woman in a studded leather choker comes to the door to vet her.

"Hi, I'm a friend of Rick's. He invited me." Saskia's voice sounds girly and loud.

The woman silently motions her in and takes her downstairs to the sparsely decorated basement with flaking walls. There's an amp alongside a couch with busted springs and an upright piano that's missing some keys. As she searches for Rick among the throng of people, it dawns on her that she's the youngest person there by a decade, even two. She doesn't know why, but it didn't occur to her that there would be so many old-timers at this party. She stands there, feeling pretty conspicuous in pink, among this edgy downtown crowd.

She spies Rick, with his hair in a ponytail and wearing a leather vest over a T-shirt, choosing a record with the help of a bottle blond. She starts toward him, but then goes all upside down inside when he caresses the woman's arm. She ducks behind an insulated pipe to watch. The music is too weird and she's too sober for this. Turning to go, she stumbles and kicks an empty beer bottle over.

Rick hears the glass make contact with the floor and hastens over to greet her with a kiss. "Hey, Shirley Temple. I was waiting for you. Let me get you a drink."

"Who's the blond?" She feels like she could stamp her foot clear through the floor to the ground below.

"Her? She's my manager."

"Really now?" Saskia covers his rainbow with her hand.

"Is that my charm you're wearing?" Rick asks, teasing the strap of her tank top.

She pretends to study a row of pot plants that are grouped beneath a Grow Light.

"Have you been thinking about me half as much as I've been thinking about you?" He takes her hand to lead her to the kitchen area, to search for a clean glass amongst the dirty dishes piled in the sink.

"You're the only one here tonight that I wanted to see," he says, pouring her a coffee mug of neat room temperature vodka.

"But isn't this your party and aren't these your friends?" Her eye is drawn to the disconnected stovetop, on which awaits a store-bought cake adorned with a twenty-three made out of an assortment of pills. "Wait a sec." She laughs nervously and downs the vodka. "You told me you were turning twenty."

"Age is just a number." Rick softly tugs the charm and pulls her closer to him. "I didn't want to spook you."

Leave. Stay. Split. Her mind twists this way and that. *He's protecting you. He's lying to you. He's into you.* Then desire bends all reason, and her hips give way to his. Rick gives her a prism of a smile and fetches himself a beer from the fridge.

The bottle blond beckons for him from the curtained alcove next to the kitchen. "I'll be right back," Rick says, and seeing that she's finished her vodka, hands her his can of beer.

"Where are you going?" Saskia exclaims.

"I have to get something for my manager."

The evening turns like a knife. She starts to leave.

"Hold on. You've got the wrong idea. I'll only be a minute. Do you want me to introduce you, Sasha?"

"*Sasha*? My name is *Saskia*."

"I know," Rick says, brushing aside one of her stray curls. "That's just my little endearment for you. Now wait here. I'll be right back."

With her stomach hugging her rib cage, she downs the beer to stop her hands from shaking and mooches a cigarette off a fat man with a ponytail who's chopping lines on the stainless steel counter. Ten minutes and two cigarettes later, she turns to leave for real, subway token in hand.

"Would you like one for the road?" The fat man winks and offers her a rolled-up bill.

"Hell, why not." Saskia takes the note and snorts three lines in rapid succession.

There's a windstorm of a second before her head erupts like Krakatoa. The subway token slips out of her hand and rolls away, disappearing into a crack in the floorboards. She lurches backward, knocking into the fat man who laughs as she blinks, trying to pull focus.

"Angel dust will always make your brains bust," he says with a chuckle.

Her head seems to be a mile above her neck. It feels like her skin is separating from her body. She hugs herself to keep from peeling and collapses into a nearby chair. Seconds and minutes and hours cascade around her, as a tsunami takes hold of her senses. Everyone keeps on drinking and dancing, as though this puddle of a girl weren't here, leaking across the floor.

Rick props her up to make her dance with him to a Lou Reed song. Her mind is too melted to tell him that she wants to go home. She's on a chair, and then she's splayed on the couch, drifting in and out of consciousness. The music gets louder and more discordant and a strobe light repeatedly punctures the air.

Time returns, and her body and brain thereafter. By now,

the basement is nearly empty. A woman has passed out next to her on the couch and Rick is nowhere to be seen. She finds her sandals, which have been kicked across the room, then staggers toward the door.

"Hey, baby." Rick emerges from a curtained alcove. "You can't leave without saying goodbye."

"What time is it?" Saskia mumbles, wiping the dried snot from her chin. "Is it still Tuesday? I need to get home."

"I was waiting for you to come to."

"I'm not sure what happened there." Saskia looks at him bashfully. "I bet you think I'm dumb now."

"Not at all. In fact, I've been looking after you all night."

"You were?"

"Why sure, don't you remember? I made you all nice and comfortable on the couch," Rick says soothingly. "Do you want to go?"

She anchors herself to his muscle-bound arm and teeters up the darkened stairs, her ankles buckling in her kitten-heel sandals. She starts to open the door leading to the street, but Rick pulls her back into the dank vestibule.

"Now I need to hear you say it."

"Say what?" She rubs her eyes to clear her thinking. "I don't understand."

"What's there to understand?" Rick says. "Just say, I want to go."

"I am going," she says, perplexed.

"Say it."

"I want to go."

"Okay then. Let's go, together." He leans into her. "You and me, you tender, sweet young thing."

His moustache tickles her philtrum and she moans as she

kisses his pillow-like lips. So this is her destination. He is the certainty behind the maelstrom of the evening. He is her hard-earned happiness.

He twirls her around and leans against her. She giggles and tries to turn back around for another kiss, but he presses her face against the raw brick wall, his breath quickening as he struggles to undo his fly. He reaches across her waist to undo her pants. When she balks, he presses her so hard to the wall that the cement particles snag her cheek and draw blood.

He yanks down her pants, his sweat clinging to her mouth like cellophane. The clammy air drenches the back of her legs, which start shaking when he wrenches her underwear down. She bucks against the weight of his body, wanting to be back in happy-land again, until he twists her arm tightly behind her back and spits into his hand.

The touch of his cock seems to scald her. She jerks away but he tugs the leather string of her pendant like a leash, until it snaps and the rainbow falls to the floor. He forces her head still, making her choke on the brick particles that fall into her mouth. She claws at him with her free hand, but his body keeps slapping up against hers, smothering her in the heat of his flesh. Just as Rick succeeds in prying her legs apart, a door slams in the stairwell. Light cuts across the darkened entrance and footsteps come pounding down the stairs.

Rick lets go of her arm. With a hoarse cry, she ducks past him to the street. She pulls up her pants and starts running, not knowing where she's going, but certain that she's headed away from him. She stumbles on the cobblestone and loses a sandal, but keeps on going in a lopsided gait.

Like in a miracle, she sees the yellow light of a cab coming up West Broadway. She waves it down with both arms, clambers in, and gives the driver her address.

"What on earth are you doing out by yourself at this time of night on a school day?" the driver asks, in a heavy Polish accent.

She huddles in a corner of the back seat and cries uncontrollably. I can't go on like this. Look what happens when I try to give my virginity away. I can't go on, she thinks. The cab whizzes past Lincoln Center where, light-years ago, Mom used to get them orchestra seats for *The Nutcracker*.

When the cab stops for a red at Ninety-Seventh Street she counts up to Toby's floor and sees a single lit window in his apartment. If only she could follow that beam and leave all this crap behind.

Once home, she asks the driver to wait until she's inside the building, holding the remaining sandal like some damaged Cinderella. The night doorman looks aghast when he sees her bloodstained face, and hands her a tissue. She takes the stairs and dumps the remaining sandal in the hall garbage before creeping into the darkened apartment. She double-locks the front door and goes to the kitchen to drink milk straight from the carton.

Mom is where she left her, fast asleep in her room. Saskia is briefly consumed with the desire to climb in bed next to her. But it's too late for that, she thinks. I'm not that girl anymore. And she's not that mother.

She can't risk waking Mom by showering so she takes a wet washcloth and sponges the blood from her cheekbone before changing into her discarded pajamas. She then burrows through Mom's medicine cabinet until she finds her sleeping pills. Tapping three into her palm, she hesitates, then wraps two tablets in a piece of toilet paper, which she places in her breast pocket, before cupping water in her hand to swallow the remaining one.

There's no way she's going to make it to school in a few hours, so she turns off the alarm on her bedside table before dropping into a dreamless sleep.

I Promise Nothing

"Are you all right? Why aren't you getting ready for school?" Mom picks her way past last night's clothes scattered on the floor. Saskia crawls to consciousness, nostrils sticky from last night's drugs, brain stickier still.

"Water. Aspirin. I don't feel so good." She wipes her nose on the sheet, with fingers that reek of cigarettes.

"What happened to your cheek?" Mom comes back with a glass and some tablets.

"I got it when I was out walking." Saskia gulps down the aspirins and hides her scraped knuckles and chafed neck beneath the sheet.

"Do you want breakfast?"

Saskia rolls onto her belly and covers her head with the pillow.

The grandfather clock is ringing the half hour when she next opens her eyes, tacky with sleep. Through the rain-swept windows, she can't tell if it's afternoon or morning. She staggers to the foyer and sees that it's 2:30. Mom's pocketbook is missing from the hope chest, so she double-locks the front door and crawls back under the covers. Even though the room is warm, her feet are cold, and she starts shaking. She tugs the delicate thread of her scab that has formed on her cheek and examines the blood as if it weren't hers. Such a small amount to show for last night's wounds.

Look at that shameful, stupid girl staring at her from the mirror on the closet door. She doesn't think she can ever view her in the same way again. No tears can ever cleanse her. Her heart feels like an airplane's black box lost on an ocean floor. Turning her back to her image, she curls her knees to her chest and plunges back to sleep with the pills from her pocket stash. No dreams, no thinking. Just the welcome descent into nothingness.

The next time she stirs is when Mom comes in the following morning with a bowl of oatmeal and a thermometer.

"Do you want to tell me what's going on?" Mom strokes her forehead while taking her temperature. "I don't know what's got into you recently."

You can say that again, Saskia thinks as she clenches the thermometer between her teeth and slaps Mom's hand away. She rolls over while Mom reads her temperature and pulls the sheet up to her chin, beckoning oblivion.

The next time she opens her eyes, late-afternoon lavender shadows are zigzagging across her wall. She struggles to keep her thoughts tightly packed while she sneaks to Mom's medicine cabinet for another sleeping pill, which she swallows before tottering back to bed.

She wakes up hollow with hunger on Friday morning.

"Are you feeling any better?" Mom enters with a breakfast tray and a bunch of peonies.

Saskia shoves the bouquet to the floor and tucks into the scrambled eggs.

"Is this the way it's going to be, then?" Mom's eyes wrestle with tears as she picks up the flowers and arranges them in a vase.

Saskia wolfs down the food and then reaches for the glass of orange juice.

"I made that fresh for you this morning."

Saskia stops drinking and tips the juice into a nearby potted plant, burping loudly.

Mom seems unable to get the words to her mouth. "How long are you going to keep this up?"

Saskia turns away from Mom and covers her ears with her hands.

"I see how it is." Mom's face wilts as she hurries from the room.

Saskia wakens a few hours later to the sound of the phone ringing and goes to answer it.

"Mrs. Soyer, is that you?" Recognizing Emerson's voice, she disconnects the call and takes the handset off the cradle before returning to bed.

She rises later that afternoon, stiff from being in bed days on end. Hair matted and body funky from wearing the same pajamas, she takes a hot shower and mechanically soaps herself, resisting the touch of her own skin. She furiously scrubs her scab until she exposes the patch of shiny pink skin. She gets out of the shower and covers her cheekbone with a Band-Aid, angling the bathroom mirror so that she can't see her steam-smudged self.

Saskia drifts into the empty kitchen and finds a brownie on a plate with a note from Mom that reads, "Truce? I'll be home later with dinner." Spending the evening with Mom is the last thing in the world she wants. She needs sympathy, a shoulder to cry on, or, failing that, some booze will do. Andy is her best bet, since she's on the outs with Tabitha and Florence, so she tests the waters by calling him.

"Where did you disappear to?" Andy tuts. "Florence and Tabitha told me you cut class, and Emerson said that someone hung up on her when she phoned."

"What a surprise. I'm in the doghouse again." Saskia picks

at the remains of some fried chicken she's found in the fridge. "What are you doing later?"

"We're going to Florence's."

"I don't want to see those twats. Can I meet you earlier on our own?"

"Well, color me Kissinger. I guess I'm going to have to broker a peace deal between you guys. Seven at Abingdon Square, then?"

"Seven it is." Saskia hangs up the phone and puts the TV and radio on full volume. She finds the pink carpenter pants she wore with Rick and picks them up, as if they could detonate, to dump in the hall garbage.

Everything she tries on makes her feel cheap. It's too tight, too bright, too girly. She settles on a simple blue gingham dress and no makeup. She stubs out her cigarette in the brownie and scrawls a note for Mom that reads, "Too late. I've left." The sun is starting to set as she walks down the street to the subway with her head bowed, a far cry from that rowdy girl who ripped into the night just three days ago.

Saskia rolls up to meet Andy with some Rolling Rock from the local deli, whose Korean owner always looks the other way.

"Well, well, if it isn't Miss After School Special," Andy says. "What happened to your face?"

"I don't want to talk about it." Saskia uses her key ring to open the bottle and takes a swig.

"No, really. What's with the Band-Aid?"

"Are you deaf? I said, I don't want to talk about it."

"Let's discuss your frock, then." Andy tries to get a rise out of her. "What color is it? Is that what they call stillborn-baby blue?"

"Gee, thanks. You sure know how to make me feel like a

million bucks."

"Seriously, you're pushing your luck, laughing girl," Andy says. "Emerson is so going to fry you."

"I don't give a rat's ass."

"You can't cut school for three whole days. Not even at the Collective. We were all worried something had happened."

"Worried?" Saskia scoffs, and then sucks back her drink. "More like gossiping. It's always three against one nowadays."

"The alcohol genie sure is casting its spell on you. Come on. Let's start over again. Is there anything I could get you?"

"A father." Saskia finishes off her bottle and reaches for his.

"Whoa. Slow down." Andy holds his beer behind his back. "Everything seems worse when you're wasted."

"Not worse, more real. This is how I've felt ever since Daddy died. I hate myself, I hate my life, but most of all I hate my family. They act like he was something that just happened to us, and that I'm the loser for wanting things the way they were. I wish they'd all died instead of him."

"Don't say things you don't mean," Andy tells her sternly.

"But I do mean it. I'm the walking opposite of everything I once was. He made me right. He was one of one, and now I'm no one. I'd rather be dead. Then at least I'd be with Daddy."

"So, Einstein, let me get this straight. Killing yourself is going to solve your problems?" Andy scolds. "Think again."

"If I was with him, I'd be happy."

"So you'd be happy as Larry if you were six feet under?" Andy says. "Oh, *puh-lease.*"

"You don't know the first thing about what I've been through." Saskia throws her empty bottle toward the garbage can and misses, sending it shattering to the sidewalk.

"While we're on the subject, I can't think of the last time you asked me anything about myself," Andy snaps. "You never even asked about my long weekend in Paris."

"That's different," Saskia snaps.

"Is it?"

"Don't turn this on me," Saskia snarls. "I'm sick of being bad-mouthed all the time. I thought you were my friend."

"I am. I love you."

"Yeah, right. That's one of the three biggest lies, right up there with 'the check's in the mail' and 'I won't come in your mouth.' Now run along and report back to Florence and Tabitha. I know how you guys get off on feeding on my shit." Saskia would rather be by herself than be with this moron and storms off.

She heads toward Washington Square Park, but the prospect of running into Rick sends her up Fifth Avenue instead, bumping into people deliberately as she slam-walks to the Cinema Village to see what's playing there. She gets there only to find that *Taxi Driver* commenced an hour ago.

Alone and adrift among the Friday night bridge-and-tunnelers, she stumbles along for a few more blocks and then collapses on a bench in Union Square. Heart in the dumps and soul in the sewer, she starts to sob.

The bells in the Con Ed clock tower begin to chime, as though they're ringing just for her. At the third stroke, she gets up and hurries toward Tammany Hall. "I want to go home," she intones through her tears. "I've had enough of this crap and I want to go back to my real home, right now."

The bells make time disappear. Her past rises up to greet her as she dashes up Irving Place. The crescent moon looks like it's dangling from the tree branch in Gramercy Park and the crowd from Pete's Tavern spills onto the sidewalk. She could be five, or fifteen. It's all the same. She's coming home now, running in haste to get there.

She spies Mikey catching a cigarette in front of her building and calls out to him. He doesn't seem to hear her so she shouts his name again. Then he removes his cap to scratch his head, revealing a shock of red hair. She realizes that it's not Mikey but a new doorman.

She counts up to the sixth floor and sees a man's silhouette in the warmly lit window of her once-home. She stares at him, transfixed. For a riotous second, she believes that love has conquered time. The world as she knew it has shown itself again. And then the man snaps the curtains shut.

The crushing realization that there's no going back melts her to the spot. As if from a distance, she hears a horn blast as a truck with a tatty purple teddy bear strapped across its fender comes speeding toward her. In that instant, she surrenders, sick of the chaos of her wasted world, and steps off the curb, closing her eyes in readiness for the impact. She pictures Daddy and smiles in sweet anticipation of leaving this life. This is the way her world will end. This is where her circle closes. She holds her breath and waits for eternity to descend.

"Are you blind, bitch!" the driver shrieks and swerves past her, the shock waves slamming her against the hood of a parked car.

Her eyes flutter open. Instead of having been absorbed in some winkle of time, she is face-to-face with a Chinese food menu trapped under the windscreen wiper. She coughs from the stench of burning rubber and slowly rights herself. Grasping the fender, she starts shaking and retches as adrenaline swamps her body. She wipes her mouth on the menu and staggers to a nearby stoop.

The full force of the jagged city comes up to meet her with an almighty push, as Manhattan, her island nation, plugs her back into its grid. This crowded sliver of a place isn't ready to give up on its rattled little citizen yet and releases her pull to nothingness.

Saskia envisages Mom collapsing with grief-crazed eyes if the police had to notify her of her death, and her compassion returns. They belong together. She still loves what's left of her mother and has to forgive her for not being able to be the person that she once was. She's tried not caring, but she can't give up on that brittle and limited woman, or her twisted siblings. Her anger is fierce, but her love for them is as big as the everythingness of every day.

She's come this far, but she still has to go one step farther. She crosses the street and approaches her building, with her stomach lurching like a Slinky.

"Can I help you, miss?" the new doorman politely inquires.

"I used to live here, and wondered whether you'd let me sit inside for a minute?"

Saskia walks into the mirror-lined lobby as though entering a church and perches on the edge of the leather banquette by the elevator. Closing her eyes, she clasps her shoulders and retreats in her mind's eye to that distant winter night. She pictures herself arriving home in her school uniform, out of breath from having run the last three blocks in time to see Daddy off.

Toby and Arthur wave to her from the living room while she tosses her knapsack onto the hope chest. The warmth of the apartment, ripe with the goodness of Odessa's cooking, makes her numbed hands tingle. Saskia rushes to her bedroom to get the Valentine's Day card she made for Daddy and hastily kisses Mom, who is helping Naomi do her hair for the dance. She compliments Naomi on her dress, then rushes to her parents' bedroom to slip the card into the suitcase she helped Daddy pack the night before.

Saskia follows the telephone cord into the bathroom, where Daddy is shaving while he makes their dinner reservation at Luchow's. She puts her arms around his waist and leans against his crisply starched shirt, feeling his chest hum with the vibration of speech.

"How do I look?" He inspects his reflection.

"Do you want a polite answer or the truth?" Saskia finds him a towel.

"Go easy on me, kid."

"Not bad, considering you belong in a museum." She hands him his Royal Copenhagen aftershave and wipes a spot of shaving cream off his earlobe.

Daddy goes next door to fetch his wristwatch from the bedside table. Saskia helps him fasten the strap and then winds it up for him.

"Thanks, sweetheart. Where would I be without you?"

"Don't ask." Saskia gets his jacket from the back of a chair and collects his suitcase. "Come on. You're going to be late."

Daddy checks his pockets for his wallet and opens the bedroom door. "After you, missy."

Mom, Naomi, and Toby come out to the foyer to say goodbye while Daddy puts on his coat. "Are you sure you don't want me to come with you?" Mom asks, while fixing his collar.

"Sure I'm sure, Duchess." Daddy draws her to him and whispers something in her ear that makes her beam. Then he turns to his kids and says, "Now listen to your gorgeous mom nd don't give her any hell when I'm gone."

"Whatever you say, Pops," Toby says with a hug. "No fast ars or fast women for me."

"Yes, Father dearest. *Mais oui, Papa.*" Naomi covers his ace in kisses while Daddy strokes her hair.

Odessa comes in from the kitchen in time to hand Daddy is gloves.

"I could get used to this Cadillac treatment. Are those neringues I smell?"

"Yes," Odessa says with a smile. "Would you like one for he ride?"

"No, I've already started my fast for the operation. Save ne some, will you?"

"Of course I will, Mr. Soyer."

"When are you going to start calling me Larry?"

"When you get back from the hospital. Now Godspeed."

Daddy kisses Mom tenderly and playfully salutes his family n parting when the elevator arrives.

"Earth to Daddy." Saskia grabs his fedora from the hope hest and follows him into the elevator. "You almost forgot his."

Mikey is waiting for them when they reach the lobby. Your taxi's outside, sir."

Seeing as she left her coat upstairs and it's snowing outside, he helps Daddy button his up, before he gets into his cab. Promise you'll open my card first thing tomorrow morning?"

"That goes without saying."

"And promise you'll take me shopping when you get ack?"

"I promise nothing." Daddy hugs her tightly, their paired eflection in the opposite-facing mirrors bouncing into a never-ending point. She pulls him toward her, as if she could reconfigure time and make this happen.

Opening her eyes, she half expects to see her old self in a headband, pleated uniform, and knee socks. Instead, her present self, ricocheting into an endless vortex in the double mirror, seems to demonstrate that the two aren't inseparable.

She stands up to take a closer look at that eager, edgy girl and kisses her reflection lightly in forgiveness.

The doorman hovers close by, looking at her as though she's a suicide bomber. "Are you okay there, miss?"

"I'll be on my way now, thanks." Saskia starts for the door and then pauses to take in the lobby one last time. There is no place like home, this is no longer her home and she will never have cause to return.

Once outside, she heads west for Florence's. One of Florence's neighbors is leaving as she gets there, so she is able to clamber up to the fourth floor, where she knocks. Florence opens the door and stares at her coolly until Saskia flops her hands at the wrist and whimpers like a dog.

Florence is the first one to speak. "What do you've to say for yourself, Scarface?"

"I'm a dumb bitch?"

"That's a start." Florence ushers her in and they tiptoe past her mom, who has fallen asleep in front of the TV with her glasses on, to make their way to her bedroom, which is covered in arty black-and-white posters.

Tabitha is rolling a joint while Andy pores over a contact sheet of Florence's work. They stop and give Saskia the dead eye when she comes in.

"I'm sorry I've been the Queen of Mean who never listens or shuts up," Saskia says. "I've barely been keeping my shi together, but you're always there to keep me up."

"They're up and I'm always helping guys to get it up," Florence quips.

"That's okay. We still love you." Andy gives her a kiss. "Besides, being a New Yorker means never having to say you're sorry."

"We've all been there," Tabitha commiserates. "My mom always says that I was the only good thing to come of a bad marriage, and tried to turn me against my dad. I went along with that for awhile, until I realized that it's their beef, not mine."

"What do you mean?" Saskia asks.

"I want to hold onto what I love about them and let the rest of it go," Tabitha explains. "I have better things to do than to fight their fight."

"Think of it this way," Andy says. "We can't choose our families, but we can choose not to be like them."

Saskia smiles sheepishly. "So, all's forgiven?"

"Yes . . . you ignorant slut." Andy pulls her down to sit beside him, while Florence whispers something to Tabitha, then reaches out the window to retrieve a bottle of sparkling wine from the fire escape.

"Wow. What's the big occasion?" Saskia asks.

Florence throws Tabitha an excited look. "Tell her."

"My short story was a runner-up in the Scholastic Art & Writing Awards," Tabitha says proudly.

"Get out of here. That's great!" Saskia exclaims.

"And they say smoking pot kills brain cells. Who would've thought?" Andy jokes.

"Ha-hem. Getting left out here." Florence hands her an envelope while Tabitha scoots off.

"What's this?"

"My first passport. I'm going to Montreal next month. It's not Paris, but it's a start."

"By the time you get to Montreal, I'll be working in L.A. My parents finally agreed to let me be a runner on their show their summer," Andy announces proudly.

"Well, la-di-da," Saskia says.

Tabitha makes a grand entrance, bearing a plate of Twinkies and a lone lit candle.

"Holy crap," says Saskia. "I clean forgot it was my birthday tomorrow."

"We were going to get you a shit pie after your little disappearing act, so this will have to suffice." Florence hands Saskia an envelope.

Saskia opens it to find a copy of the photo that Florence snapped of her the day they became friends, inscribed with, "Happy 16th birthday, ladybug. It's your time to fly."

Sixteen, Saskia thinks flatly. She isn't anything like her friends, who know what they want. She's floundering far behind, and is miles from knowing who she'll be.

Then, like a bug on its back, her soul turns over. This summer will be her time, she thinks. Time to slow down on the one hand, speed up with the other. Time to redress her brain. Time to re-dream. Time to learn to be her own friend, when her friends are away. Time, with all the gladness it holds.

"What are you going to wish for?" Andy asks.

"Let me guess," Tabitha says. "A whipped-cream-covered Ethan with your cherry on top?"

"Gross," Saskia protests. "I don't think so, somehow."

"Bullshit. You've been trying to jump his bone since day one," Florence exclaims.

"I kind of sort of was. But not anymore."

"Thank God," Andy says. "We thought we'd have to sedate you when we broke it to you that Becky's finally agreed to go out with him."

"What are you going to wish for?" Tabitha asks Saskia.

"To grow up, but not too fast. Just fast enough."

The four of them spend the rest of the evening talking and posing while Florence takes Polaroids of them. Come dawn, they've all crashed out except for Saskia, who puts on her shoes and tiptoes out of the apartment.

She walks past the Muhlenberg Library, basking in the beauty of her rose-colored city as she crosses Seventh Avenue to head down the stairs for the uptown subway. Then she sees it. The white limousine. And it is at that moment that one journey ends and another begins.

*   *   *

Saskia writes a page on the subway to Ocean Parkway, ignoring the curious glances of the shift workers coming and going to work. By the time she gets off the train, the sun is fully up and she can see the Coney Island Wonder Wheel gleaming in the distance. She asks a Hasidic man for directions to the cemetery. It takes her a while to find her father's grave among the line of tombstones, which are as peaceful as an outdoor library.

She traces the outline of his name on the headstone with her fingertip. It's surreal to be standing above him, so she kneels. Uncertain how to pray, she touches the cold marble and whispers, "I'm sorry it's taken me so long to get back here."

She produces the letter she wrote on the subway and places it next to a withered bunch of flowers. Spying a water-stained card in Tilly's handwriting on the bouquet, she vows to see her aunt again soon. She anchors her letter with a rock and, as an afterthought, adds the plastic hat from the Cracker Jack's she bought at the twenty-four-hour deli before she got on the train.

Filled with a mighty calm, she reviews all the events that led up to this day. She's here on earth and her father is below it, but life continues, and the truth is she'd rather be above than below. Through trial and many an error, she's found the courage, smarts, and heart to keep on going.

* * *

An hour later, she decides to walk from Ninety-Sixth Street instead of waiting for the local, such is her impatience to get home. Her feet scatter cherry blossoms across the sidewalk as she dashes down the block to her building. Seeing that the elevator dial is on ten, she takes the stairs instead.

"Mom? I'm home!" she cries and runs into the kitchen. Mom's not there and the coffeepot is cold to the touch. She bursts into her bedroom, to find her bed's been stripped down to the mattress, the peonies in the wastebasket and the window opened to air the room.

She hurries down the hall to Mom's room and finds a fastened suitcase on the tightly made bed. "Mom?" she calls again. Silence greets her.

Saskia sits at Mom's dressing table to smell her perfume and sift through her jewelry box. Tenderness spreads out all over, making her large with love once again.

She hears footsteps. Mom sweeps in, wearing sunglasses and carrying the dry cleaning. Saskia springs up expectantly, but Mom sidesteps her and snatches the jewelry box from her instead. "You won't find anything of value. That's long gone."

"Huh?"

Mom brusquely puts the jewelry box in a drawer. "If it's money you're after, then ask."

"Money?" Mom's expression leaves her cold with uncertainty. "I was just—"

"What then?" Dry cleaning, perfume, and earrings become the tools of Mom's avoidance.

"Nothing," Saskia replies. More nothingness gapes between them. She struggles to put words into the silence. "You look nice."

Mom fastens the earrings and checks her lipstick in the mirror. "You sound so surprised."

"I mean it."

"Just as well." Mom picks up the suitcase and turns to go. "I'm off now."

"Off?" They're now evaporating, everywhere at once. "I don't understand."

"Oh, really? You. Of all people," Mom replies, stern with effort.

Her throat becomes so caked, she can barely manage, "Where are you going that you can't take me?"

"As I recall, you couldn't wait to see the last of me," Mom says, her composure unfolding. "Consider it a birthday present of sorts."

There it is. The squalor of her words. *I hate you. I wish to God you'd died instead of Daddy.* She looks for a lexicon to fix them. "Mom. Wait." She hurriedly hands her another pair of earrings. "These go better with your outfit."

"Oh. So, it's Mom again?"

"Only if you want."

Mom takes off her sunglasses, eyes now naked in pain. "I

want. But I need to hear it from you."

Time triangulates. Then a new angle seems to open up. "I don't know what I'd do without you. I didn't mean what said."

Mom's lips toil to work together. A cry escapes her as sh puts the suitcase down. "I suppose it can also be said that don't always know how to be your mother."

"And I don't always know how to be your daughter." Th confession tumbles gratefully from her mouth.

"I need to be loved for who I am, and who I'm not," Mom admits. "I'm a good mother. Or at least, I can be a goo mother again."

"Then why the suitcase?"

"I saw the note and thought you'd gone to join you brother and sister. The police won't report a missing perso until forty-eight hours have passed." Mom pauses to gathe herself. "I didn't relish the prospect of spending your birthda alone in an empty apartment. So I made a hotel reservation."

"Can you cancel it?" Saskia asks. "'Cause I'm not goin anywhere."

"And here I was, thinking you'd run away," Mom replies "It seems we've both been running in circles."

Then she's there. In Mom's arms, beginning again.

"I suppose you have plans to go out gallivanting tonigh with your friends?" Mom asks, stroking her hair.

"I do have something lined up, but I could always un-hav it."

"Can we go out to celebrate your birthday and my ne job? I start as a receptionist next week."

"That's great!" Saskia says. "But would you mind if w ordered in? I just want to be here at home, with you."

Saskia forgoes going clubbing that night at Hurrah to watch *Gone with the Wind* on TV with Mom over a Cuban takeaway in bed followed by a birthday strudel from Cake Masters. The next day, she completes her overdue term paper. Then she blows out seeing a William Wyler double bill at the Thalia with her friends, in order to make Mom dinner.

That Monday morning, she's up and out of the house before Mom stirs. Arriving punctually at school for the first time that semester, she hurries into the office, where Emerson is grading papers. "Up early or haven't been to bed yet?" Emerson remarks tartly without looking up.

"Ha-ha. That's so funny I forgot to laugh. This is for you." Saskia hands Emerson her term paper.

Emerson lights a cigarette instead of accepting the paper. "Why should I even read it? If this past semester is anything to go by, I could take an educated guess and flunk you here and now."

Saskia's renewed purpose begins to slip away. "Please, give me another chance."

"Spot quiz then. Tell me what you've learned from being here?"

"Learned?"

"When we first met, you struck me as someone who sought a safe space, not a crash pad. Where did that girl go? I took you seriously, but then you took me for a fool."

"I didn't mean to…" Saskia starts.

"You've outright mocked our methodology. If we believe that the students are the school, then what do you bring to us?"

Saskia looks for an answer in the teeming bulletin board, potted plants and student artwork that decorates the cramped office. She tries to imagine what version of herself she would have been if she'd stayed at her old school. More orderly? Maybe. Content? Maybe not. She'll never know because she'll never be that person. But she does know that she possesses a stubborn hope, born of chaos. "Possibility?" She wagers. "Intent?"

"Did you *intend* to miss three days of school? Is it *possible* that in doing so, you caused us concern?"

"I'm sorry I disappeared on you."

"Is that all?"

"I got lost there for a while."

Emerson stubs out her cigarette while studying her skeptically. "How do I know that you won't pull a similar stunt again?"

"Because I won't. Ever again," Saskia says. "I'm back now. Promise."

"Are you happy now, or are you going to continue pushing the auto-destruct button?"

"Happy? I wouldn't say I'm happy, I wouldn't say I'm sad. I guess I'm just realizing that I can be both."

"That's my girl. Your Teutonic willfulness can get you anywhere in life, so long as you choose your battles wisely." Emerson takes Saskia's term paper to add to her file and chuckles. "Come. It's time for attendance. You can stun the entire student body into silence by showing up on time, for once."

Saskia asks Emerson to wait for a second while she gets an envelope and a piece of paper. She wraps her amethyst ring in a tissue and puts it inside with a note that reads, "Breakfast sometime this century?" She seals it and writes her siblings names on the outside.

She tucks the envelope in her book bag, planning on

dropping it off at their building later, and then hurriedly follows Emerson to homeroom. "Today is the first day of the rest of my life," she reminds herself, taking the stairs two at a time to catch up with her friends.

* * *

Dearest Daddy,

I'll never know what my life with you would have been, but I sure know what it's been like with you gone. It's been restless and reckless and beyond weird.

It was all kinds of perfect when you were around, but since then we became something that I don't recognize. You were our container. We worked as five but four didn't. Mom tried. I tried. We all tried, but we just couldn't manage.

I should have spotted Manny's horns and cleft feet when Toby brought him home, but looking back I think he was some kind of Rorschach in which each of us saw the thing we wanted most. He was a parasite who worked his way up our family food chain, but I don't blame Toby for that, not for an instant. We were a walking bomb, just waiting to explode.

Mom buried the best parts of herself with you, not because she's awful, but because you made her complete. Although she loves us, she sucks at being single and keeps on finding Mr. Wrong, as if to prove that no one could ever compete with you, her Mr. Right. I've been so angry with her for so many things, but I'm beginning to see that I've spent just as much time running away from her as she has from me. We've been like a pushmi-pullyu trying to go in different directions.

If Toby and Naomi ever wake from their fault-finding fest, I want to be part of their lives again. Despite the distance and dramatics, we're still a family. They're still the words of my life and in time this crazy scenario will become part of a bigger narrative.

I think of you every day. But I have to stop playing the twin tracks in my brain and focus on the here and stop it with the would-haves, should-haves, and could-haves.

If you could see me from wherever you are, I hope I would make you proud, despite my monster share of nasty mistakes and binging on my own brand of poison. I almost drowned in my well of want. Now it's time for me to get back on dry land again.

I'm sorry I was too late to say goodbye when you left. I never for a second thought that would be it. If I knew then what I know now, I would have never let you go.

x x Saskia

Acknowledgements

There are so many people I'd like to thank for keeping me strong through this seemingly never-ending process.

Firstly, it's got to be an A for Andrew, my everything and my inspiration. Thank you for making my world go round. To my sweet adorables, Esmé and Laszlo, for bringing me more joy then I ever thought possible.

To my siblings Mary and Chris, for their love, letting me raid their memory bank and for giving me their absolute blessings to reimagine our past. To Mimi, my passionate and elegant mother and my father Marvin, a talent who was taken far too young. You both live on in me.

To Sandye Wilson and Diane Wheeler, lifelong fellow travellers from way back when and Constance DeMartino, my Baedeker and best friend. To Polly Horner for being my flashlight when I couldn't see the way forward.

The biggest heartfelt thanks to Karol Silva, Sophie Kotch, Dani Karas, Catarina Raacke, Jane Bustin, Chiara Menage, Dominic Berning, Alexandra Stone, Margaret Glover, Jocelyn Jones, Ed Prichard, Amanda Souter, Adrian Dannatt, Tamara Argamasilla Fabian, Rachel Howard, Justine Asprey, Sonya Desai, Tim Osmond and Chris Fagg for their eyes, ears, encouragement and expertise. To the tender memory of Ida Simpson, Emily Alfred and Wilma Muhlenberg. To Nick Marston, for being a force of positivity. To my friends and teachers in the Seeger community, and the wild times that were had. To Christine Vachon and Charles Pugliese for nudging me down this narrative road. To Anne Horowitz, whose insight took the book to the next level and to Jamie Keenan for totally crushing the cover. And thank you Moshe Schulman, for circling back to me.

Last but far from least, Barbara Rose Haum, Maureen Mullen, Gillian Steen, Andy Rose, Mary Vaughan – I wish you all were here to see this day.

Printed in Great Britain
by Amazon